Judge Not
Lest You be Judged

2019

Judge Not
Lest You be Judged

Dr. Robert E. Zee

Judge Not
Lest You be Judged

Third Edition. Unabridged Version. June 2020
ISBN 9781676049081

Copyright © 2019, 2020 by Dr. Robert E. Zee

All Rights Reserved. No part of this publication may be stored in a database retrieval system or website without the prior written permission of the author.

Scripture quotations taken from the New American Standard Bible® (NASB), Copyright © 1960, 1962, 1963, 1968, 1971, 1972, 1973, 1975, 1977, 1995 by The Lockman Foundation. Used by permission. www.Lockman.org

The electronic version of *Judge Not, Lest You Be Judged* can be found at www.eddiethemechanic.com.

Disclaimer

This is purely a work of fiction and fantasy. Any names, characters, schools, businesses, places, events and/or incidents are either the products of the author's imagination or used in a fictitious manner. Any resemblance to actual persons, living or dead, or actual events is purely coincidental.

Within the storyline, medical advice is given to fictional characters by other fictional characters. While the health conditions discussed and solutions offered are based in reality, many factors come into play when determining any one person's potential treatment for any of the conditions presented. The scenarios presented are not to be construed in any way as medical advice to anyone suffering the same or similar conditions. Please consult a qualified healthcare practitioner with any questions regarding a medical condition that you suspect you may have.

Within the storyline, the character "Joe" delivers several talks based upon the Bible. Joe's talks are not fiction.

Contents

New Beginnings 1

A Few Surprises 17

Really, Now? 33

Joe's Story 45

Jenny's Story 63

A Bump in the Road 75

Amy's Story 87

A Trip to the Beach 97

Ed's Story 107

Back to the Beach 115

The Invitation 123

Heading Home 135

Appendix I
    Mr. Frazier's
    Motivational Speech 147

Where Are They Now? 155

Week One

New Beginnings

The alarm abruptly goes off, playing an annoying tone that simply cannot be ignored. Jenny springs out of bed as if the building were on fire, quickly silencing the alarm. Stumbling her way to the bathroom, Jenny's mind may be fully awake, but her body is still half asleep. Over the last two years, Jenny has mastered the art of getting ready for class, having it down to a science. As a junior at the University, Jenny has gained extensive experience in time management.

Walking out of the bathroom, Jenny yells out to her roommate, Amy, "come on, girl! Get up! We're like going to be late for class!" Amy slowly gets out of bed, wondering where she is. Managing to get herself together in record time, Amy asks Jenny, "do we have time for breakfast?" Jenny replies, "no way, girl! Just grab a bar, and eat it in class."

Amy quickly gathers her notebook, phone, a bar, and her water bottle, throwing it all into her backpack. Looking around the dorm room, Amy, who just transferred to the University from a community college, casually comments, "I wonder if I got everything." Jenny confidently replies, "don't worry about it, girl. It's like only the first day of classes. All the professor is going to do is hand out the syllabus, take attendance, and pretend to teach something." Jenny and Amy rush out the door, hoping to make it to class on time.

Arriving at the classroom with absolutely no time to spare, Jenny and Amy take a seat at a table in the back of the room. As the professor, Dr. Jill Lawrence, passes out the syllabus, she announces, "this is CS 3150. Please check your schedules and make sure you are in the right place." Dr. Lawrence takes attendance, leaving Amy nothing better to do than to take a good look at her new surroundings.

Now fully coherent, Amy, pointing to a guy sitting one table over, whispers to Jenny, "who's the hot guy with the blonde hair?" Jenny whispers back, "that's Ed Becker. He's a really nice guy. And, he's got it all together. The guy sitting next to him is Pete Darby. He's also really nice." Jenny quietly giggles, and whispers to Amy, "they like schedule their classes around times they go to the gym. And, Ed is a personal trainer at a gym somewhere." Vividly recalling the song that Amy considers to be the theme song of her life, she looks over at Ed, quickly concluding that Ed is probably way out of her league.

Once Dr. Lawrence is finished with her administrative tasks, she begins lecturing about the mathematical concepts of countably infinite and uncountably infinite. After all, in a boolean algebra class, these concepts are seemingly very important. Not everyone seated in the class finds the value in acquiring such knowledge. Instead of listening to Dr. Lawrence's lecture, many students check social media, text each other on their phones, or sleep. What students do in class does not seem to bother Dr. Lawrence in the least bit.

Closing out the one and a half hour torture session of pure boredom, Dr. Lawrence announces, "this class meets again on Thursday at the same time. Please be sure to purchase the textbook for this class. The material you will be tested on will be derived from the book." Jenny tells Amy, "that's like really good news." Amy asks, "how is that?" Jenny explains, "the test material comes straight from the book. We don't have to pay too much attention in class." That is certainly good news to Amy, who is definitely not a morning person.

With a half-hour break before their next class, Amy and Jenny take their time walking to the student center. Amy can't help but to comment again, "that blonde guy that was sitting at the table next to us is really hot." Jenny informs Amy, "Ed and Pete come to our Interdenominational Campus Fellowship. You'll probably see Ed there on Friday night." Amy, who has been following the Lord, replies, "I'm definitely coming." Jenny warns Amy, "you'll be the new girl on the block. Everyone's going to be like really checking you out, girl."

Amy Amherst and Jenny Radcliffe have been very good friends since they met in fifth grade. After high school, Jenny went to the University to study computer science. Amy, who was undecided in her career path, attended the local community college for two years. Taking a few computer classes, Amy discovered something she enjoys doing. Now choosing a career in the computer field, Amy is enrolled in the same program as Jenny, and have many classes together.

Thursday morning arrives, and so does the second session of CS 3150. Getting to class a bit early this time, Amy and Jenny walk by the table where Ed Becker and Pete Darby are seated. Pete asks Jenny, "are you coming tomorrow night?" Jenny replies, "yeah. For sure. I'll be there. Do you like know what time we're getting started?" Pete replies, "probably at seven o'clock, like last year." Ed, who has already known Jenny for two years, looks over at Amy, and cordially says to her, "hey." Amy smiles, and replies, "hi."

Jenny and Amy take a seat, having a few minutes before class starts. Amy asks Jenny, "what's tomorrow?" Wanting Amy to meet a group of like-minded Christians, Jenny replies, "it's the first meeting of our Interdenominational Campus Fellowship this semester. And, you're coming, girl." Totally overwhelmed during the first week of classes, Amy replies, "oh yeah. That's right! I almost forgot." Jenny reminds Amy, "it's your first week here, girl. You're on overload mode." Sitting back in her seat, Amy watches as most of the students have their eyes glued to their phones.

While they are waiting for the professor to arrive, Pete asks Ed, "are you still heading to the pool tonight?" Ed replies, "tonight's the night, bro! I wouldn't miss it for the world." Pete tells Ed, "I think I'll go for a swim after my workout. What time are you planning to get there?" Ed replies, "I plan to hit the pool at about five o'clock." Pete tells Ed, "I think I'll join you." Overhearing Pete and Ed's conversation is Amy, who just made plans of her own to go to the pool later this afternoon.

Amy's immediate problem is that she has no idea where the pool is. Wasting no time finding out, during Dr. Lawrence's lecture, Amy googles a map of the campus on her phone. Pleased to find out that the pool is close to her dorm, Amy smiles. Jenny texts to Amy, who is sitting right next to her, "What's up?" Amy texts back, "I'm going swimming later." Jenny texts, "Want company?" Amy texts back, "Sure. Five o'clock?" Jenny texts in return, "Perfect."

Class comes to a close. Heading to the door, Jenny mentions to Amy, "you'll like really love our pool. It's awesome!" Amy explains, "it's been a long week for me. Maybe if I get some exercise, it will help me to relax more." Jenny replies, "I totally get that, girl. It's your first week here. You've been like on serious overload mode all week."

Amy asks Jenny, "hey. I'm heading to the bookstore. Do you want to come?" Jenny replies, "no. I can't. I got to run back to the dorm for a minute," and tells Amy, "I'll catch you later." Amy, already having a few one-piece swimsuits, heads to the campus bookstore to buy the beautiful bright yellow designer two-piece swimsuit she spied two days earlier when she was buying her books.

Later that afternoon, Jenny and Amy head to the pool. In the locker room, Jenny tells Amy, "this has been a long week, girl. And, it's not over yet. Maybe after swimming a few laps, I'll like sleep better tonight." Amy replies, "I don't see how you won't, especially since we must get twenty-thousand steps a day in around here." Jenny tells Amy, "this campus is big. I lost like five pounds my freshman year just walking around."

Walking out of the locker room and into the pool area, Jenny, sounding a bit like a cruise director, tells Amy, "welcome to our indoor Olympic pool. To the left, through the huge glass doors, is our outdoor Olympic pool and sundeck." Amy, who was expecting to see a six-lane, twenty-five-meter pool, exclaims, "wow! I mean, like, this place is seriously awesome!" Jenny tells Amy, "yeah! I know, right? Let's like find a lane. We're going to exercise!" The girls each dive into an open lane, and begin swimming a few laps. Every few strokes, Amy looks around the natatorium, seeing if she can spy Ed, who, if all goes well, should be arriving any minute now.

Ed walks into the natatorium and does not head to the swimming lanes as Amy expected, but rather heads straight for the diving boards. Amy stops at the end of her lane and takes off her goggles, watching as Ed climbs the ladder to the high board. Setting the fulcrum and testing the board, Ed gives Amy the clear impression that he's been on a diving board at least once before.

Ed, taking four well-choreographed steps forward perfectly in sync with Rita Ora singing *Falling to Pieces* over the radio, takes two strong bounces on the board. Propelled high in the air, Ed does two and one half forward somersaults followed by one twist in the pike position[1], and enters the water perfectly vertical. Amy, quite impressed with what she just saw, whispers to herself, "wow! Not bad!" But, Ed's warm-up dive is nothing compared with what Amy is about to see.

Seeing Ed getting out of the water and heading straight for the diving boards again, Amy waits to see what Ed might do on his second dive. Ed climbs the ladder to the high board once again. Setting the fulcrum back slightly and testing the board, Ed prepares for his next dive. Taking five steps forward, Ed takes two strong bounces on the board, propelling himself higher in the air than during the previous dive. This time, Ed does three and one half perfectly executed forward

---

[1] Forward 2 1/2 somersaults, 1 twist, pike position - Level of difficulty 3.0.

somersaults with one twist in the pike position[2], again landing perfectly vertical in the water. More impressed than before, Amy gets out of the water and walks over to the diving area to get a better view. Taking a seat on the lone chair in the area, Amy waits to see what dive Ed will do next.

Seeing Pete arrive, Ed yells out to Pete, "did you have a good workout?" Pete yells back, "yeah. I worked out with Joe today. I pushed him really hard. He's making a lot of progress." Ed replies, "good!" Pete walks up, and asks Ed, "are you ready?" Ed replies, "yeah! Totally, bro!" Pete smiles, telling Ed, "I can't wait to see the look on his face." Overhearing the exchange between Ed and Pete, Amy wonders exactly what Ed is ready for.

Ed climbs the ladder to the high board again, preparing for his next dive. This time, Ed executes a perfect reverse two and one half somersault dive in the pike position[3], which he makes look very easy. Getting out of the water, Ed sees the expected audience developing at the far end of the diving area sitting on the bleachers. Ed knows exactly who these people are and why they are here today.

Walking back to the diving board, Ed passes by Amy, who tells Ed, "that was really beautiful and artistic! You've really put a lot of work in over the years! I'd definitely give you a 9.9 for that dive!" Ed replies, "thank you!" Amy reveals to Ed, "I used to dive, but I've never done anything quite like that before." Ed, curious to see what the really tan girl in the yellow two-piece swimsuit can do, replies, "awesome! Why don't you go ahead and take a dive?"

Suddenly put on the spot, walking at Ed's side, Amy heads over to the boards. Amy nervously tells Ed, "I haven't done this in a while. If I do a two and three quarters[4], come and rescue me." Ed now clearly knows that Amy has dived before. Almost as an afterthought, Ed tells Amy, "by the way, I'm Ed." Amy replies, "hi. I'm Amy. I transferred here this year. I think we're in some of the same classes together." Ed

---

[2] Forward 3 1/2 somersaults, 1 twist, pike position - Level of difficulty 3.7. A very difficult dive.

[3] Reverse 2 1/2 somersaults, pike position - Level of difficulty 3.0.

[4] Two and three quarters: "Three quarters" is divers' talk for landing flat on your back. "One quarter" refers to landing on your belly.

replies, "I knew you looked familiar. You're dressed a little differently than when you're in class."

Arriving at the diving board, Amy realizes she has no way out of doing this dive. Climbing the ladder to the high board, Amy quickly realizes that she's missed springboard diving. Amy pushes the fulcrum forward a bit and tests the board. As she backs up on the board, Amy's heart starts racing, but not because the dive she has planned is very difficult. Amy is being watched by someone who can clearly qualify for the Olympic springboard diving team. Not to mention, Amy is quite attracted to Ed.

Standing on the board, Amy feels a sudden return of the great confidence that she once had. Totally unaware that the crowd that has developed across the pool is the University's springboard diving team, Amy becomes quite relaxed. Making her approach, Amy takes two bounces, and executes a perfect forward two and one half somersault dive with one twist in the pike position[5], followed by a perfect entry into the water.

Underwater, Amy suddenly realizes her new two-piece swimsuit is quite inappropriate for springboard diving. Quickly fixing her top before resurfacing, Amy wonders whether anyone caught her wardrobe failure. Impressed with Amy's dive, Ed mentions to Pete, "wow! Not bad!" Pete replies, "she's obviously dived before." Ed replies, "yeah. I know. That was really impressive."

Amy gets out of the water, telling Ed, "I'm still alive!" Ed replies, "that was awesome! I'm guessing you've done this before." Now totally relaxed and with a sense of humor, Amy replies, "yeah. Once or twice. It looks like you might have done this before too." Ed confesses, "no. Today is my first day diving. I read the diving board manual in the locker room right before I came out here today." Amy laughs, clearly getting the message that Ed has an unusual sense of humor.

Interrupting Amy and Ed's conversation, Pete informs Ed, "he just walked out." Ed abruptly tells Amy, "I got to go. Don't go anywhere." Taking a seat in the chair, Amy wonders what the big emergency is as Ed makes a beeline to the high board. Realizing that Amy is no longer swimming laps, Jenny walks over to where Amy is seated. Jenny asks Amy, "what's up, girl?" Pointing to Ed climbing the ladder to the high board, Amy replies, "watch this."

---

[5] Forward 2 1/2 somersaults, 1 twist, pike position - Level of difficulty 3.0.

Quickly setting the fulcrum, Ed takes five steps forward, takes a check bounce followed by two strong bounces on the board, propelling himself high in the air. Executing a perfect forward three and one half somersault dive with one twist in the pike position[6], Ed enters perfectly vertical into the water. Jenny tells Amy, "wow! I like never knew! He's like really, really good!" Stating the obvious, Amy replies, "yeah. In more ways than one." Ed quickly swims to the side of the pool, gets out of the water, and again heads straight to the diving board.

Clearly in the spotlight, Ed has caught the attention of the entire diving team and the diving coach. Preparing for his second dive, Ed makes a minor adjustment to the fulcrum, backs up, and carefully surveys his audience. Seeing the diving coach looking right at him, Ed makes his approach, taking a check bounce followed by two very strong high bounces. In the air, Ed executes a back two and one half somersault dive with two and one half twists in the pike position[7]. Landing perfectly in the water, Ed is finished diving for the day.

Amy, the diving team, and the diving coach all know exactly what they've just witnessed. Ed gets out of the water, and walks over to Amy. Ed tells Amy, "the diving team is here to practice now, so we have to leave." Amy asks Ed, "aren't you on the diving team?" Ed replies, "no." Ed then tells Amy, "but, we can still swim in the lanes." Amy smiles, and replies, "sure! Let's do that. I haven't swam since I got here this semester." Ed tells Amy, "there's no better time to start than now."

As Ed, Amy, Pete, and Jenny are walking away, the diving coach, Dr. John McRae, rushes over toward Ed, yelling out, "hey! Where are you going?" Ed turns around, and calmly replies, "I'm not on your team." Paying little attention to the diving coach, Ed nonchalantly continues to walk away.

The coach runs up to Ed, telling him, "hey! I'm Dr. McRae, the diving coach. Can I please have a moment with you?" Pointing to Amy, Ed tells Dr. McRae, "this is Amy. Amy is my diving coach. She just told me to swim laps, so that's what I'm doing. So, I can't talk right now." Catching on to something she does not fully understand, Amy interjects, "yeah. Ed needs to swim his laps now." Ed walks away,

---

[6] Forward 3 1/2 somersaults, 1 twist, pike position - Level of difficulty 3.7.

[7] Back 2 1/2 somersaults, 2 1/2 twists, pike position - Level of difficulty 3.8.

leaving Dr. McRae wondering who the guy is that is a far superior diver than anyone on the University's diving team.

Finding an open lane, Ed jumps into the water. Pete and Jenny jump into an open lane and begin swimming laps. Even though there are more open lanes at the other side of the pool, Amy asks Ed, "can we share a lane?" Ed replies, "sure, coach. No problem." Amy was certainly glad to hear that Ed is open to sharing his lane with her.

Amy jumps into the water, curiously asking Ed, "what was all that about back there?" Ed laughs, and explains, "a year ago, I was going to try out for the diving team. Before the team came out, I made a few practice dives. I slipped on the board and had a really bad dive, which the coach saw. So, the coach yelled out at me, 'hey, you! We're having diving practice. You'll have to leave.' So, I told him that I wanted to try out for the team. He laughed at me and said, 'get out of here and go play in the kiddie pool.' Today, I hit him with a reality stick." Amy laughs hysterically, and tells Ed, "that's kind of funny, but sad in a way. His loss."

A half hour later, after a good workout, Ed gets out of the pool. Truth is, Amy was having a really hard time swimming for that amount of time because her mind was focused on Ed, not on swimming. But, Amy had a lot of fun and had a good workout today.

Amy gets out of the pool, walking over to Ed, Pete, and Jenny, who are having a conversation while they watch the diving team practice. Ed asks Amy and Jenny, "have you guys had dinner?" Amy replies, "no. Not yet." Putting an invitation out on the table, Ed tells the girls, "we're heading out to get pizza, if you guys want to join us." Quickly accepting Ed's invitation for both her and Jenny, Amy replies, "sure! We'd love to join you!" Ed tells Amy and Jenny, "great! We'll meet you in the hallway outside the locker rooms."

The pizzeria, only two blocks off campus, is a short walk from the University's athletic center. Getting in line, each one places their order for dinner. Finding a booth with a window, the group brings their drinks to the table as their pizza is cooking in the oven. Pete strategically sits next to Jenny, and Ed sits next to Amy.

Sitting across the pizzeria at a table together is Dana McPherson, Donna Ruff, and Theresa Harris, who also attend the University. Dana, whispering to Donna and Theresa, informs her friends, "crap! Don't look now, but it looks like Ed and Pete have new girlfriends." Not inconspicuous in the least bit, Theresa abruptly turns around, wondering who the new girl on the block is. Theresa comments, "and, will you just take a look at that! Jenny is having a glass of wine. Can you even believe that?" Dana replies, "it looks like she's enjoying that glass of wine way too much." Theresa, whose back is to Ed and his group, asks her two friends, "what's the rest of them drinking?" Dana, who suddenly seems very depressed, replies, "fountain drinks, I suppose."

Trying to cheer up Dana, Theresa tells her, "maybe they're all working on a project together. After all, the three of them are computer science majors. I'm not sure about the new girl, though." Dana replies, "yeah, right. It looks like they're having way too much fun for working on a project. And, Jenny is running her tongue along the rim of her wine glass. That's hardly working on a project." Donna, who was hoping to land a date with Pete sometime this year, sarcastically comments, "unless the project is Pete."

It is hard for Dana, Donna, and Theresa not to notice Jenny's new look. Seeing Jenny sporting the famous haircut from the movie *Pulp Fiction*, Donna whispers to Dana and Theresa, "dang. I so want Jenny's haircut." Theresa advises Donna, "if you want that haircut, you'd better get it real soon. Or else, it will be real obvious that you're copying her." Dana, whose hair is wavy and quite prone to getting tangles in a two mile per hour wind, comments, "that really is a nice haircut. But, that won't work on me." Theresa informs Dana and Donna, "that's the *Pulp Fiction* haircut. In the movie, Uma Thurman, who played Mia Wallace, was wearing a wig. That wasn't even her real hair." Donna sarcastically replies, "well, that's Jenny's real hair. And, that haircut looks way too good on her." It is easy to conclude that a bit of jealousy is being verbalized among the three women.

Theresa, seeing Dana and Donna are somewhat upset, reassures them, "I'm sure none of this is anything to worry about," which neither Dana nor Donna believes in the least. There is far too much laughter coming from Ed's table, to which Dana pays way too much attention. Dana takes her cell phone and zooms in to get a close up of Jenny drinking from her wine glass. Donna incorrectly assumes that, for some reason, Dana is taking a picture of Jenny's haircut. Dana snaps a quick photograph, totally unaware that she was caught in the act by Jenny, who smiles for the camera. Dana will see Jenny's smile later when she is alone and takes a closer look at the photograph.

Back at Ed's table, the pizza has arrived and everyone is enjoying dinner. Eager to hear why Ed decided to attend the University, Amy asks him, "so, how did you land at this University?" Ed explains, "when I was in high school, I wanted to be a sportscaster. But, the Bible clearly says there are no sportscasters in Heaven. So, I picked computer science instead." Quite surprised at Ed's reasoning, Amy exclaims, "wait a second! Where does it say that in the Bible?" Ed replies, "in Revelation, chapter 8, verse 1, after the Lamb broke the seventh seal, it states, 'there was silence throughout heaven for about half an hour.' Can you even imagine a sportscaster being silent for a half hour?" Laughter breaks out at Ed's table, which does not go unnoticed over at Dana's table.

More seriously, Ed relates, "actually, I really wanted to be a personal trainer. But, personal trainers don't make much money, certainly not enough to live on. And, I thought I'd also coach a high school sport on the side, preferably diving. But, I ended up here at the University in the computer science program." Pete mentions, "Ed is a personal trainer at the gym over on Spring Street." Jenny, somehow, already knew that. Ed tells Amy and Jenny, "that's my part-time job. People pay me to work out with them." Amy realizes that Jenny was spot on in the sense that Ed schedules his classes around the times that he goes to the gym.

Pete then mentions, "it was a real bumpy road for me to get to this University." Jenny asks, "really? How so?" Pete explains, "when I first drove here, my car broke down." Ed, who has heard this story many times before, laughs and interrupts, saying, "no! Not this one!" Pete smiles, and continues, "so, as I was saying, my car broke down, and something went wrong with the exhaust manifold. So, I prayed for the manifold wisdom of God, and I was able to fix the exhaust system and get on my way." Amy and Jenny laugh, which again deeply bothers a few people over at Dana's table.

Amy mentions to the group, "there's a lot in the Bible that people just don't see." Jenny asks, "really, girl? Like what?" Amy explains, "well, like Jesus clearly predicted the invention of aircraft. It's right there in black and white, or red and white if you have the red letter edition." Expecting that a convoluted interpretation of the Bible is on the horizon, Ed smiles, and asks, "oh really? Where's that at?" Amy replies, "when Jesus was talking about the end times, in Matthew, chapter 24, verse 20, Jesus says, 'But pray that your flight will not be in the winter, or on a Sabbath.'" The group laughs, with Ed particularly finding Amy's interpretation of that verse quite funny. Ed tells Amy, "I look for this stuff all the time! I can't believe I missed that one!"

After finishing his pizza, Ed pulls a handful of pills out of his pocket, and downs them with a glass of water. Before anyone can ask, Pete announces, "those are his vitamins. Ed has to keep that high-performance body of his in peak working condition." Ed tells Pete, "you got to stay on top of the competition, bro." Over at the other table, Dana watches as Ed takes a hand full of pills. Dana will most likely come to the wrong conclusion as to what type of pills Ed is taking.

The light and airy conversation at Ed's table does not escape notice by those sitting at Dana's table. Theresa tells Dana, "cheer up, girl. Ed will probably be at the fellowship meeting tomorrow night. You'll get to see him then." Dana sighs, and replies, "yeah. You're probably right." Theresa confidently informs Dana, "of course I'm right. He's never missed as far as I know." Dana comments, "I just hope she's not there," greatly emphasizing the word "she".

Finishing their dinner and enjoying every minute of it, Ed and his group heads out. Dana, and her crowd, hung around after dinner a bit more than necessary only to watch what transpired at Ed's table. Dana suggests to her friends that it is time to go, strategically leaving the pizzeria at a time when she can follow Ed and his group back to campus at a comfortable distance.

Ed and Pete walk Amy and Jenny back to their dorm. Once back in their dorm room, Amy asks Jenny, "were we just out on a double date?" Jenny warmly replies, "we can only hope." Amy tells Jenny, "those guys are really nice." Jenny tells Amy, "Ed was really checking you out when you were diving. I saw it from the lanes. He definitely likes you, girl." Amy smiles, sincerely hoping that Jenny is right.

Giving Amy some inside information, Jenny, who is a bit wired, informs Amy, "by the way, you should know that Ed and Pete don't exactly fit in around here." Amy asks, "how do you mean?" Jenny explains, "this is not a party school, girl. The guys generally fall into like three categories. The first category is the geniuses. The geniuses can design a space shuttle but, when the power goes out, they can't figure out why their cell phone won't charge. The second group is the socially inept. They think a date is like texting back and forth. And the third group is the frat boys. Well, most of them anyway. They're like drunk all the time and think they're God's gift to women. Half of them probably won't even graduate. So, Ed and Pete don't really fit in." Amy replies, "that sounds like a good thing, not fitting in." Jenny confidently tells Amy, "you got that right, girl!"

Jenny then informs Amy, "you'll also find that the women on this campus fall into two categories. The first group is those who are here to learn something and get a job when they graduate. The second group is those who are here only to get their Mrs. degree. They're like just fishing for a husband. There are a few of them who attend our Interdenominational Campus Fellowship. It's pretty obvious who they are. You'll figure it out, girl."

Jenny asks Amy, "did you notice how empty the athletic center was?" Amy replies, "yeah. What's up with that?" Jenny explains, "there are twenty thousand students enrolled in this University. How is it that there were like barely a hundred people in the entire athletic center this afternoon? It's only the beginning of the semester, girl, and everyone has their face stuck in a book already. When midterms come around, the athletic center is going to be like totally empty."

Amy asks Jenny, "so, not fitting in is a good thing around here?" Jenny replies, "you got that right, girl. So, don't even try to fit in." Amy tells Jenny, "I'll have no problem in that department. I never did quite fit in anyway." Amy then tells Jenny, "I'm going outside for a few minutes." Jenny replies, "okay, girl. I got a little homework to do."

Friday evening at 6:45 p.m., Jenny and Amy arrive at the student center, meeting room 307, where the Interdenominational Campus Fellowship meets weekly. The meeting room, with a stage up front, has no seating, except for a few chairs in the back of the room next to a small table. One lone chair in the front of the room serves as a seat for the group's leader should he or she decide to use it. During the fellowship meeting, everyone can be found either standing or sitting on the floor.

Not quite knowing what to expect, Amy asks Jenny, "what usually goes on?" Jenny explains, "someone opens with prayer, then we sing a few praise songs. Then, one of the students like usually shares something with the group, which can be anywhere from a testimony to a Hell, fire, and damnation sermon. Then, after that, we sing like one or two more songs. Sometimes we break into groups to pray. We're supposed to start at seven o'clock, but we like rarely ever get started on time. And, after the fellowship meeting, most people go out and do their own thing."

Dana, Donna, and Theresa walk in together, wasting no time to check out who is present this evening. Seeing Amy standing in the back of the room with Jenny, Dana's heart sinks in her chest like the proverbial lead balloon. Hoping to have never seen Amy again, Dana is completely out of luck. Dana looks Amy over carefully, clearly noticing Amy's rather perfect figure, muscular build, extremely dark tan, flawless complexion, and brunette hair of which every strand of her reverse bob is lying in its perfect place.

Walking in next is Rodney Steele, who is a senior this year. With his military haircut, perfectly ironed button-up shirt, and polished shoes, Rodney looks like the poster child for the ROTC program. Last year, Rodney has often taken a leadership role in the fellowship mainly because not many students like to get up in front of a group and speak.

Rodney converses with Dana, Donna, and Theresa for a while. Dana occasionally glances over at Amy and Jenny, hoping that, when Ed walks in, he does not move to that side of the room. Armed with her photographic evidence, Dana informs Rodney that she caught Jenny drinking a glass of wine, and Ed was taking pills. Playing the part of a deacon in training, Rodney looks very concerned that Jenny was consuming alcohol, but is totally blind to the fact that Dana is spreading gossip.

Too busy gossiping about Jenny and Ed, Dana has completely missed Ed and Pete walking in. As Pete walks up starting a conversation with Jenny, Ed walks up to Amy, telling her, "you made it!" Amy replies, "I did! And, I really enjoyed our dinner last night! Thank you so much for inviting us." Saying exactly what Amy was hoping to hear, Ed replies, "we'll have to do it again sometime real soon."

Waiting for the meeting to begin, Amy asks Ed, "how long have you been diving?" Ed replies, "ever since middle school. I dive mostly for fun. Last year, I thought I could make the diving team as a walk on. You know how that ended. How about you?" Amy explains, "I was on my high school swimming team. Our county pool had a diving area, so I spent my Summers teaching myself to dive. When I was in community college, diving was how I dealt with my stress."

Ed jokingly asks Amy, "stress? Never heard of it. What's that?" Amy replies, "stress? Well, let's see. Stress is when you do two and a half somersaults from the three-meter board[8] and, in mid dive, you suddenly realize you've just left the one-meter board." Completely understanding Amy's analogy, Ed laughs, and replies, "oops. Yeah. I'd say that's stress!" Amy and Ed have a nice fifteen-minute conversation, suddenly interrupted by Rodney Steele asking for everyone's attention.

Rodney takes the stage and opens the meeting, praying, "Heavenly Father, thank You for bringing us together again this year. We ask that, during this time of fellowship, that Your Name be exalted." As Rodney continues to pray, not paying one bit of attention to Rodney's prayer is Dana, whose eyes are glued to Ed and Amy. Standing next to Dana is Donna, whose eyes are glued to Pete and Jenny. Catching Dana and Donna off guard, Rodney concludes his prayer, "it is in your Son Jesus' name we pray. Amen." Dana and Donna quickly regain their composure, pretending to act normal.

---

[8] Forward 2 1/2 somersault in the tuck position - Level of difficulty 2.2. A relatively easy dive.

The praise band members walk to the front of the room, where the drummer takes his seat, the guitarist makes a few last-minute adjustments to the settings on his guitar, and the keyboardist pushes a few buttons on her keyboard. Dana McPherson, the lead singer, takes her place in front of the band, where she announces, "our first song to open this year is *Agnus Dei*, which I'm sure all of you know." The band begins to play and, following Dana's lead, the group sings.

As the band plays, putting on an obviously fake smile, Dana leads the singing as she carefully watches Amy. During the number, Rodney walks around the room, seemingly bothered by something or someone. Meanwhile, Amy stands next to Ed, and Jenny stands next to Pete, all singing from their heart. After his casual trip around the room, Rodney takes a seat on the lone chair at the front of the room.

After two more numbers, Rodney addresses the group, "welcome back this year to our multi-denominational fellowship. I'm Rodney Steele, and somehow I got coerced into taking the job of leading our group this year." Truth is, Rodney, a senior this year, wanted to lead the group last year. After making a slew of announcements, Rodney instructs the group, "I see there are a lot of new faces with us this year. Let's go ahead and take the time right now to greet our new members and visitors." A few students come up to meet Amy, most of them friends of Ed, Pete, or Jenny.

After the brief welcoming period, everyone takes a seat on the floor. Misinterpreting Dana earlier this evening, and believing that Jenny was drinking wine immediately before tonight's meeting instead of yesterday, Rodney announces to the group, "I smell alcohol. Has someone here been drinking?" Quick with a comeback, one student replies, "so what if they were?" Another student comically comments, "Rodney wants some." The group laughs at the student's response, leaving Rodney to conjure up his own response. Out of luck, Rodney comes up pretty much empty handed with a comeback. Rodney, desperately trying to avoid landing in the hole that he just dug for himself, moves on.

In the back of the room, Ed whispers to Amy, "that's Rodney Steele. Rod Steele, as in a rigid steel rod. He's one of our group's Pharisees. Every so often, he manages to put his foot in his mouth." Overhearing Ed's comment, Pete chimes in, correcting Ed, telling Amy, "what Ed meant to say is that, every so often, Rodney manages to take his foot out of his mouth." Amy and Jenny laugh hysterically, leaving Rodney wondering what could possibly be so funny at the back of the room.

Earlier in the evening, after learning of the news that Jenny had a glass of wine, Rodney was walking around the room like a drug-sniffing

German Shepard trying to see if Jenny, or anyone else, has alcohol on their breath. Although Rodney did not detect the scent of alcohol on anyone's breath, he nevertheless purported that he did. Rodney, who is always a bit paranoid, is certain that Jenny and Amy were laughing at him. Rodney would be correct, but not exactly for the reasons he thinks.

Rodney then preaches a ten-minute sermon, followed by the band playing two more numbers to which the group sings along. During the first number, an offering plate is passed around the room for those who would like to contribute to the fellowship's funds. Amy asks Jenny, "what's the offering for?" Jenny explains to Amy, "part of it is for our party. There's like a party right before we break for Christmas. And, the group does other things too. Like, last year, we bought a few Christmas presents for a needy child. But, don't feel like you have to give anything."

Rodney then closes the meeting with a prayer and the group then officially breaks for the evening. Some members head home. A few couples go out on a date or go out to eat together. Most of the members, however, stay around and socialize for a while.

Catching the attention of a good friend before he leaves, Jenny excitedly tells Joe Sugarman, a Ph.D. biochemistry student, "I got my DNA results back over the Summer! What do I do next?" Joe replies, "go ahead and email me the raw genetic file, and I'll take a look at it." Jenny tells Joe, "I can't wait to find out what's wrong with me." Joe assures Jenny, "don't worry. If it's in your genes, I'll find it." Joe reminds Jenny, "but, remember. It's going to cost you." Jenny replies, "that's okay. I'll gladly pay." Jenny then gives Joe a hug, and tells him, "thank you so much for looking at it for me. I'll email the file to you right now." Using her phone, Jenny emails Joe her raw genetic file.

Once Joe has left, Amy asks Jenny, "what's all this about your DNA?" Jenny explains, "I did one of those DNA tests at the end of last year. Joe is going to look at my DNA, and hopefully he'll find out why I can't sleep well at night." Jenny then whispers to Amy, "unless I have a glass of wine like once or twice a week, I don't sleep very well. Last year, if I went three weeks without a glass of wine, I'm like up all night long and falling asleep in class." Amy whispers back, "I can totally get that."

Amy then tells Jenny, "I did one of those genetic tests about two years ago. I wonder if Joe can take a look at my DNA sometime." Jenny replies, "I'm sure he will. Joe is a really nice guy. And, he's kind of like a genius. But, I'll warn you. Joe doesn't do this stuff for free." Amy asks, "how much does Joe charge?" Jenny asks, "do you seriously want to know, girl?" Preparing for the worst, Amy replies, "sure. Tell me."

Trying to keep a straight face, Jenny informs Amy, "well, girl. Joe is like from New York, and he's a businessman. He'll probably hit you up for two slices of pizza. And, he's going to want the real stuff, from the pizzeria, not those hockey puck pizzas that places deliver. And, Joe likes a party. So, you'll have to invite at least a half-dozen people to go with you." Amy laughs, and tells Jenny, "that, I can do!"

Ed, Pete, Amy, and Jenny hang around after the meeting and talk for quite a long while. After an hour or so, Amy and Jenny head back to their dorms, escorted by Ed and Pete. Also hanging around after the meeting, walking aimlessly around the student center the entire time that Ed, Pete, Amy, and Jenny were talking, is Dana and Donna. Stealthily following Ed and his group back to the dorms, Dana and Donna conclude that Ed and Amy are just friends as are Pete and Jenny.

Week Two

A Few Surprises

Monday morning, earlier than anyone on campus really wants to wake up, Amy and Jenny get ready for another class of CS 3150. Today, however, Amy and Jenny wake up early enough to actually get breakfast, but arrive only marginally on time for class.

Taking their seats just as Dr. Lawrence begins today's lecture, Dr. Lawrence greets Jenny and Amy, telling them, "I'm glad you two can join us today." Amy and Jenny smile, as they sit back in their seat, waiting to hear what Dr. Lawrence will speak about today.

As she usually does before she gets into the prescribed course material, Dr. Lawrence gives a bit of computing history that cannot be found in textbooks. Orating to her class, Dr. Lawrence lectures, "back in the 1960s and 1970s, there was an unofficial race between supercomputer manufacturers to develop the world's fastest computer. Now, mind you, during that era, a supercomputer had a clock speed of somewhere around 40 megahertz. Compare a 40 megahertz clock speed with the computers of today." Amy whispers to Jenny, "that seems really fast." Jenny whispers back to Amy, "she said megahertz, girl, not gigahertz." Realizing that she misunderstood the professor, Amy giggles, attracting the attention of those in the back of the classroom.

Dr. Lawrence continues, "one such example of a supercomputer from the 1970s was the Control Data Cyber 70 and 170 series. A Cyber 170-series system, for example, consists of one or two CPUs that run at either 25 or 40 MHZ, and is equipped with up to twenty peripheral processing units, and up to twenty-four high performance channels for high-speed I/O. Now, before you laugh, the central processing unit of the 170 can execute ten instructions in parallel when properly programmed at the assembly language level."

Giving the class a visual example of what she is speaking of, Dr. Lawrence states, "I am going to pass around a picture of the CPU and backplane of the Cyber 170. Please realize that the CPU in this picture is seven feet high and about nine feet wide. It is not one inch square, like the CPU in your laptop or tablets. Please take note of the Freon cooling unit on the bottom right. This CPU is Freon cooled. And, also, please take note of the wires on the backplane, which are actually coaxial cables. The wires are all the same length as to prevent timing problems. So, whether the wire has to go five inches or eight feet, the wire length is the same."

Dr. Lawrence then informs her class, "this may come as a surprise to many of you, but a Control Data Cyber 170 configured with 20 peripheral processors, running at a clock speed of 40 megahertz, can run circles around your laptop that has a far greater clock rate." Many in the class are surprised, including Amy and Jenny, who are actually now paying attention to the professor.

Tying supercomputer hardware and software together, Dr. Lawrence asks her class, "now, let me ask you this. How many computer programmers do you think are responsible for writing the operating system of the Control Data Cyber series?" One student answers, "about a hundred." Dr. Lawrence quickly and emphatically replies, "not even close." Another student not very confidently replies, "two hundred?" Dr. Lawrence replies, "you're going in the wrong direction." Realizing the class has no idea of the answer, Dr. Lawrence tells them, "one! His name is Greg Mansfield. And, I might add, the entire operating system was written in assembly language."

Wanting her class to have a better understanding of why she brought this topic up, Dr. Lawrence then exclaims, "one person was largely responsible for writing the operating system for a Control Data supercomputer! Greg Mansfield had far less to work with, hardware wise that is, than you do! Please remember that when you enter the working world! You, as an engineer, are expected to perform far better than the people who spent three to six months earning a certificate telling the world they are now a computer programmer, which, I might add, they are not."

As Dr. Lawrence moves on to her course material for the day, Amy whispers to Jenny, "I guess that guy was born to program computers." Jenny whispers back, "you got that right, girl. God definitely gave that guy a gift." Sitting one table over, Ed also contemplates what Dr.

Lawrence just conveyed to the class. Ed also concludes, in his own mind, that Greg Mansfield must have been born to program computers.

After class lets out, Amy, Jenny, Ed, and Pete walk to the student center together. On the way, Amy asks Jenny, "have you heard anything from Joe about your DNA yet?" Jenny replies, "no. It's like probably going to take a few days." Pete half comically mentions, "Ed has the diving gene." Amy replies, "I can definitely see that." Pete replies, "and, the interesting part is that Coach McRae now knows it." Returning Amy's complement, Ed tells the group, "it looks like Amy has the diving gene too."

Sitting outside the student center, Ed and the group relax for a while before heading to their next class. During the conversation, seeing three women walking up the steps to the student center, Amy asks Jenny, "aren't those the three girls from the campus fellowship?" Jenny looks to her left, and replies, "yup. They are. And, Donna like copied my haircut again! I can't believe she even did that!" Pete assures Jenny, "that haircut looks much better on you than on Donna anyway." Jenny replies, "Donna did that last year, too, when I had my Cleopatra haircut. Then, she like let it grow out to her usual middle school girl haircut." Catching on, Amy tells Jenny, "maybe she was waiting to see what you came back with this year." Jenny replies, "yeah. Exactly, girl. That's Donna for you." With the top of the hour approaching, the group heads off to their next class.

Thursday afternoon, an hour before the diving team begins practice, wanting to get some diving in, Ed and Amy head to the pool. The University's divers are not stupid. By now, they know that Ed and Amy can take on the University's diving team in a meet, and win. So does the diving coach, Dr. McRae, which is somewhat of a sore point with him.

Thirty minutes before diving practice begins, a diver on the University's team comes over to Amy as Ed is taking a dive off the high board, and mentions, "I've noticed you two guys over the last week. You guys are seriously good." Amy cordially replies, "thank you for noticing. We've been practicing a lot." Formally introducing himself, the guy tells Amy, "I'm John Klement. I'm on the diving team. What's the chances that I can get you to help me with my triple somersault." Amy replies, "I'm Amy, and sure. We can do that. But, first things first. I'm going to do a triple somersault, actually a forward three and a half somersault in the tuck position[9]. Watch me carefully."

---

[9] Forward 3 ½ somersault in the tuck position - Level of difficulty 2.8.

As Ed gets out of the water, Amy climbs the ladder to the high board. Leaving the diving board and executing a forward three and a half somersault in the tuck position, Amy demonstrates to John exactly how the dive is executed.

Getting out of the water, Amy tells John, "okay. First show me your two and a half, and we'll see what we need to do to get your three and a half down." John climbs the ladder to demonstrate his two and a half somersault in the tuck position, knowing that he is being watched by someone who is clearly far more skilled than his diving coach.

As John sets the fulcrum, Ed asks Amy, "what's up with that guy?" Amy explains, "he's on the diving team. He wants us to help him do a three and a half. I told him to show me his two and a half first. Here he goes. Watch him." John executes a forward two and a half somersault dive from the high board[10], which both Ed and Amy see that he has down to a science.

John gets out of the water, and walks over to Amy. After introducing Ed to John, Amy tells John, "that was really good." Educating John on the basics of springboard diving, Amy explains, "from the time you leave the diving board to the time you hit the water, you have one and a half to two seconds. So, to convert your two and a half to a three and a half, you only have two variables to adjust. Those are your time in the air and your rotational speed. Practically, though, it's really going to be a combination of both. So, let's start with this. Get more height, as if, say, you're going to do a two and a half with one twist, and increase your angular velocity by tucking faster and tighter." John asks Amy, "it's that simple?" Amy replies, "it sure is. Go ahead and give it a try. Remember, more height and a much faster tuck." Now armed with information, John is willing to give it a try.

As John climbs the ladder, Amy whispers to Ed, "I hope he doesn't crash." Ed whispers back, "he's got to learn sometime. If he never tries, he'll never move forward. That's the problem with this team. They keep practicing what they can do, and never attempt what they can't do." Amy asks Ed, "how do you know that?" Ed replies, "I watched them last year."

John takes three high bounces and, as he leaves the board, Amy counts, "one. Two. Three. He got it. Well, almost." Slightly overshooting the dive, John's entry was slightly past vertical. Ed tells Amy, "that wasn't too bad."

---

[10] Forward 2 ½ somersault in the tuck position - Level of difficulty 2.2.

John exits the pool, asking Amy and Ed, "how was my entry?" Amy replies, "you went slightly past vertical. But, you did it! Good job." Ed tells John, "you're almost there. Go ahead and give it another try."

Ed and Amy work in with John, each taking a few dives. John makes a few more attempts at the dive that has been a sticking point for him, making some overall progress. John, wanting to move up to the next level, a forward three and a half in the pike position[11], is advised by Ed that he will need even more height and deliver more torque as he leaves the board. John climbs the ladder, making his first attempt at the dive in the pike position.

Watching as Ed was giving instruction to John, Coach McRae comes over to John and Amy, asking, "what's going on here?" Amy, who is a self-taught diver, tells the coach, "we're explaining to one of your divers how to do a triple somersault from the high board." Coach McRae replies, "it looks like John finally got it down." Amy replies, "I can see why he was having difficulty with it. The diver's mass is quite high, kind of like Ed's, so he has to deliver a whole lot more force when going into the spin."

Knowing first hand that John has had a problem executing any form of a forward three and a half dive for more than a year, Coach McRae, with quite a puzzled look on his face, asks Ed and Amy, "who are you people, anyway?" Ed smiles, and replies, "I told you last week. Amy is my diving coach." Realizing that Ed is messing with the coach again, Amy tells Dr. McRae, "I can tell you what John's problem was, if you want." With nothing to lose, Coach McRae replies, "I'm all ears."

Amy explains, "as I mentioned, John has a really high mass for a diver. The diver has to leave the board in a way that allows torque to change the angular momentum from zero to some number greater than zero, thereby giving the diver rotational motion. All the inertia the diver has is acquired when he or she leaves the board. After leaving the board, the diver can't change the angular momentum, but they can change the moment of inertia or the axis of rotation by making adjustments to the distribution of their mass."

John, a sophomore engineering major, walks over, listening to Amy's technical explanation of the mechanics of diving. Now having everyone's attention and realizing that she has center stage, Amy continues, "the moment of inertia depends on two things. The first is the mass of the diver, and the second is the location of the diver's

---

[11] Forward 2 ½ somersault in the pike position - Level of difficulty 3.1.

mass relative to the central axis of rotation. The further the mass is from the central axis of rotation, the greater the moment of inertia. So, by pulling the legs and arms closer to the point of rotation, the moment of inertia decreases and the angular velocity increases. So, a quicker and tighter tuck means a faster rotation, thereby getting in three and a half somersaults during the two seconds the diver has to complete the dive."

Applying the same principles to ice skating, Amy then points out to Coach McRae, "if you've ever watched ice skating, you'll see the same thing. When a skater is in a spin, they can increase the rate they are spinning by bringing their arms and legs closer in to the axis of rotation. It's the same principle. By pulling their arms and legs closer to the axis of rotation, the moment of inertia decreases and the angular velocity increases. If the skater moves their arms away from the axis of spin, their rotational velocity decreases."

Quite impressed with Amy's explanation, Ed stays out of the conversation for the moment. Coach McRae looks at Amy as if she were from a different planet, asking, "how do you know all this?" Amy smiles, and replies, "I took physics. The entire time I was in physics class, I was applying everything the professor was saying to diving." Coach McRae whispers under his breath, "amazing."

Amy then tells Coach McRae, "well, it looks like your team is here. We're going to go and swim our laps now." Putting out an offer, Coach McRae asks Amy, "are you sure you don't want to join the team for practice?" Amy replies, "thank you. But, not today. We need to get our aerobic exercise in." Amy and Ed head for the lanes, as Coach McRae walks over to his team in amazement.

Once they are far enough away from the coach, Ed tells Amy, "wow! That was a really impressive explanation." Amy reveals to Ed, "that's kind of all I did with my free time when I was in community college. I had no diving coach, so I had to figure it all out myself. It kept me busy. I lived in my own little world. And, what's really funny is that I probably would have failed physics class if it weren't for diving." Ed asks, "why is that?" Amy replies, "because, I wasn't really good at physics. But, since physics applied to diving, I spent a whole lot more time on it than I would have. And, I asked a lot of questions in class about how physics pertains to diving, which was driving the professor crazy."

Ed and Amy find an open lane, and begin to swim their laps for the day. Off to the side, Coach McRae questions John, trying to discover the little secret Amy revealed that allowed John to break through his performance barrier.

Later that week, Friday evening at 6:45 p.m., Jenny and Amy arrive at the student center again and head to meeting room 307, where the Interdenominational Campus Fellowship meets weekly. Just a few minutes later, Ed, Pete, and Joe arrive, and walk up to Amy and Jenny. Jenny wastes no time asking the guys, "does anyone know who's giving the talk tonight?" Joe smiles, and replies, "I am." Jenny replies, "oh, good." Jenny is secretly glad that Rodney, the group's leader this year, is not giving tonight's talk.

Dana, Donna, Theresa, and Rodney walk in together, checking out who is present this evening and what they are wearing. Seeing Amy again standing in the back of the room with Ed, Dana immediately gets into a bad mood. As Rodney converses with Dana, Donna, and Theresa, Donna constantly fixes her hair, making sure it is up to spec for tonight's meeting.

Right on time tonight, Rodney takes the stage and opens the meeting, praying, "Heavenly Father, thank You for bringing us together again this week. We ask that, during this time of fellowship, that Your Name be exalted." As Rodney continues to pray the same prayer he prayed last week, Donna checks out Jenny's haircut and continues to check herself out in her pocket mirror. Dana, likewise, pays no attention to what Rodney prays, but rather has her eyes glued to Ed and Amy, who are standing with their eyes closed. Rodney concludes his prayer, saying, "it is in your Son Jesus' name we pray. Amen."

The praise band members walk to the front of the room. Dana, the lead singer, takes her place in center stage, and announces, "our first song to open this week's meeting is *How Great is Our God*, which I'm sure all of you know." The band begins to play and, following Dana's lead, the group sings.

As the band plays, Jenny catches Donna looking her way several times. It is no secret to Jenny why Donna is looking her way. During the number, Rodney walks around the room, again seeking out the scent of something that may not meet his strict approval. After completing his assumed job as the morality police, Rodney takes a seat on the chair at the front of the room.

After one more number, Rodney addresses the group, "welcome back this week to our multi-denominational fellowship. I'm Rodney Steele, and I'd like to welcome everyone to tonight's meeting. Let's go ahead and take the time right now to greet each other." Most everyone in the group says hello to those whom they haven't seen all week. Oddly, Dana and Donna step outside the meeting room for a moment. It is anyone's guess what their private conversation may be about. Rodney steps outside the meeting room, joining Dana and Donna.

After the longer than usual meet and greet session, Rodney reenters the room, again takes the stage, and announces, "tonight, if I am not mistaken, Joe Sugarman will be giving the talk tonight." Hearing that Joe is giving the presentation tonight, the members of the fellowship clap and cheer. The group is looking forward to Joe speaking to them tonight. Some members of the group are equally looking forward to not hearing Rodney speak tonight.

Joe walks up to the stage, thanking his audience for the warm welcome, telling them, "thank you. Thank you. Good evening all of my friends. Thank you for the opportunity to allow me to speak with you tonight. I sincerely hope I say something tonight to encourage all of you."

Joe begins by asking the group, "by a show of hands, how many of you believe *once saved, always saved*?" Half the students raise their hands, leaving Joe to wonder whether the other half do not believe in the principal of *once saved, always saved*, or whether they are just being lazy. Joe then asks, "okay. By a show of hands, how many of you do not believe in *once saved, always saved*?" About a quarter of the students in the room raise their hands, leaving Joe to conclude that another quarter of the students are being lazy tonight.

Joe announces, "I have some news for all of you. *Once saved, always saved* is not in the Bible anywhere. Salvation is a process, not a one-time event. When your salvation is complete, then you are saved. The real question is 'when is your salvation complete?'." Joe now has the attention of everyone in the group, particularly those who have been taught that once you are saved, you are always saved.

Laying some preliminary groundwork, Joe explains, "in Christianity, we throw around terms such as justification, sanctification, glorification, and a few others. But, no one really takes the time to understand what these terms really mean. Let me take a moment to define those terms for you. Justification is the freedom from the penalty of sin. Sanctification is the freedom from the power of sin. And, glorification is the freedom from the possibility of sin."

Joe then explains, "salvation is a process. Justification, sanctification, and glorification, in that order, are the three stages of salvation. All three comprise salvation, not just any one of the three. When your salvation is complete, you are free from all sin, and restored to the perfect image of God that we see in his Son, Jesus. So, salvation is a process, not an event."

With the room now so quiet that you can hear the proverbial pin drop, Joe exclaims, "preachers always preach the comforting verses, not the whole word of God! These preachers are giving their congregations a false sense of security. A false sense of comfort and security is a very dangerous thing. There are about eighty passages in the New Testament that give a warning to not let the process of salvation stop. These passages clearly give instruction to not lose what was found in Christ. Now, let me point out the obvious to you. If we are instructed to not lose something, there must be a distinct possibility that it can be lost. Tonight, I am going to look at a few of the eighty passages that give definitive evidence that *once saved, always saved* has absolutely no theological basis to it whatsoever. These eighty passages indicate that the process of salvation can be interrupted, halted, and therefore not completed as God originally intended." Many members of the group sit back, peacefully waiting to hear what Joe has to say. Others, including Rodney, are getting a bit agitated.

Addressing his first example contradicting the belief of *once saved, always saved*, Joe explains, "okay. The first passage. The pastor of the church down on Spring Street likes to quote John, chapter 10, verses 28 and 29 to prove his belief that once a person is saved, they are always saved. In those verses, Jesus says, 'and I give eternal life to them, and they will never perish; and no one will snatch them out of My hand. My Father, who has given them to Me, is greater than all; and no one is able to snatch them out of the Father's hand.' That sounds pretty clear, doesn't it?" A lot of students reply affirmatively, as Joe exclaims, "nothing in that passage says or implies that you cannot leave under your own initiative! That verse refers to the external threat of being snatched, not the internal threat of you potentially walking away."

Giving his second example, Joe explains, "in the book of Romans, chapter 8, verses 38 through 39 read, 'For I am convinced that neither death, nor life, nor angels, nor principalities, nor things present, nor things to come, nor powers, nor height, nor depth, nor any created thing, will be able to separate us from the love of God, which is in Christ Jesus our Lord.' One thing, however, is left out of that list - ourselves. Now, listen to this. Just a few chapters down, in Romans, chapter 11, verse 22, Paul wrote, 'Behold then the kindness and severity of God; to those who fell, severity, but to you, God's kindness, if you continue in his kindness; otherwise you also will be cut off.' That verse clearly states that you can be cut off. And, if you are cut off, it will be likely of your own choosing."

Many members of the fellowship are surprised at Joe's presentation tonight, never having heard any of what Joe is saying from the famous pastor of the church down on Spring Street, where many of the fellowship members attend church. But, Joe is not finished.

Running over his allotted time, Joe continues, "here's a verse that we're all probably familiar with. In the book of Revelation, chapter 3, verse 5, John writes, 'He who overcomes will thus be clothed in white garments; and I will not erase his name from the book of life; and I will confess his name before my Father and before His angels.'" Joe pauses for a moment, then exclaims, "to not erase your name from the book of life clearly implies that your name can be erased! If you don't want your name erased from the book of life, you must overcome. The question you have to answer for yourself is what in your life do you need to overcome. I can tell you this. What needs to be overcome is probably some type of sin in your life."

Asking for group participation, Joe then asks, "will someone please read Hebrews, chapter 6, verses 4 through 6 to all of us?" Pete stands, and reads to the group, "For in the case of those who have once been enlightened and have tasted of the heavenly gift and have been made partakers of the Holy Spirit, and have tasted the good word of God and the powers of the age to come, and then have fallen away, it is impossible to renew them again to repentance since they again crucify to themselves the Son of God and put Him to open shame." Joe tells Pete, "thank you, Pete."

Joe then exclaims to the group, "did you hear what Pete just read? The scripture reads, 'it is impossible to renew them again to repentance'. That means that, at one time, they repented, and subsequently, at some point after that, turned away. Here's a stern warning to everyone. There is a point of no return. You don't ever want to get to the point of no return."

Concluding with his examples from scripture, Joe then reads, "in the book of First Corinthians, chapter 9, verse 27, Paul wrote, 'but I discipline my body and make it my slave, so that, after I have preached to others, I myself will not be disqualified.' When Paul wrote that letter to the Corinthians, he must have been well aware that he could be disqualified in receiving the prize, that is his salvation. Wherever there is a verse in the Bible that says that He is able to keep us, there is a verse nearby that instructs you to keep yourselves. Your job is to keep yourself in the faith and not disqualify yourself. Nothing could be clearer."

Joe then announces, "now, here's the good news. When Jesus appears the second time, it will not be to deal with sin. Sin has already been dealt with on the cross. When Jesus returns it will be to complete the salvation of those who follow him. God will create a new reality, a new Heaven and a new Earth. The new realm will be free from sin. His new family of believers will live there with him. Our responsibility is to endure to the end. Those who endure to the end will be saved. Many people start salvation, but never finish. Those who finish in faith will be saved."

Finished with his talk, Joe tells the group, "thank you for listening to me this evening. Again, I sincerely hope that I said something to encourage someone here tonight." Joe steps down from the stage and waves to the audience as he walks to the back of the room, receiving a standing ovation from the group.

Hastily walking to the front of the room, Rodney, clearly disturbed by something that Joe said tonight, announces, "I'm sure many of us were happy to hear Joe's opinion on the matter. Since Joe ran a little over, we'll only have enough time for the band to play one number." The band takes the stage once again, where Dana announces the evening's final number.

While the band plays and the offering plate is passed around, Jenny asks those with her, "what's up with Rodney tonight? He's like all bothered about something." Ed replies, "Rodney is always bothered about something. Joe probably took an extra thirty seconds of his time." Pete suggests, "Rodney's underwear must have shrunk in the dryer." Ed, Amy, and Jenny laugh, leaving many wondering what could be so funny at the back of the room. Once the final number is over, Rodney closes the meeting with prayer.

Dana, finished with her official duties as lead singer, makes her way to the back of the room with Donna and Theresa. Rodney joins them, along with a few others. Not paying one bit of attention to the conversation within her own group, Dana overhears Ed telling Amy, "the athletic center is open until midnight tonight. Would you like to head over to the pool, and then go out for dessert?" Suddenly excited, Amy replies, "sure! I'd really love that!" Ed mentions, "there's a restaurant a few miles from here that has really good desserts." As they head out the door together, Amy replies, "that sounds really great! And, I have a surprise for you."

A bit upset at how the fellowship meeting went, Dana, who has been trying to catch Ed's attention all evening, also leaves. Following Ed and Amy at a distance as they walk back to the dorms, Dana is totally shocked when she sees Amy light up a cigarette. Waiting for Amy to walk under the security light, Dana takes a picture of Amy with her cell phone. Dana wastes no time texting the photo of Amy smoking to Donna, Theresa, and Rodney, adding the caption, "Look what I just saw." Dana then texts to the same people, "I'm going to the pool."

Amy and Ed arrive at the dorms, get their swimsuits, and head to the pool together. Dana, clearly in a rage of jealousy, continues texting gossip about Ed, Amy, and Jenny on her way back to her dorm. During Dana's meltdown, Donna is having her own emotional breakdown watching Pete and Jenny leave the meeting together. Arriving back at her dorm room with her mind racing and in a panic, Dana grabs her swimsuit and rushes to the pool hoping to beat Amy there, but she will have no such luck. Meanwhile, Ed, Amy, Pete, and Jenny are completely oblivious to the strife that is going on among Dana, Donna, and a few others.

At the diving boards, Amy takes out a necklace she bought for Ed that she hid in the bra cup of her swimsuit. Amy stands behind Ed and, placing the necklace around Ed's neck, tells him, "this is your surprise." Not really knowing what to say, Ed replies, "thank you so much!" Amy tells Ed, "I really hope you like it." Ed replies, "it came from you, so I love it!" Ed takes a few steps over to the closed folding doors to the patio and, using the glass as a mirror, takes a look at his necklace. With a big smile, Ed tells Amy, "it's beautiful! Thank you so much!" Ed gives Amy a hug and a kiss. Amy melts in Ed's arms, feeling something she has not felt in a very long time.

Standing at the door to the locker room watching Ed and Amy embrace, Dana breaks out in tears. Not handling the situation well, with no plan, Dana rushes back into the locker room where she has a full-blown panic attack and meltdown. In a frenzy, Dana texts a few indecipherable messages to Donna, Theresa, and a few others who were not intended to be on the distribution list.

Amy tells Ed, "I also brought my camera, just in case you wanted me to get a few pictures of you diving." Ed exclaims, "really? Sure! That would be really awesome!" All excited, Amy tells Ed, "let me run back to my locker and get my camera. Don't go away." It is not like Ed is going to go anywhere. He was really looking forward to this evening with Amy. Amy quickly jogs over to the locker room as fast as she can without attracting the lifeguard's attention.

In the locker room, Amy passes by Dana who is sitting on a bench hiding her tears while contemplating her next move. Dana's next move should be to go back to her dorm room and go to sleep but, with her jealousy raging, that is simply not going to happen. Amy heads straight for her locker, grabs her camera, and walks right by Dana on her way back to the pool. Amy does not recognize Dana, but Dana, without a doubt, recognizes Amy. Dana attempts to compose herself as she follows Amy at a safe distance back to the pool area. Hiding in plain sight, Dana jumps into an empty lane and stands against the pool wall, punishing herself as she spies on Ed and Amy.

Amy returns to the diving area, seeing that Ed has already been in the water once. Ed walks over to Amy, telling her, "wow! That's a really nice camera." Taking a closer look, Ed asks, "is that a film camera?" Showing Ed the back of her camera, Amy replies, "nope. It's my Nikon Df. It kind of looks like a film camera, but it's totally digital." Ed tells Amy, "I'll go and take a dive. I'll try to smile for the camera."

While Ed climbs the ladder to the high board, Amy gets into position to take the photograph. Making a minor adjustment to the fulcrum, Ed backs up and makes his approach. Amy aims her camera and, holding the shutter release down, gets multiple pictures of Ed as he executes his dive. Ed delivers a back two and one half somersault dive with two and one half twists in the pike position[12], the identical dive he demonstrated to the diving coach. Entering perfectly in the water, Ed wonders how well Amy's photos came out.

At the side of the pool, Ed asks Amy, "how did the photo come out?" Amy replies, "I took a few. We can take a look at them now, if you want." Eager to see Amy's work, Ed replies, "sure. Let's take a look." Seeing no place to sit down other than the lone chair used by the diving coach to watch his divers during practice, Ed takes a seat and Amy sits on his lap. Dana watches Ed and Amy from the end of her lane, hiding her tears by splashing water onto her face.

As Amy scrolls through the photos, Ed tells Amy, "these are really great! This is way better than video! How did you get so many pictures?" Amy explains, "I put my release mode on continuous. So, when I hold the shutter release down, I can shoot about five frames per second." Amy scrolls through the photos, stopping at one in particular that catches Ed's eye. Ed tells Amy, "there I am, going into the twist." Amy tells Ed, "that one came out really good!"

Amy asks Ed, "I've always wanted a photograph of me diving. Can you take some photos of me? Please?" As Ed dries off, he replies, "sure. What do I do?" Amy explains, "it's really simple. The camera is already set, so you just aim it at me, press the shutter release halfway down, and it will autofocus. Then, hold the button all the way down and follow me through my dive." Ed replies, "got it."

Amy climbs the ladder to the high board, being watched carefully by Ed and, from a distance, Dana. Ed focuses the camera on Amy as she makes her approach. Taking two bounces on the board, and executing a flawless forward two and one half somersault dive with one

---

[12] Back 2 1/2 somersaults, 2 1/2 twists, pike position - Level of difficulty 3.8.

twist in the pike position[13] followed by a perfect entry into the water, Amy's efforts are well documented by Ed using Amy's camera.

Amy gets out of the water, anxious to see how Ed's photographs of her came out. As Amy dries off, she tells Ed, "let's take a look!" Amy again sits on Ed's lap, as she scrolls through the photographs that Ed took. Complimenting Ed on his work, Amy tells Ed, "this is really great!" Ed replies, "I know. That was a perfect dive." Amy smiles, telling Ed, "I meant your photos. You did really good." After reviewing Ed's photographs of Amy, they again head to the diving boards, getting a few more photographs of each other diving.

A half hour later, Theresa walks into the pool area and, seeing Dana standing in the water at the end of lane three, sits on the tile floor at the side of the pool. Recalling that Dana was very upset earlier this evening, then receiving an undecipherable text message, Theresa asks Dana, "are you all right, hon?" Trying to suppress having another breakdown and acting more like a high school student, Dana replies, "no! I wanted Ed, and she's got him. It's not fair! It's just not fair!" Not knowing what to say to comfort Dana, Theresa tells her, "maybe they met each other over the Summer."

Trying not to shed any more tears, Dana tells Theresa, "I just don't see what Ed sees in her." Interjecting some logic into the conversation, Theresa replies, "they both looked really impressive coming off the diving board. Maybe they're on the diving team." Theresa's commentary on Ed's and Amy's diving skills is the last thing Dana really wanted to hear. Stumbling over her words, Dana bluntly informs Theresa, "she was sitting on his lap. And, they kissed." Having Dana's best interests at heart, Theresa tells Dana, "standing there and watching them is doing you absolutely no good. Come on, hon. Let's get out of here."

As Dana gets out of the water and dries off before heading to the locker room, Theresa takes a picture of Amy sitting on Ed's lap with her phone. Theresa's photo will likely be circulating around social media before Ed and Amy leave the athletic center.

Ed and Amy, finished with diving for the evening, dry off a bit before they head to the locker rooms. Amy picks up her camera, holding it in one hand, and Ed's hand with her other. Ed tells Amy, "I'll meet you in the hallway. Then, we can go out for dessert." Walking

---

[13] Forward 2 1/2 somersaults, 1 twist, pike position - Level of difficulty 3.0.

into the women's locker room, Amy smiles, and tells Ed, "see you in a few."

In the women's locker room, Amy walks by Dana and Theresa, recognizing both of them from the fellowship meeting earlier this evening. Amy greets the two girls, telling them, "hi there." Theresa replies, "hey." Amy would stop and talk, but she is on cloud nine, looking forward to dessert with Ed. Once Amy is a few lockers down, taking a jab, Dana tells Theresa loud enough for Amy to hear, "that's the girl that was smoking." Ignoring Dana's comment, Amy gets dressed, eager to meet Ed. Amy meets Ed in the hallway, and the couple heads for the door.

Walking back to their dorms to drop off their stuff, Ed and Amy are trailed once again by Dana. Dana, far more upset than before, mentions to Theresa, "there they are again, holding hands." Theresa whispers to Dana, "let it go already. There's a lot of other guys on this campus." Dana, who is pretty much cried out for the evening, explains to Theresa, "Ed is the perfect guy. Last year, we had physics class together. He even sat next to me in class and he was my lab partner. I really thought he liked me. I was so looking forward to this year." Dana and Theresa take a seat on a bench outside the dorms, where Dana spills her heart out to Theresa. Theresa offers to pray with Dana, but Dana is too much of an emotional wreck to do anything but babble at the moment.

Ed and Amy walk out of the dorm, and head to Ed's Jeep Wrangler. Sitting on a bench outside the dorm with Theresa, Dana watches as Ed pulls out of the parking lot. It is hard for Dana not to notice the glowing smile on Amy's face. Ed drives down the street, totally unaware that Dana is watching. Ed's Jeep fades away in the distance along with Dana's hopes of dating Ed anytime soon.

Week Three

Really, Now?

Monday morning, Amy and Jenny walk into class, finding Ed and Pete sitting at adjacent tables. Amy smiles, knowing that the guys sitting at separate tables can only mean one thing. Amy takes a seat next to Ed, telling him, "that's a really beautiful necklace. Where did you get it?" Ed replies, "my girlfriend gave it to me." Amy's heart melts, as she tells Ed, "thank you for a wonderful weekend. I really enjoyed our time together."

One table over, Jenny tells Pete, "hey, sweetie." Pete replies, "hey there. I've missed you." Jenny, after spending most of her weekend with Pete, warmly replies, "I really enjoyed spending my weekend with you." Jenny pulls her chair close to Pete's and, leaning her head on Pete's shoulder, tells him, "I probably shouldn't tell you this, but I was up like half the night thinking about what a wonderful weekend I had." Pete puts his arm around Jenny, communicating far more than words could ever express.

Interrupting all the texting and checking of social media, Dr. Lawrence begins today's lecture. As she customarily does before she gets into the prescribed course material, Dr. Lawrence gives a bit of computing history that cannot be found in textbooks. Dr. Lawrence's secret is that she gives a bit of computing history for five or so minutes before she starts her lecture because a few students usually stumble into class a little late.

Dr. Lawrence informs her class, "last week, I mentioned to you that one person was largely responsible for writing the operating system for the Control Data Cyber supercomputers. I also made mention of these modern-day certificate sellers who teach a six-month coding class, and try to place their graduates on the same level as you. Today, I am going to briefly discuss the difference between you and these certificate buyers who get their worthless certificates from certificate sellers."

With absolutely no real world experience, the students are curious to hear what Dr. Lawrence has to say to them today. Giving an actual example, Dr. Lawrence explains, "many years ago, there was a professor here on campus who received a contract to write a parser for a particular computer language. That professor is no longer with this University. One of this professor's graduate students worked on the project, and received a master's degree for her work. Instead of using graduate students to do the actual coding, this professor took what he thought was a short cut, and hired a team of fifteen certificate buyers to do the coding. Big mistake."

Now having everyone's attention, Dr. Lawrence expounds, "at that time, the graduate student that was working for this particular professor was taking my graduate level compilers class. When I was going over parsers, in class, she asked me how I would write a parser for that particular computer language. Using her question as an example, I wrote the code for a generic table-driven LL(2) parser on the board, which that particular language requires. The parser was thirty or forty lines of recursive code. It took me less than fifteen minutes to write the parser." Some students, who are currently taking the undergraduate-level compilers class, are now listening intently.

Dr. Lawrence then asks her class, "how long do you think the certificate buyers spent writing the parser that they never completed?" One student answers, "a month?" Dr. Lawrence replies, "no. Not even in the ballpark." Another student answers, "a year?" Dr. Lawrence replies, "pretty close. Fifteen certificate buyers and eleven months later, they still couldn't complete the task. So, the graduate student asked me if she can use my code. I responded, 'sure. Go ahead. I don't care.' But, she had to write the tables for the language, which took her less than a week."

Dr. Lawrence then concludes, "so, that's what a company gets when they hire certificate buyers. You are far more valuable than certificate buyers who went to a weekend coding class. Please remember that when you hit the working world." Dr. Lawrence then moves on to her prepared lecture for the day.

Today, Ed and Amy pay little attention to Dr. Lawrence's lecture. Instead, Ed and Amy talk about diving, specifically planning to go diving before dinner again today. Once their plans are set, Ed asks

Amy, "after we go diving, do you want to go out and eat?" Amy replies, "sure! I'd really love that. I'm kind of getting tired of campus food." Ed replies, "I totally get that. And, we can't just live on pizza." Amy replies, "hmm. Living on pizza. You have to admit, it's a nice thought though."

An hour and a half later, class lets out. Pete gently rocks Jenny, telling her, "hey. Wake up, sleepy head." Jenny slowly wakes up, telling Pete, "wow! I must have like fallen asleep or something. What did I miss?" Pete replies, "she talked about the various boolean algebra laws, and went over their AND forms and OR forms." Still half asleep, Jenny replies, "that sounds like really complicated." Pete informs Jenny, "I took good notes. And, it's in the book." As they walk out of the classroom, Amy tells Pete, "she just needs a glass of wine. That will reboot her brain, and she'll be back in sync with the rest of the world in no time."

The following Friday, the Interdenominational Campus Fellowship meets once again. Dana, intentionally arriving early, sits on the edge of the stage having a conversation with Rodney Steele. It would be nice to believe that the two leaders are discussing tonight's program but, instead, they are gossiping about Ed, Pete, Amy, Jenny, and perhaps a few others in the group. Within no time, Donna and Theresa join in on the gossip, sharing a few photos that they've taken of Amy and Jenny over the last week.

Totally oblivious to the fact that they are being gossiped about, Ed, Amy, Pete, and Jenny walk in and sit on the floor against the wall at the back of the room. As they are talking among themselves about their day, there is a lot of laughter and bubbliness accompanying their conversation. It is hard for Rodney not to notice the light and airy conversation in the back of the room. It is also not hard for Dana to realize the group settling in the back of the room is getting bigger and bigger.

Ed casually mentions to Amy, "I have a surprise for you after the meeting." All excited, Amy asks, "really? What is it?" Ed smiles, and replies, "I'm not saying." Overhearing Ed and Amy's conversation, Pete tells Amy, "you might as well give up now. You'll never get it out of him." Now even more excited, Amy asks Ed, "how long do I have to wait?" Ed looks at his watch, and replies, "if we stay for the meeting, an hour and a half. If we leave now, maybe ten or fifteen minutes." Jenny advises Amy, "stay. The longer you have to wait for it, the better the surprise will be." Ed laughs, and tells Jenny, "maybe I'll give it to Amy tomorrow then." Amy replies, "okay! I'll wait however long it takes. But, I want my surprise before Jesus returns."

Joe Sugarman walks in, also taking a seat in the back of the room. Jenny wastes no time at all asking Joe, "did you get a chance to look at my DNA yet?" Joe replies, "I did. I'm almost finished. I should have it done by early next week." Jenny tells Joe, "thank you so much for looking at that for me. I really appreciate it." Joe replies, "no problem. I'm seeing a side of you that no one has ever seen before." Jenny laughs hysterically, and tells Joe, "it's not like you're looking where the sun don't shine!" A dozen or so people in the back of the room laugh hysterically at Jenny's comment. Joe smiles, and replies, "well, in a way, I am." Jenny makes tentative plans to meet with Joe to find out what he has discovered.

Interrupting all the fun at the back of the room, Rodney announces, "okay, everyone. It's time to get started." Everyone in the room stands up and quiets down, and Rodney opens the meeting with a prayer. As Rodney prays, Jenny holds Pete's hand and Amy holds Ed's hand. The wandering eyes of Dana and Donna once again take notice of the hand holding and smiles at the back of the room as they hear not a word of what Rodney is praying. Rodney concludes his prayer, and the praise band takes the stage.

Jeff Gilbert, the praise band's guitarist, announces, "our first number tonight will be a solo, sung by our own Dana McPherson. Dana will be singing her rendition of *You Say*, by Lauren Daigle." Dana takes center stage, carefully surveying the room as the band plays the introduction. Dana begins her solo, trying to ignore Ed and Amy whispering to each other during her performance. And, taking a break from his officiating duties, Rodney walks around the room, stealthily seeking out the scent of alcohol, tobacco, herbal teas, or any other substance that doesn't meet his strict approval.

After Dana's solo, the fellowship group sings two more songs together. Rodney stands up and takes the stage, telling the group, "that was a really nice solo by Dana. Please join with me in giving Dana another round of applause." The group applauds, expressing their appreciation of Dana's performance. Dana would gladly trade all the applause she receives for one date with Ed, but that's not the way the world works, at least not Dana's world.

The applause subsides, and everyone takes a seat on the floor. With today's message, Rodney begins addressing the group, "social media is a big part of all of our lives, perhaps a much bigger part than it should be. There is one fact that we cannot escape from. That fact is that we all probably spend way too much time on social media than we should. Imagine if we spent as much time praying as we do staring at our phones during class, checking out what was posted on social media since our last class. Tonight, I'd like to talk about what I've seen on social media over the last few weeks. Now, please don't take what I have to say as judging anyone." Ed whispers to Pete, "here it comes. The wrecking ball is about to hit." Pete laughs, and whispers back to Ed, "be sure to duck when it comes this way."

Rodney continues, "over the last week, I've been pleasantly surprised at the number of prayer requests that I've seen online. As Christians, this is exactly what we should be using social media for. In today's society, how else would we know each other's prayer needs?" Jenny rolls her eyes at Rodney's last comment, and whispers to Amy, "how about like talking with someone face to face? Did he ever think of that?" Rodney speaks for a few minutes regarding a few prayer requests that he's seen online, while many of the fellowship members sit patiently waiting for the praise band to take the stage again.

Moving on to part two of his sermonette, Rodney continues, "so, what else have I seen on social media this week? I really hate to bring this up, but, I feel that I need to. I've seen pictures posted online of some of you drinking alcohol. I've seen pictures of some of you smoking. There are even pictures online of one person taking a hand full of pills. I can't even imagine how any of that could glorify the Lord. I even ran across one picture of someone scantily dressed sitting on someone else's lap out in public. Some of the pictures I've seen in this regard have been very suggestive in a way. Now, please don't get me wrong. I don't want to be seen as the morality police."

As Rodney continues his pontification, Ed quietly laughs, and whispers to Amy, "I think he's talking about us." Amy, who knows exactly who took and posted the pictures which Rodney is referring to, whispers back, "he is. I saw the pictures that were posted." Ed whispers to Amy, "it's not like you can go diving in jeans and a T-shirt." Amy giggles, and tells Ed, "and, he said something about sitting on someone else's lap. It's not like you can sit on your own lap." Ed laughs, momentarily catching the attention of Rodney.

Hearing Rodney's pinpointed accusation, Jenny, who did not sleep well last night, asks Pete, "would you like to go out after the meeting and get a slice of pizza? I want a glass of wine." Pete smiles, and replies, "sure. I'd love to." Jenny tells Pete, "it's a date!"

Rodney continues his sermonette, judging others yet vehemently claiming that he is not. Realizing that Rodney has singled out Amy on more than one occasion, Ed whispers to Amy, "if you want, we can leave early and I can give you your surprise." Greatly appreciating that Ed recognizes that she is in the firing range of Rodney's verbal machine gun, Amy whispers back, "that's okay. He can say whatever he wants. His little temper tantrum isn't bothering me in the least bit."

Amy lays her head on Ed's shoulder, waiting for Rodney's well-prepared tirade to end.

   Finishing his fourteen-minute, thirty-two second presentation that could not have ended soon enough, Rodney tells the group, "if any of you here would like to give your testimony, or share with our group what the Lord is doing in your life, please let one of our leaders know and we can put it on the schedule. I don't want to be the only one up here on the stage every week." No one believes Rodney for a minute. If Rodney had his way, he'd speak for an hour every week and lock the doors so no one can leave.

   Joe Sugarman stands up, and announces, "I'll be glad to give next week's talk." Rodney announces, "thank you, Joe. I'm sure we'll all be glad to hear from you again." In the back of the room, Jenny springs up, announcing, "I'll give the talk two weeks from now!" Looking at Jenny as if she were from a different planet, Rodney tells the group, "okay. In two weeks, we'll hear from Jenny, and what the Lord is doing in her life." Jenny is the last person Rodney ever expected to volunteer. Truth is, Rodney was hoping that no one volunteered so he can have center stage all to himself.

   Rodney leaves the stage, expecting applause but getting none. Amy whispers to Ed, "I know Rodney's problem." Whispering back, Ed asks, "what's that?" Amy replies, "someone baptized him in pickle juice." Ed laughs, prompting Pete to ask Ed, "what's so funny?" Ed tells Pete, "Amy says Rodney was baptized in pickle juice." A few people standing in the back of the room laugh, again leaving Rodney wondering what could possibly be so funny. Rodney, seeing the group that is laughing, concludes that the group is laughing at him.

   The praise band takes the stage again, and uplifting energy once again fills the room. The offering plate is passed around and, after two numbers, Rodney takes the stage once more, this time to close the meeting. Following Rodney's closing prayer, the group splits into smaller groups, when many either hang around socializing, head out to eat, or plan to do something together.

   Jenny was also the last person Pete expected to volunteer for speaking to the group. Pete asks Jenny, "why did you volunteer to speak?" Jenny succinctly replies, "seriously, now. Do you really like want to listen to Rodney every week?" Ed laughs, and tells Pete, "she does have a really good point." Not overly impressed with Rodney's presentation today, Amy suggests, "if we all fill up the schedule, we won't have to listen to Rodney spitting out his emotional guilt trips." It is not hard to figure out that Rodney is not exactly everyone's favorite speaker.

Dana walks to the back of the room with Donna and Theresa, intending to eavesdrop on Ed and Amy's conversation. Seeing Dana a few feet away, Amy compliments Dana, telling her, "that was a really beautiful solo you sang earlier. You have a really nice voice." Putting on a fake smile, Dana replies, "thanks." Trying to be friendly, Amy mentions to Dana, "I saw you at the pool last week. Do you like to swim?" Attempting to gaslight Amy, Dana replies, "you must be mistaken. It wasn't me." Dana continues her conversation with Donna and Theresa, secretly listening in on what Pete is discussing with Ed. Deep inside, Dana is beginning to have another meltdown.

Totally oblivious to Dana's presence, Pete tells Ed, "me and Jenny are going out for a slice of pizza. Do you guys want to join us?" Amy tells Ed, "if you want, we can do that. My surprise can wait." Ed suggests to Pete, "how about in twenty minutes, bro? Will that work?" Pete replies, "sure. No problem. That will work." Ed energetically tells Amy, "let's go get you your surprise." Amy smiles, grabs Ed's hand and rushes out of the meeting, eager to see what surprise Ed has waiting for her.

On the way back to the dorms, Ed takes a minor detour. Amy asks Ed, "where are we going?" Ed replies, "your surprise is in my Jeep." Amy asks, "oh, really? How is your surprise in my Jeep?" Ed laughs, and tells Amy, "your Jeep? You sound a little excited." Realizing what she said, Amy laughs, and tells Ed, "okay! Let me try this one more time. How is my surprise in your Jeep?" Ed replies, "because, I wanted you to be the first to see it. And, besides, I just picked it up earlier today."

Arriving at Ed's Jeep, which he intentionally parked under a bright security light earlier today, Ed tells Amy, "okay. Close your eyes and turn around." Amy turns around, hearing Ed unlock his Jeep. After a few seconds of silence, Ed tells Amy, "okay. You can turn around now." Amy turns around, seeing a beautiful 24 by 36-inch poster size picture of her in mid air, executing a dive that she did while she and Ed were at the pool last week. Showing tears of happiness, Amy exclaims, "wow! It's so beautiful! Thank you so much! I love it!" Amy gives Ed a big hug and kiss, expressing her heart felt appreciation.

Taking a closer look at the photograph, Amy exclaims, "wow! It looks like a painting!" Ed explains, "I took the image that we downloaded from your camera to the camera shop. They printed it on canvas and put it in a frame." Amy exclaims, "it's so beautiful! I really love it! Thank you so much!" Amy asks Ed, "what made you think to get this for me?" Ed explains, "when we were at the pool, you said you always wanted a picture of you diving." Amy cries more tears of happiness, telling Ed, "you remembered!"

Ed hands Amy a self-adhesive wall hook, telling her, "here's your other surprise. You can hang the picture on your dorm wall." Amy asks, "can we go and do that now? Please?" Ed replies, "sure. We got a few minutes."

Amy and Ed walk over to Amy's dorm, where they hang the poster size photograph on the wall over Amy's bed. Amy tells Ed, "that looks perfect! I like it! Thank you so much again!" Ed asks Amy, "you do know what everyone is going to ask you now, don't you?" Amy replies, "no. Tell me." Ed tells Amy, "everyone who sees the photo is going to ask you if that's you." Proud of the one significant accomplishment she's had in her life, Amy replies, "and, I'll tell them, 'yup! That's me!'"

On the walk to the pizzeria, Ed asks Amy, "do you know what?" Amy replies, "tell me." Ed tells Amy, "you were the first person I've ever run across who understood how much work I put into diving." Amy asks, "how is that?" Ed explains, "when I met you at the pool that day, you said my dive was beautiful and artistic. Then, you mentioned that I put a lot of work in over the years." Amy replies, "well, it really was beautiful and artistic!" Amy then laughs and tells Ed, "and, you don't learn how to dive like that by reading the diving board manual!"

Ed asks Amy, "don't you just love it when you do a two and a half with one twist, and someone who has never dived before asks you, 'can you show me how to do that?'" Amy laughs, and replies, "yeah. You really want to tell them, 'just jump off the diving board and do it.'" Ed and Amy walk into the pizzeria, seeing that Pete and Jenny have already arrived.

The two couples take a seat in the same booth where they sat once before. Once everyone decides what they are going to have, Ed and Pete go up to the counter and place the order. Returning to the table, Ed and Pete bring the drinks as their pizza is cooking in the oven.

Jenny takes her glass of wine, telling the group, "watch this." Running her tongue along the rim of her wine glass, Jenny imitates exactly what Dana once caught on camera and posted all over social media. Pete jokingly tells Jenny, "you'd better be careful. The alcohol police are probably right around the corner." Ed tells Pete, "don't look now, but the alcohol police just walked in." Seeing who just arrived at the pizzeria, Jenny runs her tongue along the rim of her wine glass once again, and takes a sip of her wine.

Seeing more people walking in after Rodney, Jenny comments to her group, "oh wonderful. DDT and the praise band have joined the Pharisees for dinner." Amy asks, "what's DDT?" Jenny replies, "Dana, Donna, and Theresa. DDT. In case you haven't noticed, they're kind of toxic. Donna and Dana were eavesdropping on us after the meeting, which is why they ended up here. They wanted to see if I would have a glass of wine." Catching Donna's eye, Jenny takes another sip of wine, and whispers to Amy, "and, the other girl with them is Leesa Iron. She's a Pharisee in training. Rodney is making a proselyte out of her. She's like the perfect match for Rodney Steele. Get it? Iron and Steele." Pete laughs, and tells Jenny, "I never thought of it that way before."

Somewhat naive about the situation, Amy casually asks Jenny, "they eavesdrop on us?" Taking another sip of wine, Jenny replies, "yeah, girl. They do. And, they like don't think I know it. They're all like watching me right now." Pete tells Jenny, "you might have a point. Every time you turn around, those three girls are there." Thinking about what Pete said, Ed comments, "hmm. Amy and I were at the pool a week ago, and I took pictures of Amy diving from the high board. That girl, Dana, was standing in the water at the end of her lane, staring at us." Amy adds, "I saw Dana and Theresa in the locker room that night. After the meeting tonight, I told Dana that I saw her at the pool. She denied it, and told me she wasn't there." Jenny tells Amy, "that's because Dana is like the classical dark triad. She's gaslighting you, girl."

Ed recalls, "I wonder what happened. Last year, Dana was my lab partner in physics class. She acted so sweet. But, I ended up doing all the work." Jenny interjects, "see there? More dark triad. She'll like do anything to get what she wants. And, everything about Dana is always status dramaticus."

Briefly interrupting the conversation, the waiter brings the order to the group's table, and asks, "can I get you guys anything else?" Jenny replies, "I'd like another glass of wine, please." The waiter asks, "is everyone else good?" Looking around the table, seeing no one needs anything else at the moment, Pete replies for the group, "the rest of us are good." Jenny jokingly asks Pete, "are you saying that I'm bad?" Pete laughs, and replies, "no. I'm saying that you're excellent." Jenny tells Pete, "you're so sweet."

As she takes a bite of her pizza, Amy asks Jenny, "what's this about a dark triad?" Jenny explains, "the dark triad is like a combination of being a narcissist, psychopath, and a manipulator." As if he is reading from a textbook, Pete adds, "the dark triad refers to the combined personality traits of narcissism, Machiavellianism, and psychopathy. They are referred to as 'dark' because of their malevolent qualities." Jenny exclaims, "I know, right? That was like a test question last year for Psyc class!" Pete apparently had the definition memorized.

Pete asks Jenny, "why didn't you mention any of this about Dana before?" Jenny explains, "I don't really want to gossip about people. But, when they cross the line and start stalking us, I have to like wonder why they're doing that. And, it's beginning to annoy me that they take pictures of me drinking wine, and put it all over social media."

Amy reminds Jenny, "don't let it bother you, girl. Remember, you reap what you sow." Jenny points out, "yeah. I know. But, the Bible says we're also not supposed to do things that make our brother stumble. So, I'm wondering if I should like even have my glass of wine when they're around." Amy replies, "it's one thing if you have a glass of wine, and they think it's a sin. It's another thing when they stalk you, looking for what they consider to be a sin, and then put it all over social media as gossip." Jenny sighs, and tells Amy, "yeah. You're right."

Over at the Pharisee's table, Donna tells her group, "I can't believe this. Jenny is on her second glass of wine. I just can't understand why Pete likes her." Jeff, the guitarist from the band, tells Donna, "why would you want to hang around with them, anyway? I'm kind of wondering if they're really Christians." Dana comments, "and, there goes Ed, taking a few pills again." Rodney informs his group, "I did what I could tonight during our fellowship hour. Apparently, nothing of what I said got through to any of them." Dale Gaucher, the band's drummer and perhaps the sole voice of reason in the group, suggests, "just let it go. Maybe God isn't finished with them yet. After all, a week ago, Joe explained how salvation is a process." Dale's comment is the last thing Rodney really wanted to hear tonight.

Ten minutes later, over at Ed's table, the group has finished their pizza. Amy tells Ed, "I'm going to step outside for a minute." Amy steps outside, attracting the attention of those at the Pharisee's table. It is hard for Dana not to notice Amy standing on the sidewalk lighting a cigarette, especially since Dana has had her eyes glued to Amy all night.

Not taking Dale's earlier advice, Dana comments, "there's Amy, standing outside, smoking." Donna tells Dana, "and, the way she's standing there, not even filling out her blue jeans, she looks so sexy." Dana, who is full of jealousy, replies, "thanks for pointing that out to me. I didn't really need to hear that right now." Quickly grabbing her cell phone, Dana takes a photo of Amy, which will likely be posted all over social media before Amy walks back inside the pizzeria.

As they are leaving, Jenny walks over to the Pharisee's table, and boldly tells Dana, "please don't post any more pictures of me on social media. Okay?" Gaslighting Jenny this time, Dana curtly replies, "I never posted any pictures of you online!" Taking her cell phone out of her purse, Jenny brings up a picture of Jenny drinking a glass of wine that Dana posted a few minutes ago, and shows it to Dana. Jenny, who has no problem confronting people, sarcastically tells Dana, "just in case you like forgot, I can see what you post." Jenny smiles and walks away, leaving Dana to explain her actions to those seated with her.

Week Four

Joe's Story

Early Monday morning, as they are walking to class with Ed and Pete, Amy asks Jenny, "have you thought about what your talk is going to be about in two weeks?" Jenny replies, "I have no idea. But, I'll think of something." Pete suggests, "how about speaking about when Jesus turned water into wine." Jenny laughs, and replies, "I should like really do that!" Ed comically mentions, "Rodney probably tore that page out of his Bible."

Changing the subject, Jenny announces, "oh! And, guess what? I'm meeting with Joe this week! Joe texted me over the weekend and told me that he found out why I can't sleep!" Amy tells Jenny, "I'll bet you'll be glad to find that out!" Pete asks Jenny, "does this mean no more wine?" Amy replies, "not on your life! But, I don't know. I'll see what Joe has to say first."

As they walk into the classroom, Jenny tells Ed, "by the way, that was a really awesome poster of Amy diving! Everyone on our hall was like seriously impressed." Ed confesses, "all I did was push the button on the camera. Amy did all the work." Pete suggests to Amy, "maybe you should post that pic on social media." Amy replies, "that's a really good idea! I'm going to do that like right now." Ed tells Amy, "if you want, you can post one of me diving too. Maybe the diving coach will see it." Finding her favorite photograph of Ed diving, Amy asks Ed, "how about this one?" Ed replies, "sure. That's a really good one." Amy posts the picture of her diving and Ed's favorite picture of him diving on a few social media sites, wondering if anyone will notice.

Dr. Lawrence walks in, and announces, "please recall from your syllabus that, on this coming Thursday, there will be an examination. Please be sure to be here on time. The first forty-five minutes of our ninety-minute session will be allotted for the examination. If you have been attending class and paying attention, the examination should take you no more than twenty minutes to complete." Ed whispers to Amy, "especially since there are old copies of the tests floating around." Quite surprised, Amy asks Ed, "do you have copies of old tests?" Ed searches through his backpack and, finding copies of a dozen old tests for CS 3150, hands them to Amy, and tells her, "yeah." Amy looks over the tests, realizing that some of the questions are a bit difficult.

Class lets out. Amy suggests to Ed, "we should get together and study old test questions." Not getting the news yet, Jenny asks Ed, "wait! You have old tests?" Ed replies, "yeah. I got them from Mark Johnson." Jenny replies, "I should have known." Amy asks, "who's Mark Johnson?" Ed replies, "he's a senior in computer science. He has a huge collection of old tests. He hands them down to me every semester." Pete mentions, "I keep thinking we're going to get in trouble if we get caught with them. But, those tests have saved our butts several times."

Late Monday evening, Ed and Pete get together with Amy and Jenny in the study room on the lower level of Amy and Jenny's dorm. With a few tests coming up this week, social activities have taken a back seat to studying. Going over the old tests for several of their classes, the group thinks they will ace their upcoming examinations.

Midnight comes along, and Pete mentions, "wow! It's really getting late." Jenny replies, "I like see that. And, we have an eight o'clock class tomorrow morning." Ed and Pete gather their stuff together and, after saying good night to their girlfriends, head back to their dorm.

Amy tells Jenny, "I'll be up in a few minutes," and walks outside. Amy sits on a bench in the back of the dorms, smoking a cigarette before she gets her shower and goes to bed. Checking social media, Amy again finds out that pictures of her and Jenny are being again posted online. Another picture of Jenny drinking a glass of wine has been posted where all their friends can see it. And, a picture of Amy smoking outside of the pizzeria has also been posted online. It is no secret to Amy who took and posted those pictures.

Staring at her phone as she walks down the path to her dorm, Amy catches a glimpse of a familiar face hiding out on the far side of the bushes. Wanting to catch the person in the act of spying on her, Amy gets her cell phone camera ready. Amy suddenly calls out, "Dana!" Not immediately recognizing the voice of who called out her name, Dana abruptly turns around. Amy snaps a quick photograph of Dana as she is in the act of exhaling a plume of vapor. With a bit of sarcasm, Amy tells Dana, "wow! Dana! I didn't know you vaped!" As Amy casually walks away with the photographic evidence, in a panic, Dana yells out, "no! Wait! Come back! I can explain! Wait! Please!" Amy cordially tells Dana, "I got an eight o'clock class. Gotta run."

Amy walks back into her dorm, leaving Dana outside. Dana repeatedly bangs on the door, yelling out, "please open up! We have to talk! Please!" In a complete panic, Dana, who lives in another dorm, runs from entrance to entrance, looking for an unlocked door. Out of luck, Dana sits alone on a bench, having a massive emotional breakdown. Continually checking social media, Dana fears that the picture Amy just took will go viral any minute now. But, Amy is in the shower, thinking about her evening with Ed, and how peaceful it was studying with the group.

Wednesday evening, the day before two tests, Pete and Jenny join Ed and Amy at the pool. Ed has convinced Amy that, by exercising the day before the test, she'll do a lot better. Amy is willing to give it a try. Ed has been trying to convince Pete that working out the day before a test will result in a better grade. But, hearing the same message from Ed over the last two years, Pete still has his doubts.

Walking out from the locker room, Pete asks Ed, "are you sure we shouldn't be studying rather than swimming?" Ed replies, "I'm totally sure, bro. If you don't know the material by now, another day of cramming isn't going to do you any good. All you'll do is confuse yourself." Pete tells Ed, "maybe I'll look at it later tonight." Ed replies, "you're wasting your time, bro. We already went over the old tests. Stop worrying so much. You got this."

Amy and Jenny walk up, interrupting the guy's conversation. Amy asks Ed, "are we diving or swimming?" Ed suggests, "how about both? It looks like the diving team is just finishing up for the day." With a renewed interest in diving, Amy exclaims, "let's hit the boards!" Pete tells Ed, "we're going to swim some laps." Ed replies, "we'll join you guys in a while."

Ed whispers to Amy, "the diving coach is watching me. I'm going to mess with him again." Ed climbs the ladder to the high board, and sets the fulcrum. With the diving coach's full attention, Ed executes a reverse two and one half somersault dive in the pike position[14] with a perfect entry. Getting out of the water, Ed quickly heads to the high board again. For his second dive, Ed does three and one half perfectly executed forward somersaults with one twist in the pike position[15], again entering perfectly vertical in the water. This is Ed's favorite dive to perform for the diving coach, for no diver in the University's division can successfully execute this dive.

Ed whispers to Amy, "here comes the coach. Let's really mess with him this time." The diving coach, Dr. John McRae, approaches Ed, preparing to convince Ed to join the diving team. Before Dr. McRae gets out his first word, Amy tells the coach, "I'd give Ed a 9.8 on his last dive. With a degree of difficulty of 3.7, that would be what? Thirty-six points on the rack? What do you think?" Put on the spot, Dr. McRae asks Amy, "why a 9.8?" Amy replies, "Ed's left foot was not pointed as far as his right. Please don't tell me you missed it."

Coach McRae asks Ed and Amy, "who are you guys, anyway?" Ed replies, "I'm Ed Becker. This is Amy Amherst, my diving coach." Surprised that Amy knew the degree of difficulty for Ed's dive, Coach McRae asks Amy, "you're his coach?" Acting like Ed's diving coach, Amy replies, "yeah. I'm his diving coach. And, I need to show Ed something right now." Amy instructs Ed, "watch my feet carefully as I make my entry." Amy then tells Coach McRae, "you can watch too, if you'd like."

Amy walks over to the high board as Ed and Coach McRae carefully watch. After making a minor adjustment to the fulcrum, Amy makes her approach, takes two bounces on the board, and delivers a perfect forward two and a half somersault with one twist in the pike position[16]. Pointing her feet as straight as she can, Amy makes a perfect entry into the water, leaving next to no splash. Knowing she delivered an excellent performance, Amy shows off her swimming skills and gets out of the water.

Amy walks up to Ed, asking him, "did you see what I was talking about?" Ed nods his head, and replies, "yeah. Got it." Coach McRae

---

[14] Reverse 2 1/2 somersaults, pike position - Level of difficulty 3.0.

[15] Forward 3 1/2 somersaults, 1 twist, pike position - Level of difficulty 3.7.

[16] Forward 2 1/2 somersaults, 1 twist, pike position - Level of difficulty 3.0.

tells Amy, "that was a rather good dive!" Recalling that Ed told Amy to mess with the diving coach, Amy replies, "I know. But, thank you anyway." The coach asks Amy, "would you, by any chance be interested in joining my team?" Amy replies, "um, no. I don't think you guys could pay enough."

Coach McRae turns to Ed, and asks, "are you sure I can't convince you to join my team?" Ed replies, "thank you for the offer. But, no, not this year." In a frenzy, Coach McRae asks, "what do you have to lose?" Ed replies, "my freedom. Saturday is still the Sabbath, and I go to church on Sunday. Most of your meets are on the weekends. God comes first." Realizing he will get nowhere with Ed, Coach McRae tells Ed, "when you change your mind, let me know." Ed replies, "thanks. But, I don't think I'll be changing my mind anytime soon." The coach walks away, sorely ticked off that neither Ed nor Amy is considering joining the diving team.

Once Coach McRae is far enough away, Amy tells Ed, "that was kind of fun, messing with him like that." Ed replies, "yeah, seriously." Ed then asks, "was my left foot really not pointed correctly?" Amy replies, "slightly. But, it was still a really, really good dive. I just used that as a reason to show him what I can do." Ed gives Amy a high-five, telling her, "good thinking!" Ed and Amy take a few more dives, then join Pete and Jenny over in the lanes and swim a few laps.

After a good workout, Ed tells Pete, "now, you'll do better on the test tomorrow, bro." Pete replies, "I really hope so." Jenny tells Pete, "don't worry. You'll do good. You've like already seen all the test questions for both of the tests we have tomorrow." Pete relents, telling Ed and Jenny, "okay. You guys convinced me. I'll just relax for the rest of the night." Jenny tells Pete, "I'll help you relax." Amy tells Ed, "yeah. We all need to relax tonight."

Thursday morning, nearly everyone in the class arrives early for the test. Most students are doing some last minute studying, which will not likely afford them a better grade. At the back of the classroom, Pete casually asks, "does anyone know what's up with Dana? I'm kind of worried about her." Jenny asks Pete, "like what do you mean?" Pete replies, "the word is she's missed more than half her classes and she's having some sort of meltdown. I heard she's now in the hospital or something."

Amy thinks back to Monday night and blurts out, "oops." Jenny asks Amy, "uh oh. What's up, girl?" Amy pulls up the picture on her phone that she took of Dana when she was vaping, and shows it to Jenny, Ed, and Pete. Ed comments, "wow! She looks really frightened!" Amy replies, "yeah. I know, right?"

Wondering how and when Amy got the photo, Jenny exclaims, "what? How did you get this pic, girl?" Amy explains, "Monday night, after we were studying, I went outside for a few minutes. When I was coming back in, I saw Dana hiding out behind the bushes, so I thought she was spying on me again. So, I called out her name, and she like turned around in a panic. That's when I took the photograph. I suppose I was wrong. She wasn't spying on me this time."

Shocked at what she is seeing, Jenny exclaims, asking, "has anyone else like seen this?" Amy replies, "no. I totally forgot about it until now." Amy continues explaining, "then, when I went back inside, she had some sort of panic attack and started banging on the door. I just went inside, got my shower, and went to bed." Jenny replies, "that girl is like seriously psycho. She's probably resorted to drinking."

Dr. Lawrence walks in, and the class immediately quiets down. As she is passing out the examination, Dr. Lawrence announces, "please place your books, phones, and backpacks on the floor. You will have forty-five minutes to complete this examination. If you finish early, please check your work or feel free to take a nap like some of you usually do in my class." Dr. Lawrence obviously knows that waking up for an 8:00 a.m. class is far too much to ask for some of her students. The test scores will alert her to exactly whom those students are.

Receiving his test booklet, Ed smiles, as he has seen every question on the test before. Ed also knows that Amy, Jenny, and Pete have also seen all of the questions on the test before. Knowing the answer to every question on the test, Pete might just believe Ed that working out the day before the test is far better than any last-minute studying. Finishing the test early, Amy sits back in her seat and wonders what Dana's problem really is.

Class lets out, and the consensus among the students is that the examination was a bit more difficult than expected. Ed, Amy, Pete, and Jenny, however, have a different opinion. Ed asks Amy, "so, how did you do?" Amy replies, "really good! I think I got an A!" Jenny exclaims, "I think I like got an A, too!" Pete tells Ed, "you might be right about not studying before the day of the test." Ed replies, "well, having the test questions ahead of time helps a little too." With thirty minutes before their next class, the group hangs out in the plaza in front of the student center, relaxing instead of doing some last-minute cramming for their next test.

Thursday afternoon, Jenny meets with Joe Sugarman in the school cafeteria to learn what Joe found by looking at her DNA. Walking up, Jenny sees Joe sitting at a table reviewing a few pieces of paper. All excited, Jenny announces, "hi! So, you found out what's wrong with me?" Joe replies, "I did. And, it's really very simple. Take a seat, and we'll go over it." Jenny tells Joe, "before we begin, I want to get a cup of coffee. Can I get you anything?" Joe tells Jenny, "forget the coffee. Trust me. Drink some water instead." Jenny gets a glass of water for herself and one for Joe. Returning to the table, Jenny is eager to find out why she never sleeps well.

Bouncing up and down on her seat showing her excitement, Jenny asks, "so, what did you find out?" Joe replies, "I found two problems, not one. So, that will be two slices of pizza." Jenny tells Joe, "I'll buy you like a dozen pizzas if you can fix me." Joe replies, "you don't really have to buy me a slice of pizza. That's just my personality. I always tell people it will cost them big time. Then, I enjoy seeing how they respond when I tell them the cost is a slice of pizza." Jenny tells Joe, "you're getting your pizza, Joe. You really deserve it." Truth is, Joe will go out of his way to help anyone he can.

Getting down to business, Joe asks Jenny, "have you ever heard of glutamate?" Jenny asks, "like in monosodium glutamate?" Joe replies, "exactly! I'll make a biochemist out of you yet." Joe then explains, "glutamate is the brain's primary excitatory neurotransmitter. There's an enzyme, called glutamate decarboxylase, that converts glutamate to gamma aminobutyric acid, or GABA for short. GABA is the brain's primary inhibitory neurotransmitter. Now, here's problem number one. You have a defect in the glutamate decarboxylase enzyme, so you can't convert the excitatory glutamate to the inhibitory GABA very well. So, you have too much of the excitatory glutamate, which is keeping you awake, and not much of the inhibitory GABA, which allows you to sleep and relax." Jenny replies, asking, "so, too much glutamate is like making me not sleep?" Joe replies, "exactly! You're on your way to becoming a biochemist!"

Jenny asks, "so, how do we fix it?" Joe replies, "it's simple. First, don't ever eat anything that has monosodium glutamate in it. It will keep you up all night long. Staying away from stimulants, like caffeine, will also help. To fix the problem, though, you'll have to take a supplement that has taurine, GABA, and glycine in it. Take the supplement in the evening about an hour before you go to bed. You can get the supplement at the vitamin store near the mall. And, you're in luck. There's a supplement on the market that has all three of those ingredients combined in it. You'll sleep like a baby."

Now curious, Jenny asks Joe, "then, why does having a glass of wine like always help me sleep?" Joe explains, "that's a really good question. Alcohol mimics the action of gamma aminobutyric acid in the brain. So, when you have a glass of wine, the alcohol activates the GABA receptors, which are inhibitory in nature, and you sleep better. Does that make sense?" Jenny exclaims, "totally!"

Jenny then asks, "so, why is it that when I don't have a glass of wine for three weeks, I stay up all night long and like fall asleep in class?" Joe explains, "that's a little more complicated. Not sleeping is a form of stress to the body. Stress stresses your adrenal glands, and you eventually end up with an inverted circadian rhythm. And, it's all downhill from there. But, if you take the supplement, you should never get to that point." Jenny replies, "got it."

Jenny asks, "so, what's my second problem?" Joe replies, "the expression of your MAO-A and your MAO-B enzymes are a lot less than what we would call textbook normal. That causes you to have higher activity of dopamine, serotonin, norepinephrine, phenylethylamine, and a few other excitatory neurotransmitters. God gave you a lot of excitatory neurotransmitters, but not a whole lot of the inhibitory ones. That's probably why you're so smart." Jenny asks, "what do we do about that?" Joe replies, asking, "what? You don't want to be smart?" Jenny laughs, and replies, "no! The high activity of all those neurotransmitters." Joe replies, "nothing just yet. Let's see how the supplement does first." As an afterthought, Joe advises Jenny, "oh, and don't ever take an antidepressant. By day two or three, you'll land in the emergency room." Jenny replies, "got it."

Jenny asks Joe, "can you write down the name of the supplement for me?" Handing Jenny a piece of paper, Joe replies, "I already did. Start with one in the evening about an hour before you go to bed. I think you'll notice the difference right away. You can bump it up to two if you're still not sleeping well. And, if you feel like you're really sleepy the next day, you can always skip a day."

Since Jenny's problem is obviously one of a genetic nature, Joe asks Jenny, "do your parents sleep well?" Jenny replies, "they never did. Neither does my sister." Joe tells Jenny, "that's the first law of genetics at work." Jenny asks, "what's the first law of genetics?" Joe replies, "the first law of genetics is 'choose your parents carefully.'" Jenny laughs, and exclaims, "you can't choose your parents!" Joe laughs, and tells Jenny, "I know. That's the geneticist's joke."

Jenny asks Joe, "is there any chance that you can look at Amy's DNA sometime?" Joe replies, "sure. I'll be glad to. What's Amy's problem?" Jenny explains, "I don't know how much she'll tell you, but everyone in her family like has severe depression. Amy doesn't want to go down that path. She's been really happy ever since she met Ed, but something is going on with her. I've known her like since the fifth grade." Joe confidently reassures Jenny, "if there's something in her genes, I'll find it." Jenny tells Joe, "you're so sweet, Joe. I'm sure Amy will really appreciate it."

Jenny tells Joe, "thank you so much for finding this. I'm going to the vitamin store like right now and get my supplement." Jenny then asks, "when do you want your pizza?" Joe replies, "that's okay. You don't have to do anything for me. I'm just glad I could help." Jenny tells Joe, "no, Joe. You're coming with us to get pizza after the fellowship meeting tomorrow!" Joe replies, "okay. If you insist, I'll come." Jenny replies, "I insist. So, hold off on your dinner. The pizza will taste a lot better." Joe smiles, and replies, "believe me. I know that."

Joe and Jenny talk for a while longer, but then Joe has to head to class where he teaches freshman chemistry. Again thanking Joe for his hard work, Jenny heads back to her dorm to drop off her books. Jenny then cuts class, driving up to the vitamin store near the mall to get the supplement that Joe recommended.

Friday morning, the alarm suddenly goes off, playing the annoying tone that usually causes Jenny to abruptly spring out of bed. This morning, Amy stumbles out of bed first, and shuts off the alarm. Still a bit wobbly, Amy begins to get ready for class. Amy walks out of the bathroom and, gently shaking Jenny, announces, "hey! Wake up, girl! We're going to be late for class!" Jenny slowly opens her eyes and asks, "what? What day is it?" Amy replies, "it's Friday! Come on, sleepy head, get up!" Jenny replies, "oh, yeah. Friday. I guess we have to get to class." Amy tells Jenny, "yeah. You'd better hurry up and get ready." Jenny sits up, and comments, "so, this is sleep. Wow. I never knew."

Amy and Jenny leave for class, albeit a little late. Not seeing Ed and Pete waiting for them on the retaining wall at the corner, Jenny comments, "I guess Pete and Ed left without us." Amy replies, "they probably thought that we already left for class." Jenny tells Amy, "I'm going to text Pete." Jenny texts to Pete, "Where are you?" Pete texts back, "Almost to class. I thought you left." Jenny texts back, "Nope. Overslept. On my way."

On the way to class, seeing that Jenny slept through the entire night, Amy tells Jenny, "I wonder if Joe can find my problem." Jenny replies, "I talked to him about that yesterday. He said he'd be glad to take a look." Amy tells Jenny, "maybe I'll talk to him after the meeting tonight." Jenny informs Amy, "I invited Joe to get pizza with us tonight after the meeting. You can definitely talk to him about it then." Amy and Jenny walk into class fifteen minutes late, something Jenny has never done before in her life.

Friday evening, Ed, Amy, Pete, and Jenny arrive at the student center for the weekly Interdenominational Campus Fellowship meeting. Seeing Joe standing in the back of the room, Jenny rushes up, gives him a hug, and tells him, "I slept so wonderful last night! I like never knew what sleep was until last night!" Glad to hear the good news, Joe replies, "good! I told you we'd find it." Jenny again tells Joe, "thank you so much." Jenny then asks, "and, you're still coming with us for pizza later, right?" Joe replies, "I've been looking forward to it all day."

Walking in next is Rodney Steele, who appears to be a little on the angry side tonight. Some would argue that Rodney is always a little on the angry side. They would be correct. Making a beeline toward Donna and Theresa, Rodney gives them an update on Dana. Occasionally glancing over at Amy, Rodney appears to be very concerned about something.

Ed quietly announces, "here comes trouble," as he sees Rodney head straight for Amy. In an accusatory tone, Rodney bluntly tells Amy, "Dana isn't going to be with us tonight. And, it just happens to be all your fault." Waiting to see how Amy handles the situation, Ed gives Rodney a look that sends a clear message that he'd better not cross the line. Rodney's immediate problem is that he does not know where Ed's line is. Amy replies, "good evening to you, too. And, I'm sure whatever I did is my fault. So what?" Rodney quietly exclaims, "have you no compassion?" Amy replies, "I have absolutely no idea what you are talking about. So, either explain yourself, or go away."

Rodney waves over to Donna, who briskly walks over. Rodney instructs Donna, "please explain to Amy what happened to Dana." Donna looks at Amy, explaining, "Dana is in the hospital. She had a nervous breakdown." Amy asks, "so, what does that have to do with me?" Donna continues, "she said you mentally tortured her, and that you're out to get her. She says you're trying to destroy her. And, she's so heartbroken that you're going out with Ed, and she wanted to date Ed. And, that's only the beginning." Amy rolls her eyes, not even knowing how to begin to respond to Donna's rapid fire ridiculous accusations.

Jumping into the conversation, Ed tells Donna and Rodney, "I was never interested in Dana. She's not my type. So, you can put that one to rest." Rodney responds to Ed, by telling him, "that's not what Dana has been telling us." Ed replies, "shut up, Steele. I don't care what Dana has been telling you. If you hadn't noticed by now, Dana's life is one big mess. I wouldn't date Dana if she was the last girl on this campus." Rodney tells Ed, "now, that wasn't a very nice thing to say." Ed replies, "so what, Steele. Do something about it." Apparently,

Rodney has found one line he should not have crossed. To his credit, Rodney clearly knows when to back down when dealing with Ed.

Seeing that Ed has absolutely no fear in handling Rodney, Amy tells Rodney and Donna, "well, it sounds like Dana is right where she needs to be, in the hospital. I'll put her on my prayer list." Suddenly tongue tied, Rodney wants to respond, but can't. Amy turns toward Donna, and informs her, "and, by the way, I didn't torture Dana. In case you haven't noticed, Dana is the one who has been posting pictures of me and Jenny all over social media. And, you know what? I could have posted pics of Dana too, but, unlike you and Dana, I have a sense of decency." About to pop a cork, Donna angrily, but quietly, exclaims, "what are you talking about?"

Amy grabs her purse and gets out her cell phone. Showing Rodney and Donna the photo she took of Dana vaping, Amy tells them, "I could have posted this, but I didn't." Taking a look at the pic, Donna exclaims, "wow! That's Dana! I never knew!" Shutting down the conversation, Amy tells Donna, "there's probably a lot you don't know. So, kindly stop posting pics of me online, and please stop all your gossiping." Rodney, seeing the pic of Dana vaping, for once, has nothing to say. Ed, clearly seeing that Amy is very upset, tells Rodney, "why don't you start the meeting, Steele? And, I strongly suggest that you don't bother Amy about this again. Got it?"

Rodney pulls Ed aside, and asks him, "can you please call me Rodney?" Ed replies, "sure. No problem, Steele. You got it." Now sorely irritated, Rodney asks Ed, "for once, can't you be nice?" Ed points his finger in the air and, shaking his finger several times, whispers to Rodney, "you know, Steele, you're walking a very fine line. And, I know your little secret. So, you'd better watch out." Rodney, who dares not confront Ed further, angrily walks away.

Putting on a cheery face, Rodney opens the meeting, announcing, "okay, everyone. We're ready to get started." Those in the room get quiet, and Rodney opens the meeting, praying, "Heavenly Father, thank you for bringing us together again this week. We ask that, during our time of fellowship this evening, that Your Name be exalted above all. And, we ask that You be with those who, for one reason or another, could not be with us this evening." As Rodney continues to pray, starting more rumors, Donna whispers to Theresa that Amy has a pic of Dana vaping. Rodney concludes his prayer and, with everyone's eyes now open, Donna and Theresa stop whispering to each other.

Rodney announces, "as some of you may already know, Dana couldn't be with us tonight. So, if there is someone here who would like to lead the singing, please feel free to come up to the stage."

Hearing Rodney's cue, the praise band takes the stage. No one immediately volunteers, so Rodney decides that he will lead the worship in song tonight.

During the first number, Amy whispers to Ed, asking, "what's Rodney's problem, anyway?" Ed whispers back, "he's the modern day equivalent of a Pharisee. But, I think he'll leave us alone now." Amy whispers to Ed, "good. Because, he doesn't know anything about me." Ed whispers back, "exactly. All he's concerned with is the outside of the cup and appearances, just like the Pharisees were." Amy finally understands why Ed, Pete, and Jenny call Rodney a Pharisee.

After two more numbers, Rodney announces, "I believe, tonight, we're going to hear from Joe Sugarman, and what the Lord is doing in his life. For those of you who don't know, Joe has been with our group longer than anyone else. If I am not mistaken, this is Joe's eighth year with the Interdenominational Campus Fellowship. Please give a warm welcome to Joe Sugarman." The group claps as Joe makes his way to the stage from the back of the room.

Joe thanks his audience for the warm welcome, telling them, "thank you. Thank you." The clapping subsides, and Joe begins, "good evening all of my friends. As Rodney mentioned, this is my eighth year at the University. With any luck, I'll be getting out this Spring along with some of you. Did you ever notice that no one ever says, 'I graduate in the Spring'? Everyone always says, 'I get out in the Spring', as if going to college is some sort of prison sentence." The group laughs, pleased to hear Joe's cheerful and relaxed demeanor.

Joe asks the group, "how many of you have heard of the *Eddie, The Mechanic* book series?" A few people raise their hands and, showing his excitement, Joe continues, "I started reading the series at the same time I started on my Ph.D. In the series, the main character is a guy named Eddie Bogenskaya. Eddie is the all-American guy. In high school, Eddie ran track, and was the fastest guy around. When Eddie was a freshman, he was one of the strongest guys in the high school. Eddie was even witty in the classroom. And, Eddie even got the girl that everyone else wanted. Eddie never lost! Even when it looked like Eddie was going to lose, Eddie managed to find a way to win! As if that's not enough, Eddie has several friends that are just as much of a winner as he is."

Joe then reminisces, "when I was reading the second book in the series, *Eddie, The Freshman Year*, I thought back to when I was in my high school years. When I was in high school, I would have liked to have been Eddie Bogenskaya. Who wouldn't? Eddie had everything going for him. But, back in my high school days, I was no Eddie

Bogenskaya." Many students are wondering what a fictional book series has to do with what the Lord is doing in Joe's life. Rodney, for one, sitting with his arms crossed, was expecting to hear something more of a spiritual nature.

Joe then quiets down a bit, and tells the group, "but, I had one problem. When I was in high school, I was at least seventy-five pounds overweight. I was the guy who was always last to be picked for a team in gym class. By the time I started my Ph.D. program here at the University, I was more than one hundred pounds overweight. When I weighed three hundred pounds, everyone was telling me that I should lose weight, as if I didn't already know that. When you weigh three hundred pounds, it's really hard to find clothes that fit. When you weigh three hundred pounds, your car seat wears out in twenty thousand miles. When you weigh three hundred pounds, it's kind of hard to get a date with a girl. Maybe you get the picture."

Revealing part of the storyline of *Eddie, The Freshman Year*, Joe explains, "when I was reading the second book in the series, I learned that Eddie discovers that he has every genetic quality associated with being a sprinter. But, Eddie also finds out that he has a serious genetic issue, called methylenetetrahydrofolate reductase deficiency, or MTHFR for short. Because of Eddie's MTHFR genetic issue, Eddie must take a special form of folic acid, called methylfolate, which is in the B vitamin group. Now, I won't tell you how Eddie found out that he had this problem. I don't want to spoil the story for you."

Joe then explains to the group, "so, when I finished reading the second book in the series, I decided to have my own genes sequenced. I spent countless hours going over my own genetics, endlessly searching for some reason that I could not lose weight no matter how hard I tried. After about a week, I discovered that I was born with my own genetic deficiency. What I discovered is that I have something called a renal carnitine transport defect."

Explaining further, Joe continues, "now, what exactly is carnitine? Carnitine is something the body produces that allows fatty acids to enter the mitochondria where they can be used to make energy. Without carnitine, fat cannot enter the mitochondria, and therefore cannot be used for energy. My body makes enough carnitine, but the vast majority of it goes out in my urine. Unlike all of you, my kidneys do not retain carnitine. So, fatty acids build up in the cells, which can eventually damage the liver, heart, and muscles. So, my body was able to store fat, but unable to burn fat for energy. No wonder I couldn't lose weight! There was no way for me to metabolize any of the fat that I was eating."

Explaining his solution to the problem he discovered, Joe continues, "to solve this problem, I started taking several grams of carnitine a day, started exercising, and limited the fat in my diet. But, I still like a slice or two of pizza occasionally. I'm from New York. What can I say? When I first saw the weight coming off, I was skeptical. But, after a few weeks, I dropped ten pounds and I was very encouraged. And, here I am, two years later, down ninety pounds and twenty more to go."

Joe then addresses specific members of the fellowship group, telling them, "now, I'm sure that a number of you will quote to me certain verses in the Bible that say the sins of one generation will be passed down to the third and fourth generations. I know those verses very well. If you want to look those verses up, let me help you. They are Exodus, chapter 20, verses 5 and 6; Exodus, chapter 34, verse 7; Deuteronomy, chapter 5, verse 9; and perhaps a few more. Some of you may also tell me that I should live with the genetic problem that I inherited. I'm sure the same people who tell me that I should live with my genetic issue are the same people who would accuse me of the sin of gluttony." Many members of the fellowship, knowing exactly to whom Joe is referring, laugh at Joe's comment. Ed whispers to Amy, "Joe is talking about Rodney and the rest of the Pharisees." Amy laughs, and replies, "believe it or not, I can see that now."

Addressing the larger audience, Joe continues, "but, let us all be reminded of First Corinthians, chapter 6, verse 19, where it states, 'Or do you not know that your body is a temple of the Holy Spirit who is in you, whom you have from God, and that you are not your own?' If the body is a temple of the Holy Spirit, should we not be doing everything we can to treat our bodies in the same manner as the Jewish people treated The Temple in Jerusalem during Old Testament times? Of course we should!"

Joe pauses for a moment, then explains to his audience, "so, I asked myself, 'how many other people out there have problems of a genetic nature?' We must remember that God has complete control over our genetic makeup. If God allowed me to have a weight problem and gave me the ability to find my specific solution, shouldn't I be doing the same for others? As far as where I am today, I believe the Lord is leading me in that direction."

Joe lowers his voice a bit, and tells his audience, "I've also learned the secret to keeping the weight off. This is the biggest kept secret in the world. Do you guys want to hear it?" A good number of people reply, "yes." Joe looks around the room as if he is making sure it is safe to divulge the world's biggest secret. Ed looks at Pete, already knowing the secret that Joe is about to divulge to the group, for it was Ed who told Joe the secret.

Joe then announces, "many of you don't need to hear this secret right now but, in about ten or twenty years, it might be a different story. The secret to keeping weight off is never, under any circumstances, buy any clothes larger than the size you want to be. The only exception is when a woman gets pregnant. If you have a 32-inch waist, once you buy size 34 jeans, in no time you'll be up to a size 36. Then, it's on to size 38. It will never end! And, if you are trying to lose weight, once you get down to the size you want to be, throw away all your clothes larger than that size. Do not keep them! If you keep them, you are not committed to keeping the weight off!" While the secret Joe divulged is quite simple, it, in fact, works.

Joe then concludes, "let me leave you with this. When I weighed three hundred pounds, I had a few good friends here in this fellowship. You know who you are. I just want to take this time to thank my few true friends who didn't judge me when I weighed three hundred pounds. And, I would also like to thank the two guys who help me in the gym, and push me far beyond what I would normally do myself. Thank you for listening to me this evening. I hope I said something to encourage someone here tonight."

Stepping down from the stage, Joe waves to the crowd, receiving a standing ovation from the group. Arriving at the back of the room, Joe receives a high-five from Ed and Pete, for they are the two guys who have been coaching Joe in the gym for the last two years.

Rodney takes the stage, and announces, "thank you, Joe," followed by even more applause for Joe. Rodney, a bit jealous of Joe, secretly wishes the applause were for him. Once the applause subsides, Rodney announces, "we will now continue to worship the Lord in song." The band plays, and Rodney leads the group in their final number of the evening as the offering plate is passed around. Rodney then closes the meeting with prayer, and the group breaks up for the evening.

After the meeting, Jenny asks Joe, "you're still coming with us to get pizza, aren't you?" Joe smiles, and replies, "I wouldn't miss it for the world." Joe then asks Jenny, "do you mind if Brittany comes?" Jenny replies, "of course not! We'd love to have her join us." A small group gathers around Joe, and a few others are invited to get pizza with the group. As expected, Donna and Theresa eavesdrop on those who typically hang out in the back of the room.

On the way to the pizzeria, Amy asks Joe, "is there any chance that I can get you to look at my DNA sometime?" Joe replies, "sure. I can do that." Joe then asks Amy, "what's the problem?" Telling part of her story, Amy replies, "a lot of people in my family suffer from depression. And, I don't want to take antidepressants. They just made my sister worse, and they did absolutely nothing for my father." Joe asks, "how about your mother? Is she depressed?" Amy replies, "I'm not exactly sure if she was or not." Joe reassures Amy, "if the problem is in your genes, it should be easy enough to find." Seeing how easily Joe found Jenny's problem, Amy feels very encouraged.

Joe then asks Amy, "has your DNA ever been sequenced?" Amy replies, "yeah. I did one of those genetic tests a year ago." Joe instructs Amy, "email your raw genetic file to me, and I'll get working on it sometime this weekend." As they approach the pizzeria, Amy emails her genetic file to Joe. Amy sincerely hopes that Joe can find her problem just as easily as he found Jenny's problem.

At the pizzeria, the group finds a large table, then a few guys go up and place an order for drinks and a few large pizzas. Tonight, Jenny is forgoing the wine, and having a glass of water instead. And, after Joe found out why Jenny can't sleep, Jenny is happy to buy Joe's dinner tonight. Truth is, Joe enjoys being out with the group far more than the pizza.

While they are waiting for dinner to be ready, Amy checks her phone, and mentions to Ed, "the diving pictures I posted of us have gone viral." Showing her excitement, Amy tells Ed, "I got a message from someone in the yearbook! They want me to give them permission to use the pictures of us diving in the yearbook." Ed replies, "tell them yes." Amy smiles, and replies to the message, giving the yearbook staff permission to publish her photos.

Scrolling through her messages, Amy tells Ed, "I got another message. They want me to work with the yearbook as a photographer." Ed asks, "are you going to do it?" Amy thinks for a second, and replies, "I think not. I like to do photography for fun. Once it becomes work, that takes all the fun out of it." Ed tells Amy, "kind of like me and diving." Amy replies, "yeah, exactly."

Jenny jokingly asks Pete, "didn't you invite Dana to join us? I thought she'd be really happy that I'm like not having a glass of wine tonight." With his own sense of humor, Pete replies, "you know, I forgot. Totally my fault. Shame on me." Amy asks, "would they even let her out of the hospital to get pizza?" Jenny replies, "not the kind of hospital that she's probably in, girl. They probably have her like in a straight jacket or something and pumped full of meds."

Not five more seconds go by, and Jenny announces, "dang. Don't look now, but Donna, Theresa, the Pharisees, and the praise band just walked in." Pete tells Jenny, "maybe they'll post a picture of you drinking water." Jenny laughs, and replies, "yeah. I know, right? And then, they'll accuse me of turning my water into wine!" Those at Jenny's table laugh hysterically, and are quite sure that Rodney overheard Jenny's joke.

The waiter brings several pizzas to the table, and the group digs in. Joe again tells Jenny, "thank you so much for inviting us. I haven't had a good slice of pizza in two weeks." Jenny replies, "no problem, Joe. We're glad to have you join us." Joe reveals, "I don't really go out to eat a lot. I try to keep my diet very low in fat. That's hard to do when you eat at restaurants. But, when I do go out, nothing is better than a good slice of pizza." Jenny suggests to Joe and the others around the table, "maybe we should make getting pizza after our fellowship meeting a weekly thing." Everyone at the table agrees that going out for pizza on Friday nights would be a good thing to do.

Interrupting the conversation, Rodney walks over, and asks Ed, "may I please have a word with you?" Ed replies, "sure, Steele. Have a seat." Rodney tells Ed, "I meant in private." Ed bluntly tells Rodney, "I'm in the middle of dinner right now, junior. Whatever it is, it can wait." Rodney insists, "this is extremely important!" Ed calmly replies, "it's not more important than my dinner. So, take a hike, Steele. Whatever it is, it can wait." Realizing he is getting absolutely nowhere with Ed, Rodney walks back to his group, taking a seat at the head of the table.

Amy asks Ed, "what's up with Rodney?" Ed replies, "he was about to dump a whole bunch of emotional vomit all over my dinner, so I told him to take a hike." Amy laughs, and tells Ed, "emotional vomit. That's really funny!" Ed whispers to Amy, "and, see? He really is a Pharisee. He likes sitting at the head of the table." Back at his own table, Rodney takes notice of Ed and Amy laughing and, as usual, will come to the wrong conclusion. Amy tells Ed, "Rodney sounded like he was really ticked off at something."

Overhearing Ed and Amy's conversation, Joe whispers to them, "Rodney is always angry about something. He has a deeply rooted spiritual problem. He's always trying to fix his spiritual problems using Earthly measures. You can't do that. Spiritual problems must be dealt with on the spiritual level." Ed whispers back, "that's a good point. I can see that." Joe advises Ed and Amy, "don't let him bother you."

Joe's comments to Ed and Amy regarding Rodney does not come without a history behind it. When Rodney was a freshman, Joe began working on his master's degree in chemistry. At that time, Joe taught two classes of freshman chemistry lab. Joe just happened to be Rodney's instructor for that class. What Joe has never mentioned to anyone is that, back then, Rodney quite often referred to Joe as "fat Albert". Rodney's secret was out when Joe caught Rodney yelling across the lab to his friend, "hey! Where's fat Albert today?" As it turns out, Joe just happened to walk into the lab through the back door three seconds earlier and heard Rodney's comment. Later that year, during Spring semester when Rodney joined the Interdenominational Campus Fellowship, Rodney was quite embarrassed when he saw Joe at the meeting. Rodney was, of course, hoping that Joe did not recognize him. Since then, Rodney has pretended to show Joe a lot of respect.

After dinner, the group heads back to campus. On the way, Amy tells Joe, "thank you again for looking at my DNA. I can't wait to see if you find something." Joe replies, "no problem. I'll let you know as soon as I find anything."

Pete asks Joe, "are you going to join me and Ed at the gym tomorrow morning?" Joe replies, "I'll definitely be there." Jenny replies, "so will I. That is, if I like wake up on time." Amy assures Jenny, "don't worry, girl. I'll get you out of bed in time." Until Joe found Jenny's genetic problem, oversleeping was something that was completely foreign to Jenny.

Later that night, when Ed walks Amy back to her dorm, Ed tells Amy, "Rodney has a secret." Amy asks Ed, "oh really? What's Rodney's secret?" Ed replies, "I don't exactly know. But, I know he has one." Amy asks, "how can you know that?" Ed explains, "during the meeting tonight, Rodney pulled me aside, and asked me if I can please call him Rodney. I told him, 'no problem, Steele. You got it.' He got ticked off at me, so I told him, 'Steele, you're walking a fine line. And, I know your little secret. So, you'd better watch out.' I was just messing with him. That's probably what he wanted to talk about back at the restaurant." Amy exclaims, "wow! You're right! He has to have a secret! Or else, how would he be so worried about it?" Ed replies, "exactly. And, not to mention, he fell for the oldest trick in the book."

Week Five

Jenny's Story

Monday morning, Jenny does a little better waking up for class. Ready for class before Jenny, Amy asks Jenny, "did you sleep okay last night?" Jenny replies, "I slept like a baby. And, I don't feel like taking a nap in the afternoon anymore." Amy asks, "how do people say, 'I slept like a baby'? Babies don't sleep well. They're up every two or three hours, pooping, peeing, or hungry." Jenny laughs, and replies, "you're right! I never thought of it that way before!" Checking that she has everything one last time before they head to class, Amy tells Jenny, "I really hope Joe can find my problem." As they head out the door, Jenny reassures Amy, "I'm sure he will."

Amy and Jenny meet Ed and Pete, and walk to class. On the way, Jenny asks, "can we like stop by the cafeteria on the way? I want to pick up a bar." Pete replies, "sure. I might pick one up myself." Arriving at the cafeteria, Jenny and the others in her group all grab a bar. As they are walking out, as fate would have it, the group runs into Rodney Steele.

Rodney runs up to Ed, and asks, "do you have a minute?" Stepping up his walking pace, Ed succinctly replies, "no. We're really late for class, junior." Following Ed and his group, Rodney hastily asks Ed, "can I call you later?" Leaving Rodney with an irritating and ambiguous answer, Ed replies, "I don't know, Steele. Can you?" Seeing that Ed has absolutely no intention of speaking with him at the moment, Rodney gives up and heads back to the cafeteria.

Once they leave the cafeteria, Amy tells Ed, "that was an interesting encounter. Rodney must have a really big secret." Ed replies, "yeah, seriously." Jenny asks Amy and Ed, "what's all this about a secret?" Ed explains, "Friday night, at our fellowship meeting, when Rodney was badgering us, I told him, 'I know your secret'. I was just messing with him. But, he's been in a major league panic ever since." Knowing Rodney for two years, Jenny confidently replies, "yeah. He's got a secret, all right. There's something just not right about that guy." Pete comments, "I can see that. He looked seriously worried back there." Ed replies, "I know. I'll just keep messing with him. I'll see how much he can take." Pete replies, "apparently, he can't take very much."

The friction between Ed and Rodney goes all the way back to when Ed was a freshman. Back then, Ed, a six-foot, three-inch athlete in excellent physical condition, was indirectly confronted by Rodney, who is five feet, nine inches tall, and weighed 120 pounds soaking wet. During the first sermonette that he preached to the fellowship group, Rodney addressed the sin of gluttony. During his talk, Rodney not only spoke about excessive consumption of food, but the various ways in which gluttony can be manifested. Rodney referenced Ed, indirectly referring to him as "someone in this room". To the surprise of many in the group, Rodney used Ed as an example of someone who consumes way too much food and exercises far beyond what the Lord had intended. Everyone in the fellowship knew exactly to whom Rodney was referring.

But, the confrontation between Ed and Rodney didn't exactly stop there. That evening, after the meeting, Rodney got sorely ticked off when Ed confronted him. Ed told Rodney, "nice sermon, Steele. I'm going to ignore the whole thing." Rodney brashly replied, "people like you just don't get it." The short conversation almost ended when Ed told Rodney, "that's okay, Steele. I forgive you." In a tizzy, Rodney replied, "I'm not the one who needs forgiveness here!" Ed laughed, and told Rodney, "keep telling yourself that, Steele. See where that gets you." Rodney replied, "can you please call me Rodney?" Ed replied, "sure. No problem, Steele. You got it." Since that time, Rodney has tried to be a thorn in Ed's side, albeit very unsuccessfully.

Ed, Amy, Pete, and Jenny take a seat at the back of the classroom, not quite making it to class on time. The professor, Dr. Lawrence, tells the group of four latecomers, "we're all honored that you can join us today." Amy cordially replies, "thank you. We're really glad to be here." Dr. Lawrence smiles, and hands their graded tests back to them, and whispers, "good job, guys."

Pete, who was worried about whether he studied enough for the test, looks at his grade, which is a 97 out of a possible 100. Ed, Amy, and Jenny likewise received excellent grades in the mid to high A range. Ed tells Pete, "see, bro? You need to work out the day before a test. Forget the last minute cramming." Amy and Jenny, glad that Ed shared his copies of old tests with them, are also very happy with their grades.

Dr. Lawrence then addresses the class, announcing, "up on the screen you can see the grade distribution for this test. As you can see, the average grade is a 72, and the mean is 64. Please take note of where your grade lands with respect to the standard deviation. If your grade lies in or below the lower second standard deviation, you may want to consider dropping this class. Since the average grade is in the lower C range, I'm going to hold off applying any curve until the next test." Not immediately applying a curve is Dr. Lawrence's way of making her students work harder.

As Dr. Lawrence begins her lecture, Jenny, for the first time in her life, does not feel worried or any anxiety about schoolwork. Totally convinced that Joe has discovered her problem and provided a meaningful solution, Jenny sits back and relaxes, actually making sense out of what Dr. Lawrence is teaching today.

Later that week, on Wednesday between classes, Amy's path crosses Joe's path. Amy and Joe talk for a while, then Amy gets around to asking Joe, "have you found my problem yet?" Joe's countenance suddenly drops as he tells Amy, "no. Not yet. I haven't found anything that explains what your feeling. I've checked everything that's commonly a problem with depression but, honestly Amy, this is a really tough one."

Suddenly feeling broken inside, Amy tells Joe, "at least you tried. I really appreciate it a whole lot, but I don't want you to spend all your time on me. If you can't find it, that's okay." Joe tells Amy, "I'm not giving up that easily. I'll text you immediately as soon as I know anything." Amy heads to class, and Joe heads home for the day, very motivated to discover whether Amy has a genetic issue. Amy, however, is not very hopeful that Joe will find her problem if, in fact, there even is one.

The week goes by rather quickly for everyone, except for Amy. Amy was hoping to hear something from Joe, but no word comes. Amy recalls that Joe said he'll text her immediately as soon as he knows anything. Not wanting to bother Joe any more about her DNA, Amy refrains from bothering him further. As Friday approaches, Amy has lost all hope that Joe will find anything.

Friday evening comes, and Jenny heads back to her dorm to get ready for the weekly Interdenominational Campus Fellowship meeting.

Walking into her dorm room, Jenny finds Amy sitting on her bed. Jenny asks Amy, "are you ready to go?" Amy replies, "I don't really want to go tonight." Jenny asks, "why not, girl? What's up?" Amy replies, "I just don't want to go. You guys just go without me." Perceiving that Amy is upset about something, Jenny asks, "are you okay?" In an unconvincing tone, Amy replies, "yeah. I'm fine."

Jenny bluntly asks, "okay, girl. Out with it. What's wrong?" Amy starts to cry, confessing, "there's something wrong with me. What am I doing here? I don't even belong here. What am I doing here? How did I even get here?" Giving Amy a hug, Jenny whispers to her, "it's going to be okay, girl. Tell me. What's up? What's going on?" Amy cries out, "Joe can't find out what's wrong with me. I don't want to go tonight. And, I don't want those idiots taking pictures of me anymore! Please, just go without me. I'll be okay."

Jenny tells Amy, "Ed is going to be downstairs any moment now with Pete. What am I going to tell him?" Still crying, Amy replies, "tell him I'm not coming tonight. There's something wrong with me. I don't belong here."

Glancing down at her phone, Amy suddenly springs up, rushes out the door, and runs down the hall. Jenny runs after her, but Amy is long gone. Jenny, having no idea why Amy ran out, had no idea that Amy could move that fast.

Jenny frantically texts to Ed, "Amy just ran out. Something's wrong." Ed texts back, "Where did she go?" Jenny replies, "I don't know. She didn't say." Jenny, knowing that she is giving the talk to the fellowship group tonight, rushes to get ready. Ed texts to Amy, "Where are you?" Ed receives no answer from Amy, and is now very concerned.

Arriving at the student center, Amy runs up to the third floor where Joe is waiting for her. All out of breath, Amy finds Joe sitting in a chair outside the meeting room. Amy runs up to Joe, frantically asking, "what's wrong with me? What did you find out?" Joe asks Amy, "did you run here?" Amy replies, "yeah. I guess. What's wrong with me? I want to know. Where's Ed?" Seeing that Amy is upset, Joe tells Amy, "okay. You need to calm down a little. Then, we can go over it." Joe can clearly see that Amy is very upset about something.

While Amy is attempting to calm down, Ed is frantically searching for her around the dorms. Taking two different paths, Pete and Jenny head to the meeting, looking for Amy on the way. All agree to text the others as soon as they find Amy.

Pete and Jenny arrive at the student center nearly simultaneously. After checking the lower two floors, Pete and Jenny head up to the third floor, where they see Amy sitting with Joe, as Joe is trying to calm Amy down. Pete texts to Ed, "Found her. Third floor, student center." Ed texts back, "On my way."

Jenny runs up to Amy, and asks, "what's up, girl? Are you okay?" Through her tears, Amy replies, "Joe found out what's wrong with me." Jenny asks, "what's wrong? What is it?" Amy replies, "I don't know." Joe informs Jenny, "I haven't explained it to her yet." Amy again asks, "where's Ed?" Pete replies, "he's on his way." Jenny gives Amy a hug, and tells her, "you got to calm down, girl." Amy replies, "yeah. Calm down. That's a good idea."

When Ed arrives, Amy is finally calmed down. Ed runs up, giving Amy a big hug. Amy whispers to Ed, "I'm sorry. I'm so sorry. Joe texted me and said he found my problem. So, I just ran here as fast as I could. I just had to know." Ed replies, "I'm so glad you're okay. We were all very worried about you."

Now calmed down, Amy asks Joe, "okay, so what's wrong with me? What did you find out?" Joe asks, "are you up to hearing it now? Or, do you want to wait until after the meeting?" Amy tells Ed, Jenny, and Pete, "you guys can go to the meeting. I want to hear this now." Ed tells Amy, "if you want, I'll listen with you." Amy replies, "okay." Pete and Jenny head to the meeting only because Jenny is giving tonight's talk.

Now relatively calmed down, Amy asks Joe, "so, what did you find out?" Joe explains, "it took me a really long time to find this one. I went down a rabbit hole all the way to China and back to find it. You have something called sepiapterin reductase deficiency. It's very rare."

Somewhat overwhelmed, Amy asks, "so, what does this mean? What do I do about it?" Joe explains, "sepiapterin reductase catalyzes the production of something called tetrahydrobiopterin, or BH4 for short. Tetrahydrobiopterin is needed for your body to create dopamine and serotonin." Joe then hands Amy a drawing, and tells her, "here, I drew it out for you."

After reexplaining everything to Amy using the diagram, Joe continues, "with the genetic anomaly that you inherited, you have very low levels of dopamine, and virtually no serotonin. Dopamine and serotonin are your 'feel good' neurotransmitters, so it's no secret why people in your family are depressed." Wanting to be sure, Amy asks, "so, this is how almost everyone in my family was so depressed?" Joe replies, "it is. For sure, it is. Nothing else in your genetic profile would even come close to explaining it otherwise."

Amy asks, "can it be fixed?" Joe explains, "yes. And it's actually quite simple. All you have to do is take 5-hydroxytryptophan and an herb called Mucuna pruriens. But, you have to be careful. You've never had much dopamine and serotonin in your brain before. You might end up getting too happy." Amy asks, "so, where do I get this stuff?" Joe replies, "the vitamin store near the mall carries it. But, get the Mucuna pruriens in liquid form to begin with, so you can find your right dose. Just mix it in with tea or something." Joe hands Amy a piece of paper, and tells her, "here, I wrote it down for you. Take this down to the vitamin store, and they'll get it for you."

Amy breathes a sigh of relief, saying, "so, there really is something wrong with me. I knew it! I'm not like everyone else." Joe reassures Amy, "God allowed you to be this way for a reason. You may not find out the reason for many years, like I did." Amy asks Joe, "so, I can be normal, like everyone else?" Joe pauses for a moment, carefully thinking how to word his answer. Joe then replies, "you can be the best Amy Amherst that God designed. But, trust me. You don't want to be like everyone else. Being normal does not necessarily equate to joy or happiness." Amy replies, "I'll settle for that."

Joe tells Amy, "I'm going to guess that, since you have a really dark tan, you lie out in the sun a lot." Amy replies, "every chance I get." Joe explains, "vitamin D increases the production of dopamine, and sunlight releases serotonin. So, what little serotonin and dopamine your body does make is enhanced slightly by sunlight. And, smoking releases dopamine, so it wouldn't surprise me if you quit after taking the 5-hydroxytryptophan and Mucuna pruriens." Amy confesses, "the only time I even feel halfway good is when I'm out in the sun. I really hate Winter." Joe tells Amy, "if I'm correct, this will be your best Winter ever."

Joe then reveals to Amy, "in your favor, I also found that the expression of your MAO-A and MAO-B enzymes are a lot less than normal. That will cause you to have slightly higher activity of dopamine and serotonin than you would otherwise have. God spared you from having a more severe form of sepiapterin reductase deficiency." Amy asks, "so, there are people out there with this that are a lot worse than me?" Joe confidently replies, "yes. But, remember, what you have is very, very rare."

Joe further explains, "let me tell you how I thought to look for the problem with tetrahydrobiopterin. You told me that antidepressants didn't work for your father or your sister. The reason antidepressants didn't work for them is because they likely have very low levels of serotonin and dopamine as well. Most of the common antidepressants on the market are termed reuptake inhibitors or monoamine oxidase inhibitors. The problem is that, if there are no neurotransmitters to reuptake, the medication can't possibly do its job. And, you can inhibit the monoamine oxidase enzyme all you want until Jesus returns but, if there are no neurotransmitters in the junction, the monoamine oxidase inhibitor is not going to do a thing. Are you following me?" Amy replies, "yeah." Joe then informs Amy, "if you took antidepressants, they aren't going to work for you either. That, I can absolutely guarantee."

Hearing the band starting to play their first number, Amy says to Joe and Ed, "well, we'd better get inside. It sounds like they're starting. I don't want you guys to miss the meeting." Ed asks Amy, "are you sure you want to go tonight?" Amy replies, "yeah. Jenny's speaking. I don't want to miss it. And, I'm going to stand in the back of the room and watch what normal is like."

Amy then asks Ed, "can you take me to the vitamin store tomorrow? Please?" Ed, who takes a lot of vitamins himself, replies, "sure. They open at ten o'clock. We can go right after we get out of the gym." Amy replies, "thank you. Then, tomorrow I'll be on my way to being normal." Amy suddenly feels a lot better knowing that 'normal' is on the horizon.

As they are walking into the meeting, Joe tells Amy, "we can talk about this more later. There's a few other things you should know about." Amy gives Joe a hug, and tells him, "thank you so much, Joe. I don't know how to thank you for all that you do." Joe replies, "you don't have to do anything for me. But, if you really want to do something, a slice of pizza would be at the top of my list." Amy tells Joe, "you got it."

Amy, Ed, and Joe walk into the meeting, quickly running into Rodney and Jenny who seem to be in the middle of a slightly heated discussion. Rodney continues to insist, "I want to know what you're going to be talking about before you get up on stage tonight." Jenny keeps telling Rodney, "it's a surprise. And, I'm not going to tell you." Seeing Jenny being confronted by Rodney, Amy walks over, takes Jenny by the arm, and walks her out of the room away from the confrontation, telling her, "I got some news, girl. I got to tell you." Rodney, flat out of luck in finding out what Jenny will speak about tonight, walks up to the front of the room and joins in with the singing.

Outside the meeting room in the public area, Amy tells Jenny, "I'm so sorry about before. Joe found out what's wrong with me, so I ran here as fast as I could." Jenny exclaims, "that's great! I am so happy for you! What did he find out?" Amy tells Jenny, "I'll tell you about it later. But, what's up with Rodney?" Jenny explains, "he like wants to know what I'm going to talk about tonight. And, I don't want to tell him. He like keeps insisting that I let him know." Amy tells Jenny, "he's afraid that you're going to spill his little secret." Jenny exclaims, "you're right, girl! I never thought about that!" Hearing the music stop, Jenny tells Amy, "I got to go inside. I'm on pronto."

Amy and Jenny walk back into the room, hearing Rodney announcing, "it looks like our speaker for this evening, Jenny, has left the meeting. So, I guess I'll be giving the talk today." From the back of the room, Jenny yells out, "I'm here!" Jenny briskly walks up to the front of the room as her audience claps. Jenny announces, "thank you, Rodney. You can have a seat now." The audience laughs at Jenny's candid remark, forcing Rodney to take a seat in his special chair against the side wall.

Jenny begins her talk by holding up a 24 by 36-inch framed poster of the infamous picture of her drinking a glass of wine that was taken by Dana at the beginning of the semester. Jenny holds the poster high in the air so everyone can see, and tells the group, "this is a picture of me, drinking a glass of wine. I'm sure many of you recognize this picture. It's been circulated around social media for quite some time now." Jenny places the poster on a chair where everyone can clearly see it during her talk.

Adding a notable amount of sarcasm, Jenny continues, "some of you were very considerate and compassionate by posting this picture of me all over social media. I really can't thank you enough." Sitting on the side of the room, Rodney looks very worried, wondering where Jenny is going with her talk. Dana, sitting near the front of the room, looks even more worried than Rodney, for it was Dana who took the picture and is responsible for circulating it on social media.

Jenny confesses to the group, "I have a glass of wine once or twice a week. So what? If I don't have my glass of wine or two each week, I won't sleep well at night. After three weeks without a glass of wine, I find myself lying awake all night long, and falling asleep in class. The best I could ever hope for is three hours of continuous sleep in a day. That doesn't sound too good, does it? Well, trust me. It's not. When I don't sleep, my grades all go down the toilet. How can that be good?"

Abruptly changing the subject, Amy tells the group, "when I was a senior in high school, one night in particular really stands out to me. I remember that night as if it were yesterday. The police came to our door, and notified my sister, Amanda, and I that our mom and dad died in a terrible automobile accident. Their car ran off the road, and hit a tree. It happened over the Christmas holiday when Amanda was home from college. I remember crying all night long. They think my father fell asleep at the wheel. Now, before some of you start any rumors, there was no alcohol in his bloodstream. And, they determined that it wasn't a heart attack or anything like that. And, guess what? Just like me, my father never slept well. Who knows? If my father had a glass of wine once or twice a week, maybe he would still be alive today." Everyone in the room is now silent, interested in hearing the rest of Jenny's story.

Jenny continues, "my sister, Amanda, is three years older than me. She went back to college that January. Where was I going to go? My only sister is going back to college, and both of my parents died. My aunt and uncle live like all the way on the other side of the country. They said they had no room for me in their eight-thousand square-foot, six-bedroom house. My other uncle was in the military, and still is. So, that obviously wasn't on my list of options. And, all my grandparents aren't in very good health. They can barely take care of themselves, so how were they going to take care of me?"

Explaining where she landed, Jenny continues, "lucky for me, my friend's father offered to let me stay with them. That friend is Amy Amherst, who is sitting in the back of the room today. Some of you already met Amy. Amy is a really nice person. A few of you were even so kind as to post pictures online of Amy smoking, just like you posted pictures of me drinking wine." Jenny then sarcastically mentions, "we really can't tell you how much we appreciate it." Dana, quite embarrassed, holds her head in her hands and stares at the floor.

Jenny then looks at Rodney and, recalling that Ed suspects that Rodney has a secret, tells the group, "some people have secrets. At least I didn't keep the fact that I have a glass of wine once or twice a week a secret." Hearing Jenny's reference, Rodney rests his arms on his legs, and stares at the floor for a minute or so as the sweat begins to pour from his face. If Rodney had his way, he'd give Jenny the hook right now. But, Rodney knows that would never fly. Ed and Pete would make sure of it.

Telling the group about her sister, Jenny explains, "just like me, my sister, Amanda, doesn't sleep well. I called Amanda last week. When we were talking, she told me she hasn't slept in three days, and that she can barely function at her job. Amanda told me that, for the last few weeks, she has been barely hanging on. But, I had some good news for Amanda." Looking straight on at Dana, Jenny asks, "can any of you guess what the good news was that I had for Amanda?" During the uncomfortable pause in Jenny's story, Dana, for some reason, appears to be very frightened. Jenny pauses, and tells the group, "I can tell you this. I didn't tell Amanda to have a glass of wine. But, before I tell you the good news that I had for Amanda, let me first explain something."

Before revealing the good news that Jenny gave to Amanda, Jenny explains, "I did one of those genetic tests over the Summer. My friend, Joe Sugarman, who is sitting in the back of the room next to Amy, was kind enough to look over my genes for me to see if he can find the reason that I can't sleep. And, guess what? Joe found the reason why I can't sleep."

Pulling a piece of paper out of her pocket as a reference, Jenny explains, "Joe found out that I have a genetic defect in my glutamate decarboxylase enzyme. The glutamate decarboxylase enzyme converts glutamate to gamma aminobutyric acid, or GABA for short. So, I have way too much glutamate and I don't have very much GABA. Too much glutamate is excitatory, and makes it really hard to sleep. GABA is inhibitory, and helps you relax and sleep." Jenny looks at Joe in the back of the room, and tells Joe, "I hope I pronounced all of that correctly, Joe." Joe tells Jenny, "you did fine! I'll make a biochemist out of you yet!"

Jenny continues, "and, that's why I can't sleep well. So, what does having an occasional glass of wine have to do with this?" Staring at Rodney, Jenny continues, "alcohol, which is a chemical that some of you think is going to send me to Hell on the fast track, mimics the action of GABA in the brain. So, that's why having a glass of wine once or twice a week helped me to sleep."

Explaining Joe's solution to her problem, Jenny holds up a bottle of pills containing the supplement that Joe recommended, and tells the group, "based on my genes, Joe recommended that I try this supplement. After taking the supplement, for the first time that I could ever remember, I slept through the entire night. I woke up the next morning and told my roommate, Amy, something like, 'so, this is sleep. I never knew.' I slept so well, that I was even late for class that day. So, I told my sister, Amanda, about the supplement, and texted a picture of the bottle to her. Amanda went to a vitamin store where she lives and bought a bottle. I talked to Amanda again this morning. She told me that she hasn't ever slept this well. I've never heard her so happy. In fact, she was so happy, she was crying."

Jenny then asks, "so, what does all this have to do with the Bible, God, or anything else? Well, when I was born, there was no warranty on my body. Pretty much, genetically, I was stuck with what I got. God knows exactly what I was facing for the last twenty or so years. I am just so grateful that God sent Joe into my life to find out why I couldn't sleep."

While Jenny is speaking, Dana whispers to Donna, "Jenny is a junior. The semester just started. That means she's only twenty years old. The legal drinking age is twenty-one." Donna whispers back, "I never thought about that! She must have a fake ID." Dana whispers to Donna, "you're right! And, she just said she's twenty years old." Donna whispers back, "you're right!"

Addressing those who are her true friends, Jenny continues, "I would like to thank those of you who put up with me over the last two years. You asked me to go out and eat with you, but I was too tired to go. You asked me to study with you, but my brain was so worn out that it wasn't functioning. You asked me if I wanted to go to the football game with you, but I really needed to sleep instead. When we walked from one place on campus to another, I struggled to keep up with you because I was so tired. You called me on the phone, and I didn't answer because I felt like I wasn't all there. And, I'm sorry that, when we were talking, I appeared like I wasn't paying attention. The truth is, I tried really hard, but I just couldn't. I did my best. I really did. But, this last week has been much better for me. So, I'm sure I can do a little better now."

Jenny then concludes, "thank you all for listening to me this evening. And, I'm sorry if I sounded a little scatterbrained. I did the best I can." Everyone in the room, with a few notable exceptions, stands and gives Jenny a standing ovation. As Jenny makes her way to the back of the room where her friends are, she receives a hug from everyone she passes. Arriving at the back of the room, many gather around to give Jenny a hug.

Rodney coldly announces to the group, "okay. Thank you, Jenny. I'm not sure exactly how that fits in with Jesus, but I hope everyone enjoyed that." Ed whispers to Pete, "what? Is Rodney totally inept or something?" Pete replies, "um, yeah. I'd say so." As the praise band takes the stage and begins playing, at the back of the room, the focus still remains on Jenny.

The meeting comes to a close. In the back of the room, Amy asks Joe, "you're coming with us to get pizza, right?" Joe replies, "well, if you insist. Sure, I'll come along." Joe asks Ed and Pete, "what time are we planning to meet at the gym tomorrow morning?" Ed replies, "how about nine o'clock?" Joe replies, "that sounds good to me. I'm definitely going to be there." Ed reminds Amy, "we can head straight to the vitamin store after we get out of the gym." Amy replies, "thank you so much. I would really appreciate that." Overhearing the group's plans is Dana, who always manages to show up at the pizzeria to see if Jenny has a glass of wine.

Before Ed and his group head to the pizzeria, Dana walks up to Amy and, whispering to her, asks, "did you delete that pic of me that you took that night?" In a normal tone of voice, Amy asks, "oh, do you mean the one of you vaping?" Dana whispers, "yeah. That one." Amy replies, "I haven't gotten around to deleting it yet." Dana firmly tells Amy, "you better delete it, or else!" Not in the mood for Dana's drama, Amy nonchalantly replies, "yeah, whatever. I'll put it on the list." Seeing her group heading out, Amy walks away leaving Dana in limbo.

Walking out of the meeting room together, Ed asks Amy, "are you all right?" Amy reassures Ed, "yeah. I'm good. But, I can't wait until tomorrow." Ed gives Amy a hug, telling her, "I love you." Shedding tears, Amy hugs Ed tighter, telling him, "I love you."

Week Six

A Bump in the Road

Saturday morning, Ed, Amy, Pete, and Jenny head to the gym and meet in the lobby, waiting for Joe to arrive. Joe, who lives off campus, walks through the door full of energy, and asks, "what are we doing today?" Amy suggests, "I really want to dive and swim laps but, if you guys want to lift weights, that's okay." Joe tells the group, "I have my swimsuit. I can join you." Pete suggests, "let's do that. We hit the weights really hard last week. Some cross training will be good." Joe, put through a few grueling workouts by Pete last week, is glad to hear Pete's suggestion. Pete, however, will not let Joe slack off while he is swimming laps. The group heads to the lockers, and will meet each other at the pool.

Joe walks into the natatorium, seeing Amy already on the diving board. Amy makes her approach and does a triple somersault with a perfect entry off the high board. Joe comments to Ed and Pete, "wow! That was really good. I'm really impressed." Ed tells Joe, "Amy has been diving for years. She's a way better diver than she thinks she is." Truth is, Amy is a far better diver than anyone on the diving team. And, Coach McRae knows it.

Amy walks over, joking, "it's about time you guys got here. Jenny is almost finished with her laps. And, I was thinking it's almost time to go." Ed tells Amy, "it sounds like you're getting better already." Amy replies, "I'm counting down the minutes to lunch, when I'll get to take my supplements."

Quite surprised about Amy's diving ability, Joe tells Amy, "that was a really good dive! I had no idea you were that good! Ed told me just a minute ago that you've been diving for years. Setting goals and meeting them also raises dopamine levels. Diving probably helped you out a little bit too." Amy replies, "really? Wow! Now I know how I like diving, the beach, and laying in the sun so much." Joe informs Amy, "you're doing what your genetics programmed you to do." Ed and Amy head to the diving boards together, and Pete and Joe head over to join Jenny in the lanes.

Halfway through their diving session, as Amy gets out of the water, Ed sees a potential problem. Instead of preparing for his next dive, Ed waits for Amy at the ladder to the high board. Walking up, Amy asks, "what's up?" Ed whispers to Amy, "look who just walked in." Amy glances over to the locker room entrance, seeing Dana in a swimsuit, apparently waiting for someone. Amy whispers to Ed, "Jenny was right. Dana's a stalker." Amy then jokingly tells Ed, "and, take a look at that! There's a wine glass sitting at the end of Jenny's lane." Ed laughs, and whispers to Amy, "don't look now, but the alcohol police just walked in." It is anybody's guess why Rodney is at the pool today.

Amy suggests to Ed, "let's do a synchronized two and a half with one twist off the high boards, just so the alcohol police don't think we're drunk." Ed laughs, and tells Amy, "that's a great idea! But, let's wait for them to look at us." Ed climbs the ladder to one high board. In perfect sync, Amy climbs the ladder to the other high board. Amy looks over at Ed, telling him, "they're watching us." Ed replies, "good," and asks Amy, "are you ready?" Amy replies, "yeah." Verifying the number of bounces that they will take on the board, Ed asks Amy, "on three?" Amy replies, "got it."

Amy tells Ed, "you lead. I'll follow." Amy watches Ed and, in perfect sync, Ed and Amy make their approach. Both taking one check bounce, followed by two bounces on the board, Ed and Amy leave the board simultaneously, executing a two and one half somersault dive with one twist in the pike position[17]. Also in perfect sync, after perfectly entering the water, Ed and Amy swim to the pool's edge. Getting out of the pool, Ed gives Amy a high-five. Quite impressed with what he just saw, the lifeguard even gives Ed and Amy a thumbs-up.

Walking over to the diving boards together for their next dive, Amy whispers to Ed, "oh crap. They're headed this way." Ed whispers back, "good. Let's mess with them." Ed climbs the ladder to the high board, as Amy waits for him to complete his next dive. Rodney and Dana watch Ed as he makes his approach and executes his next dive. Amy

---

[17] Forward 2 1/2 somersaults, 1 twist, pike position - Level of difficulty 3.0.

overhears Rodney whispering to Dana, "that's not too hard." As Ed gets out of the pool, Amy climbs the ladder, hearing Dana and Rodney's whispering to each other.

Amy completes her next dive. Seeing Dana climbing the ladder to the high board before Amy has surfaced, Ed advises Dana, "wait until she's out of the water before you climb the ladder." Rodney sarcastically asks Ed, "what are you? The lifeguard or something?" Ed replies, "no, junior. Before you climb the ladder to the high board, you want to make sure the pool is clear." Rodney, apparently with an attitude today, rolls his eyes. But, Ed would be correct. From the high board, you cannot easily see someone in the water directly below the diving board. Executing a dive and unexpectedly landing on top of someone in the water never ends very well.

Dana, making her approach, does a reasonably executed swan dive[18] into the water. Taking Ed's advice and waiting for Dana to leave the water, Rodney climbs the ladder to the high board. Ed whispers to Amy, "junior, up there, is about ready to take a dive. Maybe it's time to swim laps." Amy whispers back, "I agree."

Amy then tells Ed, "you've been reading *Eddie, The Freshman Year.*" Ed asks Amy, "how did you know?" Amy replies, "you're beginning to sound like Mark. Mark and Eddie call everyone who is less than skilled 'junior'." Ed replies, "I guess you've been reading it too." Amy replies, "I'm busted. I'm almost finished with it."

Walking over to the lanes, Ed and Amy stop and watch, as Rodney makes his approach. Rodney springs off the board and, attempting to do a somersault in mid air, is unexpectedly greeted by the diving board on his way down. Amy yells out, "man down!" As Rodney crashes into the water, the lifeguard grabs his radio and notifies the administrative office, "man down in the pool! Code red." From his platform, the lifeguard dives into the pool to perform the rescue.

Ed tells Amy, "that didn't go too well." Amy replies, "yeah. I'd say. It just goes to show that stupidity is more dangerous than drinking or smoking." Amy tells Ed, "let's go help out the lifeguard. He's way over his head. He can't handle this by himself."

Towing Rodney, who is unconscious, the lifeguard approaches the side of the pool. Amy quickly rushes over to procure the aquatic backboard located on the wall behind the lifeguard's station. Throwing the board into the water, Amy dives in and, with the aid of the

---

[18] Swan dive - Not a competitive dive.

lifeguard, immobilizes Rodney by strapping him onto the backboard. Taking control of the situation, Amy tells Ed, "we're going to lower his feet, and I need you to pull him up onto the deck." Ed replies, "got it." Amy and the lifeguard tilt the backboard and push as Ed pulls Rodney out of the water. Meanwhile, Dana does her part by standing around having a panic attack.

Amy gets out of the water, followed by the lifeguard. Amy checks Rodney's vital signs and tells the lifeguard, "well, he's still alive. He's all yours now." The lifeguard asks Amy, "you seemed to know exactly what to do. Are you a lifeguard?" Stating her credentials, Amy replies, "advanced open water[19]." The lifeguard quickly realizes that Amy's qualifications are far beyond his own. Seeing the emergency team arrive, Amy and Ed head over to the lanes, letting the crash crew do their job.

Ed mentions to Amy, "I didn't know you were a lifeguard." Amy replies, "yeah. That's my ace in the hole if I fail at everything else in life." Ed and Amy dive into an open lane, and begin swimming their laps as Rodney is carried away.

After the workout, Joe tells Ed, "swimming is a great workout. I'll have to do this more often. And, I sink in water now." Recalling his chemistry, Ed tells Joe, "that's because your specific gravity is now greater than one." Joe energetically replies, "I can see it now! You're all going to become chemists someday!" Pete explains to Joe, "that's good news! You sink now because your muscle mass is way up and your fat mass is way down. All that working out is paying off." Joe replies, "that really is good news."

After leaving the gym, Ed and Amy head straight to the vitamin store. On the way, Amy mentions, "hey! We're not being followed!" Ed replies, "that's because the alcohol police is out of commission for a while." Amy tells Ed, "Rodney wasn't looking very good when we got him out of the water. His head and neck hit the diving board pretty hard. That couldn't have ended too well." Ed mentions, "I don't know what he thought he was doing." Amy tells Ed what she previously observed, "he didn't even set the fulcrum and test the board. That's a dead giveaway that he's clueless." Arriving at the vitamin store, Ed tells Amy, "we're here. Let's go in and get your stuff."

It has been almost a week now since Amy began taking 5-hydroxytryptophan and Mucuna pruriens as Joe recommended. And

---

[19] Advanced Open Water: The highest level of certification a lifeguard can obtain.

Jenny, faithfully taking her supplement before she goes to sleep in the evenings, has been sleeping well for several weeks. Dana, fully recovered from her nervous breakdown, still thinks she has a chance of dating Ed. But, what very few people know is, since Amy and Ed met, they have spent nearly every last waking moment with each other. Donna, likewise, still thinks she has a chance with Pete. Unknown to Donna, Pete and Jenny have also spent quite a lot of time together since the semester started. And, Rodney, recovering from the serious concussion he received when his head hit the diving board, is trying to catch up on all the class work he missed.

Friday evening brings the weekly meeting of the Interdenominational Campus Fellowship. Arriving quite early for the meeting, Amy sits with Ed in the public area, waiting for others to arrive. Also, arriving early is Joe Sugarman. Wondering how Amy is doing since he found Amy's genetic issue, Joe takes a seat with Ed and Amy.

Joe, who checked up on Amy earlier in the week, asks Amy, "so, it's been about a week now. Are you still doing well?" Amy explains, "I am. I didn't realize how bad I was before. Thank you so much for finding that for me." Joe replies, "it was my pleasure. I'm glad you're doing a lot better." Amy tells Joe, "I told my sister about what you found. So, she started taking the 5-hydroxytryptophan and Mucuna pruriens too. She's doing so much better too." Joe tells Amy, "tell your sister to send you her genetic file. I'd be interested to see if she has the same problem as you." Amy replies, "I can do that."

Ed quietly announces, "here comes trouble," as he sees Rodney heading straight for Amy and him. Briskly walking up and getting right down to business, Rodney asks Ed, "have you been telling people that I have a secret?" Messing with Rodney, Ed replies, "which secret are you referring to?" Rodney sighs, and tells Ed, "can you please stop it? What you're doing is not very Christian like." Ed replies, "stop what? What am I doing?" Rodney replies, "you're telling everyone that I have a secret." Again messing with Rodney, Ed replies, "sure. No problem, Steele. But it would really help if I knew which one of your secrets you are referring to." Realizing he is getting absolutely nowhere, Rodney asks Ed, "and, will you please stop calling me Steele?" Ed replies, "sure. No problem, junior."

Kind of ticked off at Rodney's attitude, Ed tells Rodney, "by the way, junior, the least you can do is thank Amy for helping to save your life." Looking quite puzzled, Rodney asks Ed, "what are you talking about?" Ed informs Rodney, "Amy pulled you out of the water when you cracked your head open at the pool. But, I guess you missed that when you got knocked out." Rodney emphatically tells Ed, "she did not!" Ed tells

Rodney, "how would you know, junior? You slept through the whole thing."

Looking Rodney straight in the eyes, Amy exclaims, "wow! Dana, the queen of gossip, didn't tell you? I can't believe that!" Ed looks at Amy, and exclaims, "wow! You're right! Dana didn't even tell him!" Now wondering what the truth is, Rodney walks away, wishing that he had never confronted Ed regarding an unfounded rumor.

Once Rodney is far enough away, Joe laughs, and asks Ed, "have you been reading the *Eddie, The Mechanic* series?" Before Ed can reply, Amy laughs, and asks Joe, "how can you tell?" Joe replies, "Ed is beginning to sound a little like Eddie Bogenskaya and Mark Svoboda." Amy laughs, and tells Joe, "I've noticed that too! He's almost to the end of *Eddie, The Freshman Year*."

Ed tells Amy and Joe, "I have no idea what Rodney was talking about. I haven't been telling anyone that he has a secret." Amy adds, "Rodney is getting seriously paranoid. He must have a really big secret." Amy then asks Joe, "is there a gene that makes people paranoid?" Joe replies, "there are several genes associated with paranoia. But, if I had to take a wild guess, I'd say Rodney hit his head a little too hard on that diving board. I heard the crash from my lane when I was swimming." Amy confidently tells Joe, "minimally, he ended up with a concussion. If he's lucky, that's all he got."

Brittany Kramer, Joe's girlfriend, takes a seat, joining the conversation. Brittany asks, "what's up?" Joe replies, "we were just talking about genes." Brittany tells the group, "they haven't found it yet, but Joe has the pizza gene." Amy laughs, commenting, "I must have the pizza gene too." Joe tells Amy, "you've been a lot more bubbly than I remember. I can see you're doing a lot better." Amy replies, "I am. Thank you so much for finding my problem."

Pete and Jenny walk up, and it is time to go to the meeting. Amy asks Jenny, "where have you guys been?" Jenny replies, "we ran up to the vitamin store, and I got another bottle of my supplement." Amy asks, "like, in running?" Jenny replies, "yeah. I have a whole lot more energy now that I sleep. I wanted to make sure I like had a backup bottle. I'd hate to go back to not sleeping again." Pete adds, "that wouldn't be good. Jenny has been doing really great in the last few weeks." The group takes a seat at the back of the room, waiting for the meeting to begin.

During their wait, Amy asks Joe, "can you tell what vitamins someone needs by looking at their DNA?" Joe replies, "you sure can." Amy tells Joe, "Ed takes tons of vitamins. Now I'm wondering if all of those vitamins are really necessary." Ed tells Joe, "if I don't take them, I'm not at 100 percent. I think it's something in the B vitamin group, but I've never been able to quite figure it out." Joe asks Ed, "what do you take?" Ed replies, "a multivitamin and mineral, lots of B vitamins, amino acids, fish oil, choline and inositol, and a few other things." Joe offers, "if you want, I can take a look and see what's really necessary." Ed replies, "sure! I'd really appreciate that." Ed emails Joe his raw genetic data, now wondering which vitamins he really needs.

Rodney opens the meeting, announcing, "okay, everyone. We're ready to get started." Everyone in the room gets quiet, and Rodney opens the meeting with a prayer. After his prayer, Rodney announces, "as some of you may already know, I had a little accident a while ago. I'm a little behind on my school work so, if any of you want to give the talk over the next few weeks, there's a sign-up sheet on the table in the back of the room. Please feel free to sign up for a slot." Truth is, Rodney recognizes that his sermonettes are not well received while everyone else who gives a talk receives a standing ovation.

The band takes the stage, starting their opening number. While everyone is singing, Jenny asks Pete, "are we like getting pizza after the meeting?" Pete replies, "that seems to be our usual thing to do after the meeting recently." Jenny tells Pete, "good. I'm starving." Pete reminds Jenny, "we ran five or six miles before the meeting. And, you haven't eaten since lunch." Jenny replies, "oh, yeah. That could like be part of it."

During the second number, Amy walks over to the table, signing up to give the talk next week. Amy asks Ed, "do you want to give a talk?" Ed replies, "sure. Sign me up." Amy signs Ed up and, taking her place next to Ed, tells him, "you're on in three weeks. That should give you enough time to think of something. What are you going to talk about?" In quite a serious tone, Ed replies, "how to extend your life expectancy by staying off the diving board." Amy starts laughing hysterically, and has to leave the room.

Suddenly concerned, Jenny asks Ed, "what's wrong with Amy?" Ed explains, "nothing. She signed me up to give the talk in three weeks. Then, she asked me what I was going to talk about. So, I told her, 'how to extend your life expectancy by staying off the diving board'. She started laughing and she couldn't stop." Jenny laughs, and tells Ed, "that is like seriously funny!" Once Jenny calms down, she tells Ed, "Amy has been doing so much better. I've never seen her this happy before."

Hearing the music stop, Amy walks back into the meeting room. Standing next to Ed, Amy asks, "what did I miss?" Ed replies, "Rodney is beginning his talk. He's speaking from personal experience tonight. His subject is choosing a sport to get you to Heaven early." Amy starts laughing again, telling Ed, "stop that!" Rodney, distracted by the laughing in the back of the room, is wondering what could possibly be so funny. As Rodney speaks, Ed puts his arm around Amy, who lays her head on Ed's shoulder, not listening to a thing Rodney says.

The band begins to play, waking Amy up from her short nap. Still half asleep, Amy whispers to Ed, "I think I fell asleep." Ed replies, "you did, sweetie. But, you didn't miss too much." Ed and Amy stand and sing along with the group. Rodney then closes the meeting with prayer, and the group breaks up for the evening.

After the meeting, Amy asks Joe and Brittany, "you guys are coming with us to get pizza, right?" Joe smiles, and replies, "sure! We'll join you." Brittany tells Amy, "see? Joe definitely has the pizza gene." After socializing with a few of the other group members, Ed, Pete, and Joe head to the pizzeria with their girlfriends.

At the pizzeria, the group takes a seat, deciding what to have for dinner. The only question is what will be on the pizza. Walking up to the counter, Jenny decides that, tonight, she is going to have a glass of wine with dinner. Taking a seat at the table after placing their order, Ed announces to the group, "the Bureau of Alcohol, Tobacco, and Firearms just walked in." Rodney, taking a seat a few tables away with Dana, Donna, Theresa, and the praise band, clearly takes notice of Jenny holding her glass of wine.

Jenny comments, "aren't we special! It looks like we're being stalked again." Amy, now caring little what others do or say, replies, "yeah. By the paparazzi. We must be famous or something." Jenny smiles, and replies, "I know, right?" Catching Rodney taking out his cell phone, Jenny runs her tongue along the rim of her wine glass, suspecting that Rodney is secretly taking a picture of her as he looks over the menu.

As Rodney and his group walk up to the counter to place their order, Donna clearly takes note of Jenny and her wine glass. Instead of returning to her table with her group, Donna steps outside the pizzeria for a moment.

Ignoring the group of Pharisees, Ed and his group enjoy a peaceful dinner. Toward the end of their dinner, Ed and his group see two police officers walk in and step up to the counter. Discreetly pointing to the counter, Ed jokingly tells Jenny, "you're busted. The Bureau of Alcohol, Tobacco, and Firearms called in for reinforcements." Coming to Jenny's rescue, Amy tells Ed, "not half as busted as Rodney's head when he hit the diving board." Jenny laughs, and replies, "you know, there should be a sign on the diving board that like says, 'diving by stupid people can cause injury to the brain,' kind of like the warning on a bottle of wine to pregnant women." Laughter breaks out among the group, clearly noticed by the police officers who are walking over to the table.

The senior officer, Officer Michael Brown, announces, "I hate to interrupt your dinner, but I need to see the ID of the young lady drinking the glass of wine." As Jenny takes out her ID, Officer Brown asks, "has anyone else at this table been drinking?" Replying for the group, Joe informs the officer, "no, sir." Jenny hands the officer her driver's license and college photo ID. Expecting Jenny to get busted, everyone at Rodney's table watches closely as the two officers examine Jenny's ID. Officer Brown tells his partner, "she checks out." Officer Brown announces, "again, I'm sorry to interrupt your dinner. You guys have a good evening, and stay safe."

Walking up to the counter, Officer Brown tells the owner of the establishment, "she checks out, Tony." Tony, the owner, replies, "they've been in here a lot over the last two years. None of them have ever caused any trouble. They're good kids." The officer tells Tony, "enjoy your weekend, Tony." Tony replies, "you too, Mike."

Once the officers drive off, Jenny, sounding a bit ticked off, tells her group, "I'll be right back." Jenny walks over to Rodney's table, grabs Donna's phone off the table, holding it in front of Donna's face to unlock it. Trying to grab the phone from Jenny, Donna exclaims, "give me my phone!" Donna, however, is absolutely no physical match for Jenny. Neither is anyone else at that table, including Rodney. Quickly examining the outgoing calls, Jenny sees that Donna called 911 twenty minutes ago. Quite angry with Donna, Jenny exclaims, "so, you called the police on me!" Donna exclaims, "you had no right to look at my phone!" Jenny tells Donna, "so what? What are you going to do about it?" Tossing Donna's phone on top of her slice of pizza, Jenny walks away, again taking a seat with her group.

Obviously ticked off, Jenny tells those at her table, "when Donna stepped outside earlier, she called the police on me for having a glass of wine. Can you believe that?" Pete replies, "she probably thought you were twenty, like most of the other juniors." Joe asks Jenny, "how old are you?" Jenny replies, "I'm twenty-one. I failed fifth grade because I kept falling asleep in class. And, back then, I like couldn't sleep at night, so I was up all night long. I couldn't keep up with my schoolwork, so they like let me take fifth grade all over again." Amy comments, "that was really nice of them." Joe laughs, and mentions,

"Donna's math doesn't appear to be too good. There's probably a lot of twenty-one-year-old juniors on this campus."

As if one confrontation wasn't enough for the evening, Rodney walks over to Jenny's table, telling her, "that wasn't very nice of you, looking through Donna's phone like you did, and then tossing her phone onto her pizza." Attempting to thwart further confrontation, Ed tells Rodney, "we're eating dinner, junior. Take a hike." Rodney emphatically tells Ed, "please stop calling me 'junior'!" Ed replies, "no problem, Steele." Now getting angry, Rodney exclaims, "and, stop calling me 'Steele'!" Ed replies, "sure. No problem, junior." Amy interjects, "that concussion must have done way more damage than anyone suspected." Laughter breaks out at the table, perhaps hinting to Rodney that he should walk away.

Not taking the hint that he should leave, Rodney admonishes Amy, telling her, "what you said wasn't very nice either! Can't you be nice?" Amy gets her cell phone out of her purse, and begins taking a video of Rodney having a temper tantrum. Seeing what Amy is doing, Jenny takes out her cell phone and does the same. Ed tells Rodney, "look, junior. I told you to leave. So, why don't you go back to your table, and take a few pictures of us eating." Rodney becomes unhinged at Ed calling him 'junior' and feebly smacks Ed on his shoulder, exclaiming, "will you please stop calling me 'junior'?"

Ed stands up, throws Rodney over his shoulder, and carries him back to his seat. Rodney exclaims, "put me down!" Ed tells Rodney, "you got it." Slamming Rodney onto his chair, Ed tells those at Rodney's table, "make sure junior, here, doesn't bother us again. Next time he won't be so lucky." Ed walks back to his table, hoping that Rodney behaves himself.

Ed returns to his table, where Joe tells him, "we're going to have to start calling you Eddie, the mechanic." Taking a bite of pizza, Ed replies, "I really don't know what's wrong with Steele." Amy reminds Ed, "Rodney thinks you know his secret." Jenny comments, "that's right! I remember you guys saying something about that!" Amy tells Jenny, "it must be eating him alive." Jenny replies, "whatever his secret is, he could just confess it to the Lord, and like be done with it." Joe, a little older and wiser, suggests, "he's unlikely to confess any sin that he's not ready to give up. He'll just keep on justifying it to himself."

As the group is getting ready to leave, Joe asks, "what time are we meeting at the gym tomorrow morning?" Pete replies, "how about the normal nine o'clock?" Joe replies, "that sounds great! I think I might swim a few laps after hitting the weights." Finished with dinner, Ed and his group leave. On the way out, Amy waves to Rodney, telling him, "see you at the pool tomorrow."

Week Seven

Amy's Story

Mid week, Ed sits down in the school cafeteria with Joe, who discovered which vitamins Ed needs and those that might be considered unnecessary. After discussing Joe's progress on his workouts, Joe informs Ed, "there's about three hundred genes that control variations in the need for certain vitamins. I'm sure they'll find more in the future, but I checked all the ones that I know about. I think I got it figured out."

Ed asks Joe, "what did you find?" Joe explains, "it's pretty simple. The reason you take a hand full of vitamins a couple times a day to feel good is because you have a genetic defect in the metabolic pathway for folic acid. It's called methylenetetrahydrofolate reductase deficiency, or MTHFR for short. From what I can tell, you need between 800 to 1,200 micrograms of methylfolate every day. That's why you feel better when you take a lot of B vitamins. And, based upon a few other genes, you need to be taking a lot of the methyl form of vitamin B-12." Ed exclaims, "I knew it was something in the B vitamin group! But, I could never quite put my finger on it."

Giving Ed the good news, Joe explains, "in summary, from what I can tell, you need to take a multivitamin and mineral supplement with the active forms of the vitamins. They have that down at the vitamin store. On top of that, you need to take a total of 800 to 1,200 micrograms of methylfolate every day. And, keep taking the fish oil and magnesium that you've been taking. That should cover what I found on your genetic test. And, in addition, you can continue taking your amino acids and the other supplements that you take for building muscle."

Ed thinks for a moment, and tells Joe, "this is going to save me a lot of money." Joe tells Ed, "if you'd like, you can take some of the money you're going to save, and buy me a slice of pizza." Ed replies, "you got it, Joe." Joe then hands Ed a piece of paper, telling him, "I wrote down what you should ideally be taking. You can get these down at the vitamin store." Ed replies, "thanks!"

Joe asks Ed, "by the way, how's Amy doing?" Ed replies, "I've never seen her this good. She has way more energy now. And, from what I hear, her sister is also doing much better." Joe replies, "that's really good to hear." Joe shakes his head, and tells Ed, "I just wish we could have found Amy's problem a long time ago." Ed replies, "me too. Amy was very concerned that she'll eventually go down the path that the rest of her family did." Joe tells Ed, "it very well could have been. But, God had a different plan for her."

Seeing a lot of students suddenly leaving the cafeteria, Joe looks at his watch, and tells Ed, "it looks like it's time for me to give the freshmen their chemistry exam." Ed tells Joe, "walk around the classroom during the test. I bet you can easily get in 1,000 steps, maybe more." Joe smiles, and replies, "that's a good idea! I never thought of that!" Ed and Joe head out to class together, adding another few hundred steps to their day.

Friday evening again brings the weekly meeting of the Interdenominational Campus Fellowship. Arriving slightly early for the meeting, Amy is lying on the sofa in the public area with her head on Ed's lap as Ed reads something on the internet that Amy found earlier today. Quite relaxed considering she will be speaking in front of a group of nearly one hundred people, Amy contemplates exactly what she will say tonight.

The band begins to play. Ed tells Amy, "I guess it's time to go in." Slow to get up, Amy replies, "I suppose so." Ed tells Amy, "I've never seen you this calm and relaxed before." Amy replies, "I guess it's because my life finally makes sense to me now. I know where I belong." Ed and Amy walk in, standing with their friends at the back of the room.

After the band plays three numbers, Rodney takes the stage, and announces, "if I am not mistaken, Amy Amherst will be giving the talk today. Is Amy here with us tonight?" Disappointing to Rodney, Amy yells out, "I'm here." Not seeing Amy among the members earlier this evening, Rodney was secretly hoping that she did not show up. Unfortunately, Rodney has no such luck. Amy is standing in the back of the room with Ed.

Amy walks up to the front of the room, and stands on the stage. Amy begins by saying to the group, "hi. I'm Amy Amherst. I transferred to this University this year. Some of you might already know that. When I think back to the beginning of the semester, the song that I consider the theme song of my life came to my mind when I first met Ed Becker. My song is *Creep*, as it is sung by Chrissie Hynde. Whenever Chrissy sings anything, she puts so much energy and emotion into her performance that you can actually feel it. If you listen to my song sometime, you'll understand exactly how it is that I feel I don't fit into this world."

Dana rudely interrupts Amy, announcing, "that song has profanity in it!" Not missing a beat, Amy tells Dana, "now, how would you know that, Dana?" The audience laughs, perhaps suggesting that Dana should keep her mouth shut. Amy tells her audience, "if you don't want to listen to the song because of a few bad words, then pull up the lyrics sometime." Amy then specifically addresses Dana, telling her, "maybe there's a G-rated version out there just for you, Dana." The audience laughs again, ensuring that Dana will not interrupt the rest of Amy's presentation.

After being rudely interrupted, Amy continues, "so, as I was saying, I never fit into this world. But, that's okay. It doesn't bother me anymore. Just to let you know where I'm coming from, I'll try to explain it to you. In high school, when I went to a basketball game, everyone around me was cheering for our team. I felt absolutely no excitement at all. When I watched our high school football team, I really didn't care who won the game. I just wanted to go home. And, when we were out in a group, and everyone was having a good time, I was the quiet one. My brain just couldn't handle all the multiple conversations going on at once."

Describing her home life, Amy continues, "my home life wasn't any better. When my family went on vacation, to me it was something to be endured, not enjoyed. I tried to have fun. I really did. But, no matter how hard I tried, I didn't have any fun. When Christmas came, everyone else was full of joy. I had no joy. And, some people enjoy food. To me, eating was always more of an inconvenience. Everything I've ever done in my life was for survival. So, I never really fit in. The only time I ever felt anywhere near normal is when I'm outside in the sun. You know, like at the beach."

Amy then asks her audience, "so, how was I like this?" Taking a piece of paper out of her pocket so she can get her facts correct, Amy explains, "Joe Sugarman was kind enough to look at my DNA. Joe found that I have pretty much no serotonin in my brain, and very little dopamine. So, with next to no serotonin and very little dopamine, I was severely depressed. But, since I had no idea what normal was like, I had no idea that I was depressed. In other words, I was emotionally flatlined for years. In my case, Joe found out that it's caused by something called sepiapterin reductase deficiency. I inherited this rare problem from my parents who, now that I think back, were also very depressed. And, so is my sister, Lindsey. But, me and Lindsey didn't really know that we were depressed. For the longest time, we both thought how we are is normal. But, we both knew we weren't like everyone else."

Recalling Jenny's talk, Amy continues, "a few weeks ago, my friend Jenny told you that, when her parents died in an automobile accident, she came to live with my dad and I. What Jenny didn't tell you is that my mom died when I was fourteen. My mom got breast cancer. The doctors said it was caught very early and could easily be cured. But, hearing the news, I think my mom got scared and just gave up. She died a month later, and it wasn't from the cancer. They never did figure out exactly how she died. If you ask me, I think she died of a broken heart."

Amy then reveals, "what Jenny also didn't tell you is that, right after I graduated from high school, my dad committed suicide." Taking her phone out of her pocket where she has a copy of the note that her dad left, Amy continues, "my dad left a note that said, 'Amy and Lindsey, I'm sorry I brought you into this world and the pain that comes with it. It broke my heart to watch my precious daughters grow up and miss out on enjoying life. Now that you're both on your own, I've decided to leave. I hope that someday they can find a reason for whatever it is that is wrong with our family. I just couldn't go on. I hope you understand. I'm sorry. Love, Dad.' So, that was the future that I had to look forward to." Hearing Amy's story, tears come from a few members of the fellowship.

Amy then tells the story, "two nights ago, I was lying in bed at night, thinking about my dad. I was wondering if, just maybe, when he met Jesus face to face, he begged Jesus to send someone to help me and Lindsey so we didn't have to go through what he did. I don't know if that's how things work in Heaven or if that's even possible, but the thought did cross my mind."

Amy continues, "so, when I first came to this fellowship, I was really surprised to see how judgmental a few of you are. You took pictures of my friend, Jenny, drinking a glass of wine and posted it all over social media. You took pictures of me smoking, and posted it all over social media." Addressing one person in specific, Amy looks at Dana, telling her, "by the way, Dana, right after I started taking the supplements that Joe told me to, I quit smoking. So, you can stop taking pictures of me and posting them online now."

Looking right at Donna, Amy continues, "and, one person here even had the nerve to call the police on Jenny when she had a glass of wine. Just so you know, Jenny is twenty-one years old. So, don't bother calling the police the next time you see her with a glass of wine."

Quoting from the Bible, Amy tells the group what they all should already know, saying, "in the book of Matthew, chapter 7, verse 1, it states, 'Do not judge so that you will not be judged.' I'm sure you've all heard that verse at least once before. God's judgement is perfect and just. When we judge, we judge from appearances. God judges from our hearts. Our judgement is so convoluted that God must be laughing at us when we do judge others."

Addressing a few members of the fellowship, Amy informs a specific group, "for those of you who have judged me, I'm okay with that. I forgive you. God made me how I am for a reason, and I'm okay with that too. If you're not okay with how God made me, well, that's your problem, not mine. I'm not changing to accommodate you or your legalistic ways." Hearing Amy's convicting words, Rodney holds his head in his hands, and stares at the floor.

Addressing many members of the fellowship, Amy continues, "for those of you who have not judged me, thank you so, so much. You don't know how much I appreciate you." Amy then surprises her audience by concluding, "I'm really going to miss a lot of you. It's been really nice knowing you guys. I wish you all the best and maybe, sometime in the future, our paths will cross again."

One of Amy's few close friends, Courtney, raises her hand, and asks, "wait! What are you saying?" Amy reveals, "I won't be returning to the University next semester." Quite shocked, Courtney asks, "wait a second! Why not? What happened?" Amy explains, "on the eddiethemechanic.com website, there is an outtake entitled, 'Mr. Frazier's Motivational Speech'. I'll bring it up and read part of it to you. And, just to give you a brief background, Mr. Frazier, the track coach, is giving this speech to his University's track team."

Taking her phone out of her pocket, Amy brings up the website and reads to her audience, "moving on to the subject of success, Mr. Frazier continues, 'now, when you graduate, society has programmed you that you measure success by how much money you earn. You don't measure success by how much money you earn! You don't measure success by what kind of car you drive! You don't measure success by the size of your house! It is of no value to wake up in the morning and drive to a job you hate. It is of no value to drive a luxury car when you really want to drive a Jeep or British roadster. It is of no value to live in a mansion in the suburbs when you really want to live in a bungalow at the beach. The only measure of success is how well you follow your passion and do what you love!'"

Amy then tells the group, "you guys should read the rest of Mr. Frazier's speech[20]. When I read it, I cried. Mr. Frazier's motivational speech changed the direction of my life. And, Dana, you don't have to worry. There's no foul language in Mr. Frazier's speech, so you can relax." The group laughs at Amy's treatment of Dana this evening. This time, Dana, who wishes she can sneak out of the meeting, remains unusually quiet.

Not wanting to leave her audience hanging, Amy explains, "my passion is the beach and the water. Only five other people in this room know this, but I'm a lifeguard, and have my advanced open water certification. So, I've decided to move back to the beach town where I'm from, and get a job as an ocean lifeguard like I did over the last few Summers. If you've ever seen the reruns of *Baywatch*, that's what I'll be doing. And, I don't know how I'm going to do it, but I'm going to find a way to live in a bungalow a few blocks from the beach. I don't know how I'm going to make it work year round, but being a lifeguard is my passion. I'm going to trust God to work out the details. And, I will not come in second place. You'll have to read Mr. Frazier's speech to know what coming in second place really is. Thank you guys for everything."

Courtney again raises her voice, and asks, "wait, wait! What's all this about second place? Do tell!" Amy smiles and tells Courtney, "okay. Since Mr. Frazier makes a Biblical reference in his speech, I'll read it to you. But, your homework is to read the entire speech by next Friday." Seeing that Amy is acting a bit like some of the professors on campus, a few members of the fellowship laugh.

Amy scrolls through Mr. Frazier's speech, trying to find the reference. Finding what she was looking for, Amy reads, "Beginning his talk in a way quite familiar to the team, Mr. Frazier exclaims, 'let me remind you of something we all need not forget. In any race, there is only one winner! In the Bible, in the book of First Corinthians, in chapter 9, verse 24, the scripture reads, 'Do you not know that those who run in a race all run, but only one receives the prize? Run in such a way that you may win.' Make no mistake about it! There is only one

---

[20] See Appendix I to read Mr. Frazier's Motivational Speech.

winner! Whoever comes in second place is the first loser! If you come in second place, learn something! Work harder, learn from the situation, and figure out what you need to change to do better next time!'"

Amy tells her audience, "if coming in second place makes me the first loser, I'm changing what I am doing. I'm definitely not settling for second place. I'm going to follow my passion and win at what God has planned for me. I'm going to be the best I can at what my passion is, which is being a lifeguard. Thank you guys so much for listening and understanding."

Amy walks off the stage, receiving a standing ovation. On her way to the back of the room, Amy receives hugs and encouragement from those whom she passes. Amy can't miss the tears coming from the eyes of some of those in the fellowship. Many will be sad to see Amy go, but are happy for her that she is following her passion. With so much attention placed on Amy, the band delays taking the stage.

In the back of the room, Pete tells Ed, "wow! This is a big surprise! Did you know that Amy was leaving?" Ed replies, "yeah. Believe it or not, she just decided this afternoon. I read Mr. Frazier's motivational speech with her. She's read it a few times already. I totally get where she's coming from. I'm really going to miss Amy." Pete tells Ed, "I'm really going to miss Amy too. But, I totally get it, bro."

After ten minutes, Amy finally makes her way to the back of the room. Walking up to Joe, Amy tells him, "thank you so much for finding my genetic problem, and also for telling me about *Eddie, The Mechanic*. Mr. Frazier's speech to his team really changed my direction. And, I'm going to read the whole series." Joe tells Amy, "I am really going to miss you. You'll have to send me your address once you get settled. I'll come visit and buy you a slice of pizza." Amy replies, "you're so sweet, Joe. I'm going to really miss you."

Rodney takes the stage and announces, "I guess some of us will be sad to see Amy go." As Rodney speaks, in the back of the room, Jenny comments, "did you hear that? Rodney is as cold as ice." Joe, the biochemist, corrects Jenny, telling her, "you probably meant to say dry ice. It's a lot colder than frozen water." Jenny informs Joe, "Rodney defies chemistry, Joe. He's colder than absolute zero." Joe laughs, and tells Jenny, "I'm telling you! I'll make a biochemist out of you yet!" Joe's passion is biochemistry. Joe is one who is clearly following his passion.

The band finally takes the stage, having time to play only one number. Dana, quite happy to hear that Amy is leaving the University, energetically leads the singing as the band plays. Very few students, however, sing along. Some are in the back of the room talking with Amy. Others have googled the song *Creep* to which Amy referred earlier, and are listening to the song with their earbuds or reading the lyrics. Many students have looked up the eddiethemechanic.com website and are reading Mr. Frazier's motivational speech. And, the offering plate gets passed around, taking quite a convoluted path this evening.

After Rodney closes the meeting with prayer, acting a bit on the nice side, Dana whispers to Amy, "is there any chance that I can get you to delete that pic of me on your phone?" Amy asks Dana, "what's the big deal about a pic of you vaping?" Dana insists, "I just want it deleted. Is that asking too much?" Amy replies, "I already told you. Someday, I'll get around to it." Amy walks away, leaving Dana hanging yet once again.

After the meeting, Amy heads out to get pizza with her friends. Knowing that Amy will be gone in a few weeks, a few more people join the group today. Also heading out to get pizza is Dana along with her group of friends. Now that Amy will not be around next semester, Dana will be on her best behavior in an attempt to land a date with Ed once Amy is gone. If that were to happen, it will make Dana second string. Ed, who has made it clear that he is not the least bit interested in Dana, is not likely to settle for second string.

Amy answers the proverbial twenty questions about her plans during dinner. Sitting a few tables over, Dana, not paying attention to the conversation at her table, eavesdrops on the conversations at Amy's table. Specifically, Dana desperately wants to know whether Amy will finish out the semester or leave sometime very soon.

Jenny asks Amy, "are you like really going to get a bungalow near the beach?" Amy replies, "that's my plan. I want to buy a bungalow near the beach and get a Jeep, kind of like Ed's, so I can drive around with the top down." Jenny asks, "where are you going to get the money to buy a bungalow, girl?" Amy replies, "when my dad died, he left everything to me and Lindsey. So, I can survive for a while." Jenny takes a sip of wine, noticing that no one at Dana's table is exercising their photography skills today.

Pete, who has a tendency to worry a lot, asks Amy, "are you sure you can get a job as a lifeguard at the beach?" Amy explains, "they already want me back for next Summer. I'm going to call my former division chief next week and see if I can start in the Spring." Ed suggests to Amy, "we can take a ride down to the beach one weekend. Maybe you can meet up with him." With a sudden burst of excitement,

Amy replies, "that's a great idea! I didn't even think about that!" Ed tells Amy, "let's put it on the calender."

Courtney asks Amy, "are you going to do something else, other than be a lifeguard?" Amy explains, "I'm also a certified lifeguard instructor and CPR instructor, so I can teach classes to the high school kids who want to get Summer jobs as a lifeguard at a community pool. Those classes are usually packed in the Spring. And, I can always put my camera to use somehow."

Listening in as best as she can to Amy's conversations, Dana never finds out whether Amy will leave at the end of the semester, or just throw in the towel and leave now. This time, no one at Dana's table called the police because Jenny is drinking a glass of wine. And, a few of those at Dana's table, now realizing that Amy is a kindhearted person, wish they were sitting at Amy's table instead.

After dinner, Amy and her friends head back to campus, where Amy tells them more of her plans. Now setting a different course for her life, Amy surely has a few more challenges ahead of her.

Week Eight

A Trip to the Beach

The next week, instead of attending the weekly Interdenominational Campus Fellowship meeting, Ed and Amy skip out mid Friday afternoon. As they are packing up Ed's Jeep, Amy tells Ed, "I can't tell you how much I appreciate you taking me to the beach. Thank you so much." Ed replies, "no problem. And, besides, why wait until Spring break to hit the beach?" Amy replies, "that's a good point. If it were up to me, I'd be there every weekend. But, I don't have a car." Ed asks Amy, "why didn't we think of heading to the beach over the weekends earlier in the semester?" Amy replies, "yeah, seriously!"

Checking the oil in the Jeep before they head out, Ed asks Amy, "are you sure you have everything?" Amy replies, "I think I have everything I need. If I forgot something, I can always stop by the store." Ed, always prepared for an emergency, checks his battery, makes sure he has an extra quart of oil or two, and makes sure all the fluid levels are normal before setting out. Ed announces, "it looks like we're ready to go." Ed starts the engine, and he and Amy are off to the beach.

During the three-hour trip, Ed and Amy have a lot to talk about. Not fully understanding the details regarding their accommodations, Ed asks Amy, "where are we staying again?" Amy replies, "the lifeguards have a bunkhouse near the beach. I talked to Mitch, and he said we can stay at the bunkhouse over the weekend since the season is winding down. The seasonal lifeguards do other things over the off season, so they have to move out. I got to stay at the bunkhouse when I was in community college because I was part time over the off season. Oh, and the only catch is that we have to wash our sheets and towels before we leave."

Ed curiously asks, "why does the head lifeguard always have the name 'Mitch'?" Amy laughs, and replies, "apparently, to be division chief, you have to have the name 'Mitch'. It's a universal constant." Ed laughs, and comments, "so, if you have a son someday, and you want him to be division chief, you'll have to name him 'Mitch.'" Amy replies, "exactly!"

Amy tells Ed, "while we're down there, I want to drive around and see if I can find a house." Ed asks, "to buy, or rent?" Amy replies, "I want to buy one. And, I kind of know exactly where I want to live." Knowing Amy has no job at the moment, Ed asks, "where are you going to get the money to buy a house?" Amy explains, "when my dad died, I got about five hundred thousand dollars. If I buy my house with cash, I won't have many expenses. I can live on the cheap."

Hearing that Amy has a lot of money, Ed asks, "how come you never bought a car?" Amy replies, "you'll see when we get to the beach. The bunkhouse, the beach, the park, and the community college that I went to are all really close together. So, I have a bicycle. That's all I ever really needed. My bicycle is in the storage room at the bunkhouse." Ed replies, "wow! Such a simple life." Amy replies, "that's me. All I really need is a place to sleep, and a beach. Well, and a job so I can eat."

Amy then confesses, "maybe it's because I had no neurotransmitters that I like the simple life. All I really want to do, Ed, is to wake up in the morning, get online and look up my assignment for that day, and head to the beach. And, honestly, in my world, my biggest challenge of the day is to figure out what to do for lunch. I really don't know what I was thinking when I applied to the University." Ed replies, "I totally get that. Mr. Frazier is right. You have to follow your passion."

Amy thinks for a moment, and tells Ed, "if I didn't read Mr. Frazier's motivational speech to his team, my life would seriously be on the wrong track." Ed points out to Amy, "but, for the last few months, you've been on the right track." Amy asks, "how can you say that?" Ed replies, "God sent you to the University so that Joe can find your problem. And, not to mention, if you didn't go to the University, you probably wouldn't have run across Mr. Frazier's motivational speech anytime soon." Amy exclaims, "you're right! You're a genius!" Ed laughs, and replies, "far from it."

Amy asks Ed, "I wonder if Mr. Frazier is a real person." Ed surmises, "his character is probably modeled after a real person. Joe would probably know." Amy asks, "how would Joe know?" Ed reveals, "Pete told me that Joe's father knows the author." Amy tells Ed, "we'll have to ask Joe sometime. I really want to know." Ed replies, "so do I. And, I want to know if Mr. Zunde is a real person too." Amy laughs, and tells Ed, "Mr. Zunde is so funny!"

Out of the blue, Amy tells Ed, "Axel Braden is a real person." Ed asks, "how do you know that?" Amy laughs, and explains, "I went to high school with a guy named Jimmy Johnson. I've read most of the outtakes, and I'm almost finished reading *Eddie, The Sophomore Year*. Axel Braden sounds just like Jimmy Johnson."

About three hours after they left, Amy tells Ed, "we're here," and shuts off the GPS on her phone. Coming to an intersection, Amy tells Ed, "hang a right at the light." Amy tells Ed, "if you want pizza for dinner, there's a place a few blocks down that has the best pizza ever." Ed replies, "sure. Let's stop for dinner."

Over dinner, Ed asks Amy, "so, what's the plan?" Amy replies, "tomorrow morning, I have a meeting with Mitch to see if he'll hire me full time. After that, we can do whatever we want. But, I would really like to look at that neighborhood near the park to see if there's any houses that I like. It's all the way down on the South end of the beach." Ed tells Amy, "you seem to have this all under control." Amy explains, "when I'm in my little bubble of a world right here at the beach, it's the only time I feel like I'm in control. Everything is simple and perfect. Ed, I really belong here. I really do." Ed replies, "I can tell."

After dinner, Ed and Amy drive to the bunkhouse. Pulling into the driveway, Ed comments, "this is really nice. I was expecting something more like barracks." Amy tells Ed, "this was my home for two years when I was in community college."

The bunkhouse, a small motel across the street from the beach, was bought by the State several years ago to provide housing in close proximity to the beach for the lifeguards. The lifeguards enjoy greatly reduced rent with the understanding that they are on twenty-four hour call should an emergency situation exist.

Ed and Amy get out of the Jeep, and walk in the front door. Sitting in the living room, one of the lifeguards jumps off the sofa, and exclaims, "Amy! You're back! What happened?" Amy exclaims, "Angel! I've missed you!" Angel asks, "what brings you here?" Amy replies, "I'm only in for the weekend. I have a meeting with Mitch tomorrow morning. Mitch said I can stay here over the weekend." With great excitement, Angel asks, "what? Are you coming back? Tell me you are!" Amy replies, "that's the plan. Hopefully, there's an opening for full time."

Making introductions, Amy tells Ed, "Ed, this is Angel. Angel is one of the full-time lifeguards. Last Summer, me and Angel patrolled on the boat a lot together. Angel, this is my boyfriend, Ed. Ed drove me here from the University." Ed tells Angel, "it's nice to meet you." Wondering where Amy found such a hot boyfriend, Angel tells Ed, "it's really nice to meet you, too." Angel asks Ed, "are you staying with us?" Replying for Ed, Amy tells Angel, "Mitch said it was okay."

Hearing Angel so excited, Mike, another lifeguard, walks down the hall, yelling out to Angel, "where's the party?" Angel yells back, "you'll never guess who just walked in!" Mike enters the room, and exclaims, "wow! Amy! I totally thought you were gone forever." Amy laughs, and tells Mike, "you're only glad to see me back so you don't have to teach the beginner's classes by yourself!" Mike laughs, and replies, "guilty as charged!"

Ed, Amy, Angel, and Mike sit and talk for a while, catching up on the last few months. With a bit of hesitance, Amy asks Angel and Mike, "do either of you know if Mitch has any full time openings?" Angel explains, "well, yeah. John left for the Keys as soon as he got his captain's license. Let's see. Who else? Dan is gone. He's teaching scuba classes in the islands somewhere. So, there's at least two openings for full time. And, there's an opening for beach captain on the South side. But, you have to be advanced open water certified, and a certified instructor." Amy doesn't say anything, but she is both advanced open water certified and a certified instructor. Angel perhaps forgot those little details.

Very excited to see Amy, Angel announces, "we need to get you guys settled in. Let's find you guys an open room." Mike heads out for dinner, as Angel, Amy, and Ed head to the small office, where Angel gets the keys to two rooms, one for Amy, and one for Ed. Angel tells Ed, "house rules. Gals on the left, guys on the right." Ed replies, "got it." Ed tells Amy, "I'll go and get our stuff." Amy tells Ed, "when you get back, we're going to the beach!" Ed walks out to his Jeep, seeing quite a stark difference in Amy when she is in her element.

After getting settled, Ed and Amy walk across the street to the nearly deserted beach. After a long walk down the beach, Amy sits on Ed's lap as they watch the waves crashing onto the shore. Amy tells Ed, "I think we're going to see the moon rise!" Ed asks, "how do you know?" Pointing over the ocean, Amy replies, "over there, on the horizon, it's getting a little lighter. And, a few more people are showing up. They're probably coming here to watch the moon rise over the ocean."

Amy asks Ed, "so, what do you think?" Ed replies, "this place is really nice. I can really see why you want to come back here." Amy tells Ed, "there's only one thing wrong with this place." Ed asks, "what's that?" Amy puts her head on Ed's shoulder and, coming back to reality, replies, "you won't be here." Suddenly emotional, Amy begins to cry, telling Ed, "maybe I'm making a big mistake coming back here!" Ed holds Amy tightly, reminding her, "this is your passion, sweetie. You can't walk away from it. If you walk away from this, someday you'll seriously regret it." Ed holds Amy tightly, communicating far more than words could ever express.

Taking in what Ed said about her passion, Amy asks, "how can I know for sure that being a lifeguard is God's will for my life?" Ed asks Amy, "who do you think gave you your passion to be a lifeguard?" Amy is silent for a moment, then tells Ed, "you're right! The only reason I picked computer science as a career is because people always say that, sooner or later, you have to get a 'real job'. How is being a lifeguard not a 'real job'?" Ed tells Amy, "take your pick. Being out on the beach for the rest of your life doing what you love, or sitting in an office behind a computer screen." Amy sighs, and tells Ed, "you're right. I definitely don't belong behind a computer screen. It's not me."

Ed thinks for a moment, and reminds Amy, "do you remember when Joe said something like, 'God allowed you to be this way for a reason'. And that, 'you may not find out the reason for many years.'?" Amy replies, "yeah. I remember him saying that." Ed tells Amy, "I think you just found out why God made you like you are. The beach is where you belong." Amy stands up, and exclaims, "you're right! What's the matter with me? How come I couldn't see this before?" Ed replies, "maybe it wasn't the right time." Amy is now very confident that she knows God's will for her life.

Now more relaxed, Amy tells Ed, "Mr. Frazier must be a Christian." Ed asks, "how do you know?" Amy brings up Mr. Frazier's motivational speech on her phone, which she must have read two dozen times by now, and read, in part, to the fellowship group last week. Also wanting to hear it again for herself, Amy reads to Ed, "Beginning his talk in a way quite familiar to the team, Mr. Frazier exclaims, 'let me remind you of something we all need not forget. In any race, there is only one winner! In the Bible, in the book of First Corinthians, in chapter 9, verse 24, the scripture reads, 'Do you not know that those who run in a race all run, but only one receives the prize? Run in such a way that you may win.' Make no mistake about it! There is only one winner!

Whoever comes in second place is the first loser!'" Amy then adds, "and, in the *Eddie, The Mechanic* series, Mr. Frazier references that Bible verse quite a lot." Ed replies, "you're right. Now, I really have to know whether Mr. Frazier is a real person or not."

Amy reminds Ed of what she said last week, telling him, "so, right now, I'm in second place. I don't want to be the first loser." Thinking about what Amy just read, Ed replies, "Mr. Frazier is right. There is only one winner." Amy reconsiders, and tells Ed, "you know, Ed. I'm not in second place. If I get a degree in computer science, I'd be more like in last place. I'd be a big time loser." Ed is silent, deeply contemplating what Amy just said.

Now that Ed and Amy are a bit more relaxed, Ed tells Amy, "the moon is rising." Amy turns around, telling Ed, "the moon is so beautiful!" Ed mentions, "I think it's a full moon." Amy tells Ed, "it's a full moon. Tomorrow, the moon will rise about an hour later." Ed doesn't ask Amy how she knows. Ed has figured out that, since Amy's life was at the beach for a few years, she knows these things. With her head on Ed's shoulder, Amy watches the moon as it rises over the ocean.

Once the moon is far above the horizon, Amy tells Ed, "we'd better get back. I have to get a good night's sleep." As they are walking back to the bunkhouse, Ed asks, "what time are you meeting with Mitch?" Amy replies, "at nine o'clock, which means we have to wake up sometime between seven and eight. The main precinct is in town, a few miles up the road. We can get breakfast on the way." Ed tells Amy, "if I'm not up in time, bang on my door." Amy replies, "will do!" Walking through the door, Ed and Amy kiss good night, and they each head to their rooms.

The next morning, after breakfast, Ed and Amy head to the main precinct where Amy will have her interview with Mitch. Arriving a little early, Ed asks Amy, "how long is your interview?" Amy replies, "I'm not really sure. If you want, you can go take a look around town. I'll text you when I'm finished." Ed replies, "that will work." As Amy heads inside, Ed decides what he is going to do around town for an hour or two, perhaps longer.

Looking diagonally across the street, Ed sees a gym on the second story of a row of shops. At the street level, on the corner, is a swimsuit shop. Next to the swimsuit shop is a bicycle rental facility. A little farther down is an ice cream shop. Everything Ed sees speaks of the beach life he's heard Amy so passionately talk about. Hoping that the gym has a pay per visit program for out of town visitors, Ed decides to walk across the street, planning to get in a workout while Amy is in her interview.

Walking into the gym, Ed sees a help-wanted sign over the front desk, indicating that the open position is for a personal trainer. Not recognizing Ed, the front desk attendant asks, "may I help you?" Ed replies, "I was going to ask if you have a per visit deal, but I noticed your help-wanted sign." The attendant asks Ed, "are you a personal trainer?" Ed replies, "I am. I'm certified by the American College of Sports Medicine." Checking out Ed's athletic physique, the attendant asks, "would you like to speak to the manager?" Ed replies, "sure, if he's available."

The attendant tells Ed, "I'll be right back." As the attendant walks into the gym manager's office, Ed looks out at the floor, checking out the equipment. Looking out the wall of windows, Ed is impressed by the beautiful panoramic view of the beach. Across the street, on the beach, Ed can't help but to notice the lifeguard station where a lifeguard is watching the few people who dare to go into the late Autumn water.

Catching Ed off guard, Scott, the gym manager and owner, walks up, and asks Ed, "Denise tells me you're interested in the personal trainer position?" Ed replies, "yes, sir." Scott asks, "and, you're ACSM certified?" Ed replies, "that is correct, sir." Scott tells Ed, "come back with me, and let's talk." Ed replies, "thank you." Ed and Scott walk back into the office where Ed and the manager have a long conversation.

Emerging from the office forty-five minutes later, Scott escorts Ed around the gym, showing him the equipment, personal training area, and, most of all, the view of the beach. Ed is quite impressed, as the twenty thousand square foot facility is properly equipped and well laid out. Scott then shows Ed an unoccupied office near the personal training area, telling Ed that, should he accept the offer, this would be his office.

After the nearly one-hour interview, Ed asks Scott, "can I let you know on Monday?" Scott replies, "sure. And, if you have any questions, please feel free to call me anytime. I'll write my cell number on my card." It is clear that Scott, who is really impressed with Ed's credentials, really wants Ed to take the position. Ed thanks Scott for his time. Scott hands Ed his card and thanks Ed for coming by. Ed heads out, wondering if Amy is finished with her meeting with Mitch.

Walking across the street, Ed sees Amy sitting on a bench outside the precinct. Seeing Ed walking down the sidewalk, Amy rushes up to him, and exclaims, "Ed! I got the job! Mitch hired me full time!" Ed lifts Amy off the ground, spins her around twice, telling her, "that's awesome, sweetie! Congratulations!" Amy asks Ed, "can we drive down the road, please? I want to see where I'm going to be working!" All excited that Amy got the job, Ed replies, "sure!"

On the way, Amy energetically tells Ed, "Mitch gave me the position of beach captain on the South end of the beach! That's in the area where I really want to live!" Ed suggests, "while we're down there, we can drive around and look at houses." Still not back to Earth, Amy exclaims, "can we? Can we? Please?" Ed replies, "sure." Ed, nor anyone else, can miss Amy's excitement, for Amy has found where she really belongs.

Arriving at the far South end of the beach, Ed drives into the parking lot where the lifeguard office is located. Ed and Amy walk around the beach for a while, as Amy carefully looks over the area as if she now owns it. Finding a place to sit in the sand, Ed asks Amy, "so, this is your beach now?" Amy replies, "you sound just like a lifeguard! That's what we always say. Like in, 'that's Angel's beach', or 'this is Amy's beach'." Ed tells Amy, "I've never seen you so happy." With tears of happiness, Amy replies, "that's because I am happy, Ed! I'm really happy!"

After telling Ed about her job and talking about the beach for twenty minutes, Amy asks Ed, "so, what did you do when I was talking with Mitch?" Ed calmly replies, "I got a job." Abruptly turning around and, looking Ed in the eyes, Amy exclaims, "what? What are you talking about? Wait a second! How did you get a job?" Ed tells Amy, "I don't want to go back to the University either. I never really fit in. So, I talked to the owner of the gym on the corner across from where you were, and he offered me a position as a personal trainer."

Surprised and confused at what she is hearing, Amy exclaims, "how is that? How did all this come about? What are you saying?" Ed explains, "I don't really belong at the University either. I'm not even good at my major. The only reason I've made it this far is because Mark Johnson gave me copies of all the old tests. I would have flunked out a year ago if it wasn't for Mark Johnson. So, what am I going to do when I graduate? What I really want to do is be a personal trainer, and coach a high school sports team. Maybe, someday, I'll even get to own my own gym." Now calmed down a bit, Amy tells Ed, "I can totally get that."

Ed asks Amy, "do you remember back during the second week of classes when Dr. Lawrence talked about the Control Data supercomputers, and how one guy, Greg Mansfield, wrote the entire operating system?" Amy replies, "yeah. And, I'm surprised you even remembered his name." Ed replies, "I researched it on the internet. There's not much out there on the subject, but what Dr. Lawrence said is true. But anyway, I'll never be like Greg Mansfield. I need to do what God put me on this Earth to do. And, computer programming is not exactly very high on the list." Amy asks, "what's at the top of your list?" Ed replies, "personal training, teaching people about their body, diving, sports, maybe owning a gym someday, and that kind of thing."

Still somewhat totally confused, Amy asks Ed, "are you doing this because of what I'm doing?" Ed replies, "no." Amy asks, "then, how are you doing this?" Ed replies, "because I love you and I want to be with you. Will you marry me?" Amy suddenly sheds tears of happiness, gives Ed a hug with all her strength, and tells Ed, "I will! I will!" Amy kisses Ed, then hugs him for a good five minutes as Ed gently rocks her in his arms. Amy now knows beyond a shadow of a doubt that the beach is exactly where she belongs. And, best of all, Ed will now be there with her.

After celebrating their engagement at lunch, Amy and Ed drive around the neighborhood across from the beach. Amy mentions to Ed, "if we live here, I can walk to work." Ed replies, "this is a really nice area. And, it's only five miles from the gym. I could ride a bicycle to work." Amy laughs, and tells Ed, "until a storm rolls in. Then, you'll be calling me and asking me to come get you."

All of a sudden, Amy exclaims, "stop! Stop! Pull over!" Ed asks, "what's up?" Amy exclaims, "there's an open house! Let's go and look!" Ed and Amy get out of the Jeep, walking up the path to a cozy cottage that has been newly renovated on the outside. Walking into the home, Ed and Amy are given a tour by the real estate agent on duty. Amy is impressed by the fact that the inside has also been renovated, and no work needs to be done.

Looking around on their own, Amy whispers to Ed, "this is perfect. It's two bedrooms, and eight-hundred square feet. That's all we really need for now." With a unique perspective, Ed replies, "I like it. It's a lot nicer than the dorms or the bunkhouse." Ed and Amy thank the real estate agent, take a brochure, and head out. Ed and Amy drive around looking at houses for about one more hour, then head back to the bunkhouse.

Ed and Amy hit the beach and, without a care in the world, relax for the remainder of the afternoon. Lying in the sun taking advantage of the rays, Ed and Amy work on their suntans. Suddenly starting to laugh, Amy tells Ed, "you've got to read this sometime!" Ed asks, "what are you reading?" Amy replies, "I'm reading another outtake on the

Eddie, The Mechanic website. This one is called *Jimmy O'Brien's Folly*. This Jimmy O'Brien character sounds like Rodney, Dana, and Donna all rolled into one!"

Ed gets his phone, and starts reading the story. Halfway through the story, Ed mentions to Amy, "I'm definitely reading this whole series. This is seriously funny!" Amy replies, "I know, right?"

Once he is finished reading the outtake, Ed tells Amy, "you're right! Rodney is definitely Jimmy O'Brien!" Amy tells Ed, "when you're done with that one, read, *Jimmy O'Brien on the Track*. It's funnier than Rodney on the diving board." Ed mentions, "this stuff can't be totally made up. Some of it has to be real." Amy replies, "I definitely get that feeling too. This is not fiction." Ed moves on to the next story, clearly seeing Rodney in the character of Jimmy O'Brien. Within an hour, Ed and Amy have read all the outtakes, some of them multiple times.

The sun begins to set, and Ed asks Amy, "what's the plan for tomorrow?" Amy replies, "we can go to church in the morning. The one I used to go to is not too far from here. I really like the people there. It would be really nice to see them again." Ed asks, "what kind of church is it?" Amy smiles, and replies, "red brick and cement." Ed laughs, telling Amy, "that's my favorite kind." Amy explains, "I don't really think it has a denomination. A few of the lifeguards go there." Ed tells Amy, "I bet they'll really be surprised to see you." Amy informs Ed, "by now, Angel has texted everyone and they all know I'm back in town."

Amy then tells Ed, "after church, we can do whatever we want. But, we still have to wash our sheets and towels before we leave." Ed suggests, "if we get our laundry done before church, we can hit the beach one more time before we head back to the University." Amy smiles, and replies, "I would love that."

Week Nine

Ed's Story

Walking into class a bit late on Monday morning, Ed and Amy are both wondering why they even bothered coming back to the University. Taking a seat in the back of the classroom, Amy asks Ed, "did you tell Scott that you accepted the position?" Ed replies, "I did that first thing this morning." Amy asks, "so, we're all set?" Ed replies, "almost. I have to give notice down at the gym. I'm sure there's a few other details." Amy tells Ed, "we'll just coast for the rest of the time we're here."

As Dr. Lawrence gives her lecture, to Amy, the professor's words go in one ear and out the other, making far less sense than they did last week. Ed contemplates why he ever came to this University, wondering why he even stayed as long as he did. Jenny and Pete are in the dark, for Ed and Amy have not yet announced anything that transpired over the weekend.

After class, Jenny asks Amy, who got in very late last night, "how did it go over the weekend, girl?" Showing her excitement, Amy exclaims, "I got the job!" Jenny replies, "that's awesome, girl! I prayed for you! I knew you'd get it!" With a half-hour before they have to be at their next class, Amy and Ed fill in Jenny and Pete on the details of their trip.

Jenny asks, "what else did you guys do down at the beach?" Amy looks at Ed, who nods his head. Amy energetically announces, "Ed and I are getting married!" Jenny exclaims, "what? Are you serious? When did this happen, girl?" Amy energetically explains, "after I got the job! We were on the beach, and Ed asked me! And, Ed got a job as a personal trainer at a gym downtown. And, then we looked at houses and went to the beach a lot." Quite surprised at what she is hearing, Jenny exclaims, "what? You guys go away for a weekend, and like wow, girl! I'm so happy for you guys!" As Amy and Jenny converse, Pete cannot believe what he is hearing.

It is hard for those who walk by to not notice Amy and Jenny's energetic conversation. Among those who become aware of Amy's excitement is Dana, who just exited the classroom building. Standing in the alcove, Dana listens as Amy tells Jenny and Pete, "I'm not finishing out the semester here. I'm hanging around for a while, but then I'm out of here. But, don't tell anyone. Ed's going to make the announcement to the fellowship when he gives his talk on Friday." Jenny tells Amy, "my lips are sealed." Hearing the news, Dana's lips, however, are not. Dana immediately texts to Donna, Theresa, Rodney, and a few others, "Amy is out of here. She's not finishing out the semester."

Thanks to Dana, rumor gets around campus that Amy is leaving before the end of the semester. But, no one dares to ask Amy about her plans. By the end of the week, a few members of the fellowship know that Amy will be leaving earlier than anticipated. Even though Amy made her reasons for leaving the University perfectly clear when she addressed the fellowship, a few twists by the gossipers were added along with a few more rumors.

Friday evening, the Interdenominational Campus Fellowship meets once again. For once, Dana is in an upbeat mood. Dana will be listening carefully to Ed's talk tonight, hoping to learn exactly when Amy will be leaving. Once Amy is gone for good, Dana's plan is to make a move on Ed.

Before the meeting begins, Rodney walks to the back of the room where Ed is hanging out with the usual group. Fearful that Ed may reveal his secret, Rodney asks Ed, "are you still giving the talk tonight?" Ed laughs, and replies, "of course, junior. Why wouldn't I? You're the one that got the concussion, not me." Rodney asks Ed, "will you please stop calling me 'junior'?" Ed replies, "no problem, Steele. You got it." Those who are standing around laugh, quite amused that Rodney walks into the same trap week after week. Rodney walks away, knowing that, if the conversation goes any further, Ed will certainly out wit him.

Rodney takes the stage, and announces, "okay, everyone. We're ready to begin." Everyone in the room stands up and quiets down. Rodney opens the meeting with prayer. During Rodney's prayer, Dana has her eyes glued to Ed and, as usual, not paying one bit of attention to anything Rodney is saying. From Dana's perspective, Amy, who is standing next to Ed, does not look too happy. Amy, however, is thinking to herself that neither of her parents can attend her wedding. Once Rodney concludes his prayer, the praise band takes the stage.

After three numbers, Rodney takes the stage and announces, "tonight, we'll be hearing from Ed Becker, who I hear has some interesting news for us. Ed, please come on up to the stage." Ed walks up, wondering how Rodney knew that he has some news to disperse. Taking the stage, Ed candidly asks Rodney, "what news is that, Steele?" Realizing that he made an announcement based upon rumors, Rodney turns an interesting shade of red. Rodney knows, beyond a shadow of a doubt, that he has just been busted. And, Rodney does not dare to challenge Ed in a public setting.

Sparing Rodney from further embarrassment, Ed begins, "thank you for giving me the opportunity to share with you tonight what the Lord is doing in my life. I'll try to keep this short. First, let me tell you where I'm coming from. For my entire life, I have been told that I'm not good enough, that I'll never succeed, or that I shouldn't even bother to begin something because I'll fail. I was even told by my guidance counselor in high school to not bother applying to this University because I'll never get accepted. I applied anyway, just to prove him wrong."

Explaining where he does find his success, Ed relates, "as I searched for something that I could succeed at, I found it was sports. In high school, I played football and was on the swimming team. As some of you may already know, I'm also a halfway decent springboard diver, and I have a part-time job as a personal trainer. I'm a whole lot better at sports than I am at academics." Referring to himself as a "halfway decent springboard diver" is the understatement of the year. Even though he is not on the University's diving team, Ed, without a doubt, is the best diver in the University's division.

Making Amy's plans public knowledge, Ed explains, "two weeks ago, Amy announced that she was not going to return to the University next semester. Amy's plans have slightly changed. Last weekend, Amy interviewed for a position as a lifeguard near her hometown, and they offered her the position. Amy has decided to move on, and will not be finishing out the semester here at the University." Hearing the news, Dana smiles, quickly realizing that what she heard by eavesdropping on Amy and Jenny earlier in the week is accurate. Ed glances over at Rodney, who suddenly has a look of concern on his face. One can easily conclude that Rodney is very paranoid about something.

Taking his phone out of his pocket, Ed reads, "in First Corinthians, chapter 9, verse 24, it says, 'Do you not know that those who run in a race all run, but only one receives the prize? Run in such a way that you may win.' Right now, I'm running in a race that I cannot possibly win. The race I cannot win is right here at this University. I might end up getting a degree in computer science. But, if I work in that field, I will probably fail. Honestly, guys, I'm not very good at what I'm here at the University to study. Like Amy, I really don't belong here." Ed then confesses, "the only reason I've made it this far is because a good friend of mine gives me a lot of old tests and helps me with a lot of my projects."

Revealing his plans for the future, Ed announces, "what I really want to do in life is to be a personal trainer, and someday own my own gym. Another thing on my list is to coach a high school sports team, preferably a diving team. When Amy and I were away last weekend, I interviewed for a position at a gym as a personal trainer. I got the position, so I will also not be returning next semester." Ed's audience is quite shocked at the announcement but, in a way, not surprised. Sitting cross legged on the floor and shocked at hearing the news, Dana holds her head down as if she is carefully studying the carpet.

Ed smiles, and tells the group, "now, for the big news." Ed pauses for a moment, as Amy walks up to the front of the room. Amy stands next to Ed and, holding Amy's hand, Ed announces, "when we were away at the beach last week, Amy and I got engaged and we're getting married." Most everyone in the fellowship stands, cheering and clapping wildly for Ed and Amy. The news, coming as quite a surprise to everyone in the fellowship, is not exactly what anyone was expecting to hear today.

During the brief celebration of Ed and Amy's engagement, Dana, in tears, sneaks out of the room. Dana is followed by Donna, who hopes to console her. During the clapping and cheering for Ed and Amy, very few people see Dana and Donna leave. Those who are aware that they left pay them no attention.

Once the celebration subsides, Ed concludes, "when Amy and I went away last weekend, it became perfectly clear to us that God ultimately has a different path for us than the one we were on. And, as we always hear from our pastors, God's timing couldn't have been more perfect."

Ed then finishes his brief talk, telling the group, "thank you all very much. And, I hope all of you have a great weekend." The group applauds again as Ed and Amy walk to the back of the room. On her way back, those whom Amy passes want to see her ring, which Amy is very happy to show them.

Rodney takes the stage, who, with a very bad slip of the tongue, announces, "I'm sure we'll all be glad to see Ed and Amy go." Quickly realizing what he just said, Rodney raises his voice to a level above the sudden booing and hissing, correcting himself, saying, "I meant to say 'sad to see Ed and Amy go'! Boy, did I ever screw that one up! I'm so sorry!" It is no secret that Ed and Amy are ticked off at Rodney's slip of the tongue.

The booing and hissing continues for a while, broken by Ed yelling out from the back of the room, "hey, Steele! While you're up there, why don't you confess your secret to the fellowship?" A lot of chatter arises, as many people are surprised to hear that Rodney has a secret. Ed was, of course, messing with Rodney once again. As Rodney is standing on the stage in a panic, he clearly sees Amy whispering something to Ed.

Great fear suddenly comes over Rodney, noticed by everyone in the room, as Ed again makes his way up to the stage. With everyone now thinking that Ed is going to spill Rodney's big secret, chatter again rises in the room. About to have a major league emotional breakdown, Rodney tells everyone, "okay, everyone. Please calm down." Clearly convinced that Ed is going to spill Rodney's biggest kept secret, Rodney, in a panic, confesses, "okay, Ed. Hold on. I'll tell them. You don't have to."

Everyone in the room quiets down, waiting to hear what Rodney has to confess. Ed interrupts his trek to the front of the room and, standing with his arms crossed against the side wall, is very curious to hear what Rodney has to say. After all, Ed has absolutely no direct knowledge of any secret of Rodney's.

With a quiver in his voice, Rodney announces, "let me first begin by telling everyone that I am very, very sorry. I hope you all can forgive me." In a full-blown panic attack, Rodney pauses, wipes the sweat from his face, then continues, "over the years, we've passed the offering plate around to fund our annual functions. For the last two years, I've taken some of the money from the offering plate." Showing a few tears, Rodney again pauses for a few seconds, and continues, "I am so sorry. I really hope you guys can forgive me. And, I'll be returning what I took." Now sobbing, Rodney continues, "and, effective right now, I'm resigning from my position as treasurer of our fellowship. If anyone wants to fill that position, please feel free." Instead of condemning Rodney, those in the fellowship clap, accepting Rodney's confession and willingness to make his sin right.

Once the clapping subsides, Ed walks up to the stage, and tells Rodney, "I wasn't going to tell everyone about any secret of yours, Steele. But, I do have one more announcement, and it has nothing to do with you." A few people laugh as Rodney steps aside, and Ed announces, "I forgot to mention this before. We're headed to the pizzeria after the meeting tonight. If anyone wants to join us, please feel free to come along." Ed returns the stage to Rodney, and rejoins his friends in the back of the room.

The band takes the stage and begins to play as the offering plate is passed around. Dana, who usually leads the singing, is conspicuously absent. Pete whispers to Ed, "so, Rodney really did have a secret." Ed replies, "apparently so. I really had no idea that Rodney had a secret. I was just messing with him a few weeks ago." Pete informs Ed, "when you walked up to the front, Rodney must have seriously thought you were going to expose his secret." Thinking back, recalling what transpired over the last five minutes, Ed laughs, and replies, "you're probably right about that."

After the meeting, waiting for an opportune time, Rodney walks up to Ed, asking him in private, "how did you know about what I did?" Ed replies, "I didn't, Steele. I was just messing with you. Everyone has secrets. Apparently the Holy Spirit convicted you of your secret. You should be happy about that." With a sudden display of anger, Rodney looks at Ed, wanting to say something, but cannot find any words. Rodney walks away, hammering his fist into the air, sorely ticked off that Ed pulled one over on him.

Ed and Amy walk out of the meeting room with their regular group, headed to the pizzeria. Dana, still having a major league emotional breakdown, seeing Amy, screams out, "I can't believe you did this to me! You stole Ed from me! I can't believe you did that! Why? Why did you have to do this to me?" Dana breaks out into an even bigger crying fit, now attracting the attention of everyone around. Rodney walks over to Dana, attempting to calm her down.

Amy asks, "what's up with Dana?" Always aware of more than meets the eye, Jenny tells her, "nothing anymore. Rodney just walked over to her. Her knight in shining armor just came to her emotional rescue. Everything about that girl is like total status dramaticus. Just as soon as she gets over it, she'll like move on to another major catastrophe." Pete comments, "let's all hope Dana never breaks a fingernail." Amy laughs, and mentions, "I can't imagine what would happen if she had a real emergency, like breaking her head open on a diving board." Pete tells Amy, "who knows? If she hit her head on the diving board, it may improve something." Joe laughs, telling Pete, "you might be right about that."

Arriving at the pizzeria, the group places their order and takes a seat near the window. Occasionally glancing out the window, Amy sees no sign of Rodney or Dana. Jenny also checks the window occasionally, also looking for any signs of trouble approaching. Fortunately, tonight, the group will enjoy a peaceful dinner. Rodney and his group have decided to eat at the student center cafeteria because Dana just can't face seeing Ed and Amy sitting together tonight.

Over dinner, Joe asks Ed, "if you don't mind me asking, who in your past told you that you're not good enough or that you'll never succeed?" Ed explains, "when I was in high school, the guidance counselor was constantly trying to get me to go to trade school. When I was a junior in high school, my parents told me that I should consider buying a truck and start a landscaping business. To use their words, they didn't think I was 'college material'. Maybe they were right. Even the pastor of the church that I attended told me that he'd hire me as a custodian and groundskeeper when I graduated from high school." Joe advises Ed, "don't listen to what anyone else tells you. You do what God would have you to do. In the end, that's all that matters." Ed tells Joe, "I think I'm on that path now."

Joe explains to Ed, "two years ago, you and Pete started helping me train. Since then, I've made a lot of progress. If it weren't for you guys, I'd still be struggling with my weight even though I solved my genetic issue. I have all this knowledge about biochemistry and genetics, but that only goes so far. I remember when you told me to take the concept of breakfast, lunch, and dinner, and throw it out the window and, instead, eat five or six small meals a day. Then, when you told me to take a double dose of carnitine an hour before I got on the treadmill, I really saw the weight starting to come off. People need your help, Ed." Ed replies, "I wasn't cut out to work with computers. Neither was Amy. You're right, Joe. I need to do what God has planned for me."

Suggesting a departure from their usual activities, after dinner, Joe suggests that the group take a long walk around campus. No one objects, and everyone gets five miles in. Joe will see a little more weight come off. Taking a long walk, Jenny is sure to sleep really well tonight. And, Ed and Amy will get a final look at the University campus together.

During the walk, Ed mentions to Joe, "Pete told me that your father knows the author of the *Eddie, The Mechanic* series." Joe replies, "he does. I don't know exactly how they know each other, but they do." Ed asks Joe, "is there any way that you can find out whether Mr. Frazier is a real person, or is modeled after a real person?" Joe replies, "I'll give it a try. It doesn't hurt to ask. I'm kind of curious myself."

Amy asks Joe, "while you're at it, can you find out if Mr. Zunde is a real person too? The further along in the book I get, the more I'm convinced that Mr. Zunde is a real person. Mr. Zunde's kind of cool." Joe replies, "sure. I'll find out what I can. And, I agree. Mr. Zunde is cool. Mr. Zunde is not one to put up with anyone's crap. Some of the characters in that series just seem too real to me." Ed replies, "I've noticed that too."

It has been clear to those reading the *Eddie, The Mechanic* series that Joe, when he speaks in front of a group, now has the energy of Mr. Frazier. It is also clear to Amy that, since Ed has been reading the series, Ed has been sounding a bit like Edward Bogenskaya and Mark Svoboda, especially when dealing with Rodney.

After their five-mile walk, everyone heads home for the night, only to meet up at the gym early tomorrow morning.

Week Ten

Back to the Beach

While making their plans to move to the beach, Ed and Amy hang around the University simply because their housing has already been paid for the entire semester. And, there are a few loose ends to tie up, such as withdrawing from their classes. Since they'll be around campus for a few more weeks, they'll still be able to attend the Interdenominational Campus Fellowship meeting and use the University's athletic center.

Mid week, Amy and Ed look online at homes for sale near the South end of the beach where Amy will be working. Finding a few possibilities, Amy makes a few notes, planning another trip down to the beach. Amy also checks her bank account, making sure she can afford the homes she plans to look at. And then, there are the wedding plans. Amy always wanted to get married on the beach. With the clock running down before they start work, Ed and Amy realize they have a lot of work to do.

Mitch, the division chief, has allowed Ed and Amy to stay at the bunkhouse as they make their transition to the beach. Mitch has told Amy that she can feel free to start whenever she wants, as long as it is before the Spring rush to the beach. Ed is a little less flexible. Ed's starting date is right at the beginning of the year, when the big annual rush to the gym begins.

Early on Friday morning, Ed and Amy pack up, ready to head to the beach for the weekend. Meeting in front of Amy's dorm, Ed asks Amy, "are you ready?" Amy replies, "more than ever. I can't wait to get out of this place." Ed asks, "do you mean permanently, or just for the weekend?" Amy replies, "well, kind of both." Amy then asks Ed, "did you see the difference between the people down at the beach, and the people here at the University?" Ed replies, "I see what you mean. Everyone down at the beach is really happy. Around here, most people are, well, you know." Amy clearly gets what Ed is saying.

Walking to Ed's Jeep with their scantily packed duffle bags, Amy is definitely looking forward to a weekend at the beach. Coming up to his Jeep, Ed suddenly drops his duffle bag on the ground, running to the other side of the vehicle. Hearing the sound of his tire punctured by a knife, Ed quickly moves in and apprehends the vandal. Ed squeezes the vandal's hand with unmerciful pressure, forcing him to relinquish the knife.

Once the situation is under control, Ed yells out to Amy, "call the police!" Amy, who videoed the altercation between Ed and Rodney, replies, "sure! No problem!" Rodney begs Ed, "please! Please, don't call the police! I'm sorry! I'll pay for the tires! I'm sorry!" Ed asks Rodney, "with what? The money you stole from the fellowship, junior?" Ignoring Rodney's apology, Amy calls the campus police, requesting that an officer meet her at the parking lot across from Ed's dorm.

Ed asks Rodney, "what was that all about, junior?" Sobbing like a baby, Rodney explains, "I'm sorry! I said I'll pay for the tires." Quite angry that Rodney slashed three of his tires, Ed asks, "suppose we showed up an hour later, Steele? Then what? Would you be sorry then? Would you offer to pay for the tires you damaged then?" Seeing that Rodney does not answer Ed, Amy tells Ed, "the only thing he's sorry about is that he got caught."

The campus police arrive. The officer walks over, announcing, "I'm Officer Branson. What's going on here?" Ed replies, "junior, here, just slashed three of my tires." Pointing to Rodney's knife, Ed tells Officer Branson, "his knife is over there, on the ground." In a moment of desperation, Rodney exclaims, "I did not! I've never seen that knife before in my life!" Amy tells Officer Branson, "he's lying," and shows the officer the video she took of Rodney with the knife in his hand. Officer Branson, who is no idiot, reviews the video, clearly seeing the evidence.

Officer Branson tells Rodney, "the young lady has a video of you in an altercation with this gentleman. During the altercation, that knife laying over there is clearly in your hand. I am going to give you an opportunity to revise your story. Go ahead. I'm listening." Rodney relents, telling the officer, "okay! Okay! But, I told him I'd pay for his tires." Hearing Rodney's confession, the officer obtains Rodney's student ID card, cuffs Rodney, and places him in the back seat of his patrol car. Rodney sobs himself a river, desperately thinking of a way to get himself out of this one.

Officer Branson explains to Ed, "this is a property damage issue. This is what I'm going to do. I'm going to take him down to the station, and get his info. This case will then be referred to the dean." Ed asks, "how about my tires?" The officer explains, "I've seen cases like this before. If he doesn't pay for your tires, the dean will expel him. And, since the perp is a senior, I strongly suspect that he will gladly pay for the damage, otherwise he won't graduate. And, if he doesn't pay for your tires, you can always take him to small claims court." Although Ed breathes a sigh of relief, he and Amy will not be getting on the road anytime soon.

Officer Branson leaves, taking Rodney away. Quite upset, Amy asks Ed, "now what do we do?" Ed replies, "I call a tow truck, and have the Jeep towed to the tire shop on Spring Street. Once I get new tires, we'll be on our way. We should be out of here by lunch. When we get back, I'll hit Steele up for the bill." Amy tells Ed, "you make this sound so easy." Ed replies, "I've been reading the *Eddie, The Mechanic* series. Obstacles are only obstacles if you let them be obstacles."

After lunch, Ed returns to campus with his Jeep and five new tires. After all, the spare tire needs to match the other four tires. Ed and Amy load up the Jeep, and head out to the beach. Meanwhile, Rodney is sitting in the police station where the campus police are in no rush to deal with him. Making Rodney wait for hours is the police department's way of sending him a strong message. While he is waiting in the holding cell, Rodney reviews the video that Amy was kind enough to email to both him and the campus police.

Ed and Amy finally arrive at the beach, albeit five hours after they planned. With the day winding down, Ed and Amy drive around and preview a few houses that Amy has picked out to look at with the real estate agent tomorrow morning. After the short tour around the neighborhood, Ed and Amy head to the bunkhouse. Once they are settled in, Ed and Amy head to the beach for the evening.

Walking along the beach, Amy tells Ed, "it's quarter after seven. The campus fellowship meeting is starting about now." Ed replies, "that's right! I wonder if Steele made it." Amy suggests, "why don't you text Pete and find out." Ed replies, "that's a good idea. I think I'll do that."

Ed texts to Pete, "Hey. Did Steele show up tonight?" Pete immediately texts back, "No. He's MIA." Ed texts to Pete, "He's probably still in the campus jail." Pete texts back, "What???" Ed stops, and texts to Pete, "Steele slashed my tires this morning. We caught him. Called the campus police. They took him away." Pete texts to Ed, "They're starting. Theresa is making an announcement. BRB." Ed shows Amy the conversation, who mentions, "wow! I wonder what's up with Rodney." Ed replies, "he's probably in his dorm room, drinking a six-pack of beer." Amy laughs, and tells Ed, "that could be!"

Continuing on their walk down the beach, Amy tells Ed, "the house we saw the last time we were down here was my favorite, from the outside, anyway." Ed concurs, telling Amy, "I agree. It's made of concrete, and far enough in from the beach that, when there's a hurricane, it will survive." Amy replies, "I never thought about that!"

Along their walk, Amy takes her camera and, putting it on a picnic table, sets the automatic timer. Using the ocean as a backdrop, Amy and Ed quickly get into position and pose for the photograph. The picture is taken and Amy and Ed rush over to take a look. Amy tells Ed, "let's get a few more. I'm going to post these online later." Amy gets a few more photographs of her and Ed on the beach, and Ed gets a very special photograph of Amy with the lifeguard station on her future beach as the backdrop.

Interrupting Ed and Amy's photo shoot, Pete texts to Ed, "Theresa says Rodney has to quit leading the fellowship. Concussion is bad. Says he can't function." Not quite believing that Rodney's concussion is the reason for Rodney resigning from his leadership position, Ed texts back, "Yeah, right. Steele couldn't function before his concussion." Pete texts to Ed, "They're asking if anyone wants to lead the group." Ed texts back to Pete, "Let me know who they pick."

Ed tells Amy, "Steele quit leading the fellowship. He's apparently blaming his concussion." With a bit of sarcasm, Amy tells Ed, "I'm sure that's it. It probably has nothing to do with pilfering from the fellowship or slashing tires. Wait a second! If I remember correctly, one of Jesus' twelve Disciple's stole from the money box! His name was Judas Iscariot." Ed mentions, "wow! That's right! Now, I'm really wondering if Steele is a believer."

Amy then digresses, and tells Ed, "we shouldn't really judge Rodney." Ed replies, "I get that. But, the Bible says, 'you will know them by their fruits'. Steele's fruit is all rotten. First, he gossips, and reposts pictures of you and Jenny online. Then, he steals from the fellowship for two years. And, yeah. I get that he confessed it. But, when I told him that I didn't really know that he had a secret and that I was just messing with him, he got really ticked off. So, the only reason he supposedly repented is because he thought I knew what he was doing. Then, he slashes my tires and then he had the nerve to lie about it to the officer. That's all rotten fruit." Amy agrees, telling Ed, "you do have a point. Whenever you see a tree, and there's rotten fruit on it, the fruit never goes back to being edible again. It just rots out more."

Ed tells Amy, "I would just like to see one piece of good fruit on Steele's tree. Just one." Amy replies, "come to think about it, I can't think of any." Ed replies, "that's because there isn't any. He's just like the Pharisees. Shiny and clean on the outside but, on the inside, he's full of robbery and wickedness." Amy replies, "I totally see that now."

A while later, as they are walking down the beach, Ed gets another text from Pete. Ed takes out his phone, seeing a message from Pete that reads, "New leader. Mike Collins stepped up." Ed texts back to Pete, "That's good news." Showing Amy the text from Pete, Ed tells her, "Mike Collins is leading the fellowship now. That's a vast improvement over Steele."

Amy comments, "I still can't believe that Rodney said, 'I'm sure we'll all be glad to see Ed and Amy go.' That was really in bad taste." Ed laughs, and tells Amy, "and, he gets ticked off because I call him 'Steele'? Then, he tells me that what I do is not very Christian like?" Amy points out, "he plays on people's emotions." Ed replies, "exactly. Dana and Donna do the same thing."

After a long walk down the beach, Ed and Amy sit in the sand and talk for a while. With no pressure to wake up early in the morning, Ed and Amy take the time to plan their wedding, pick a tentative wedding date, and plan their move to the beach. At the top of the list for tomorrow, Ed and Amy again review the homes they planned to look at. Around midnight, Ed and Amy head back to the bunkhouse, finding all five tires on Ed's Jeep in perfect condition.

The next day, Ed and Amy meet the real estate agent, who shows them the homes that Amy picked out to view. Going from home to home, in her mind, Amy keeps coming back to the home she saw during their previous trip to the beach. The home needed no work, was a few blocks from the beach, and, as Ed pointed out, is likely to survive a hurricane. By mid morning, Amy has made an executive decision and puts a contract on the cozy little cottage she just can't get out of her mind. Ed, who is used to living in a dorm room, has no objection. Truth be told, all Ed needs is a place to lay his head at night.

Before lunch, Amy and Ed head to the church that Amy attended when she lived in the area. Amy and Ed speak with the pastor, and confirm their wedding date they chose yesterday while sitting on the beach. With everything falling into place so easily, Ed and Amy conclude that God is clearly at work in their lives.

Saturday afternoon, Ed and Amy head to the beach again. Lying in the sand, Ed tells Amy, "finally, I've figured out what I want to do in my life." Amy tells Ed, "when it comes so easy, God must be at work. For a long time, I was trying to figure out what to do with my life. It was right there in front of me all the time. I can't believe I didn't see it." Ed replies, "seriously. I know what you mean. It's been right in front of me all the time too." Voicing her pet peeve, Amy explains to Ed, "and, what's really weird is that, if you find something that you really want to do, and it doesn't conform to what everyone else thinks you should be doing, it's somehow not a 'real job'."

Amy gets up, sits behind Ed and puts her arms around him, telling him, "well, Ed Becker, I guess we're stuck with our not so real jobs." Ed replies, "good. I don't want a 'real job' anyway. A real job is when you wake up way too early in the morning and drive to work, sitting in rush hour traffic. Then, when you get there, you're stuck inside all day long, chained to a desk, with a half-dozen people telling you what to do. Then, when it's time to go home, you sit in rush hour traffic all over again." Amy tells Ed, "my dad used to call that 'live to work'. He always wanted to 'work to live' instead. But, he could never really figure out how to do that." Ed assures Amy, "we'll figure it out." Amy replies, "I think we already did."

Amy abruptly tells Ed, "let's go in the water!" Ed and Amy run to the water and head out into the ocean. Only a few people venture to go out in the water during the off season, for the water is a bit on the cold side. Observing the obvious, Ed tells Amy, "there's not a whole lot of people in the water today." Amy explains, "that's because the water is getting colder. A lot of the people out here right now are Canadians or from the Northeast. The water is warm here compared with what they get up there."

After an afternoon on the beach, heading back to the Jeep, Amy exclaims, "oh, oh, oh! I almost forgot! I have a surprise for you!" Ed replies, "really? What is it?" Amy smiles, and replies, "if I tell you, it won't be a surprise anymore, now will it?" Ed asks, "when do I get my surprise?" Amy replies, "how about right now, before we have dinner? But, we'll have to drive to your surprise. And, you can't exactly take it back to the University with you." Ed and Amy get into Ed's Jeep, and Amy directs Ed to his surprise.

Arriving at the county park, Amy tells Ed, "I would tell you to close your eyes, but you're driving." Ed laughs, telling Amy, "unless you give me very precise instructions of when to turn and when to stop or go."

Amy tells Ed to pull into a parking space at the side of a building, where they get out of the Jeep. Amy instructs Ed to close his eyes, as they walk hand in hand around the outside of the building to get to where Ed's surprise is waiting for him.

Amy tells Ed, "okay. You can open your eyes now." Ed opens his eyes, seeing an Olympic size swimming pool, complete with a diving area having two high boards and one low board. Amy exclaims, "surprise! You can still dive when we move down here!" Ed exclaims, "wow! This is awesome, Amy!" Amy points out, "the icing on the cake is that there's a separate diving pool with diving platforms. I've never dived from a platform before, though." Ed replies, "neither have I. But, I dived off a cliff once." Amy tells Ed, "this is where I dived when I lived down here." Ed and Amy take a walk around as Amy shows Ed what else is in the park.

Sitting on a bench near the tennis courts, Ed tells Amy, "this is a really nice park. It has everything." Amy replies, "there's not many people here right now but, during the Summer, this place really comes alive. It's kind of like that song, *Saturday in the Park* by the group Chicago." Ed tells Amy, "I like busy parks. They feel alive. It must be really nice here in the Summer." Amy replies, "it is. It really is."

Amy asks Ed, "do you want to hear something really funny about a song?" Ed replies, "sure." Amy asks Ed, "do you know that song *Kodachrome*, by Paul Simon?" Ed replies, "yeah." Amy explains, "well, in the song, he says he likes to take a photograph. But, here's the problem. Kodachrome is a color-reversal film. It's used for making slides and movies, not photographic prints. Kodacolor is Kodak's film for making prints. But, it's kind of hard to get anything to rhyme with Kodacolor." Ed laughs and replies, "I never knew that!" Amy tells Ed, "sometimes I think I'm the only person in the world who's seen that."

Amy then asks Ed, "do you want to hear something else that's kind of funny?" Ed replies, "sure." Amy tells Ed, "Paul Simon wrote another song, called *Mother and Child Reunion*. He got the name of the song title from a Chinese restaurant menu." Ed interrupts, and asks, "how's that?" Amy explains, "in a Chinese restaurant, the dish called *Mother and Child Reunion* is chicken and egg." Ed laughs, and replies, "that's really kind of funny."

Amy tells Ed, "getting back to the park, the good part is that it's a county park, so the tourists can't use it." Ed tells Amy, "this whole area is perfect. I don't know why you ever left." Amy smiles, and replies, "to find you, Ed Becker, and to find out what's wrong with me. And, now I'm coming back to where I really belong." Ed tells Amy, "I love you so much," and gives Amy a big hug and kiss.

As they walk back to Ed's Jeep, Ed tells Amy, "once we get settled, I want to coach a high school sport." Amy asks, "do you think you can do that?" Ed replies, "I'm reading the manual." Amy quickly recalls the first time she met Ed at the pool, when Ed told her that he read the diving board manual right before coming out to dive. Amy laughs, and asks, "and, just what manual is that, Mr. Becker?" Ed replies, "the *Eddie, The Mechanic* Series. Mr. Frazier is a really great coach."

Ed then mentions to Amy, "I still want to know if Mr. Frazier is a real person or not. There's just way too much stuff in that series that sounds real to me." Amy reminds Ed, "Joe said he can probably find out for you." Ed replies, "I should ask him if he found out when we get back." After a nice tour around the park, Ed and Amy head down the road to find dinner.

After their nice relaxing weekend at the beach, Ed and Amy are totally convinced that they have made the right decision to move to the beach town near where Amy grew up. Early Monday morning, they head back to the University where they will spend the rest of the week skipping classes, going to the gym, and planning for their future.

Week Eleven

The Invitation

Returning to campus on Monday, during the early afternoon, Ed calls Rodney to collect the money for the tires that he slashed. Meeting Rodney between classes, Ed asks Rodney, "did you have a good weekend?" Hoping to get some sympathy, Rodney replies, "no. I'm falling behind in all my classes. I can't think straight since the accident." Ed points out to Rodney, "you demonstrated that on Friday when you slashed my tires." Ed's candid response was not exactly what Rodney was looking for. Ed hands Rodney a copy of the bill, and bluntly tells him, "it's time to pay up, Steele."

Rodney examines the bill, and exclaims, "why are you making me pay for five tires?" Ed explains, "because all four tires have to match. You can't just replace three of them. And, the spare tire has to match the other four. So, where's my money, Steele?" Rodney boldly informs Ed, "I'm not paying for any of this!" Ed replies, "yeah, you are, Steele." Rodney flips Ed a bird and tells him, "up yours. You can't make me pay for them." Not playing games with Rodney, Ed replies, "fine. Have it your way. I'm headed to the dean's office right now. You can deal with him. Good luck." Ed walks away, heading straight to the dean's office.

Weighing his options, Rodney quickly concludes that he has none. Rodney runs after Ed, yelling out, "okay! Okay! Hold up! I'll pay for them." Ed stops, and firmly tells Rodney, "okay. Good. Now, we're getting somewhere, Steele. You can pay for the tires, like right now." Sincerely hoping that the answer is "no", Rodney asks Ed, "can I transfer the money to you with my phone?" Ed replies, "sure. No problem, Steele." Rodney grudgingly performs the transaction, but Ed doesn't care about Rodney's attitude. Ed just wants his money.

Once he verifies the money has been transferred to his account, Ed tells Rodney, "I'll see you Friday at the fellowship meeting. Have a good week. And, I suggest you stay away from my Jeep, junior, if you know what I mean. The next time you won't be so lucky." Rodney admonishes Ed, exclaiming, "that was uncalled for! And, you know, you could have acted a little more like a Christian in the way you handled this." Ed laughs, telling Rodney, "really, Steele? I wonder how stealing money from the fellowship and slashing tires fits in with your theology. And, besides, Steele, I don't 'act' like a Christian. I am one. You're the one who seems to be 'acting' like a Christian," placing great emphasis on the word "acting". Ed walks away, leaving Rodney stewing over having to pay for Ed's five new tires.

Later that week, the Interdenominational Campus Fellowship meets at the same time in the same place. Arriving early since they have no classes, Ed and Amy hang out in the public area adjacent to the meeting room. Jenny and Pete walk over, joining them. Jenny asks Ed and Amy, "are you guys headed to the beach again this weekend?" Amy replies, "no. Not this weekend. We got a lot of stuff to do around here." Jenny asks, "really, girl? Like what?" Amy replies, "stuff for our wedding and things like buying a bed to sleep in." Jenny replies, "oh yeah. A bed would be like really nice. It would sure beat sleeping on the floor, girl."

Ed asks Pete, "who's giving the talk tonight?" Pete replies, "I don't know. Rodney still has the sign-up sheet. I'm not sure if anyone even signed up for tonight." Amy comments, "I guess it will be a surprise." Jenny tells Amy, "hopefully it won't be Rodney. Last week, he showed up like really late, and was a total space case." Amy reminds Jenny, "that's because we caught him slashing Ed's tires, and the police took him away." Jenny exclaims, "that's right! How come I couldn't put two and two together?"

Joe walks up with Brittany, asking, "how's everyone doing?" Jenny exclaims, "great! I'm sleeping so well now! Thank you again for finding my problem for me!" Amy tells Joe, "I'm doing really good too! I like normal. Thank you so much, Joe." Joe tells Jenny and Amy, "that sounds really great! I'm so happy for both of you." Amy asks Joe, "you're coming with us to get pizza later, right?" Joe replies, "sure. We'd really like to do that. You know, I had a really light lunch today. So, I am really looking forward to pizza tonight."

Ed asks Joe, "have you talked to your dad yet about the author of *Eddie, The Mechanic?*" Joe replies, "I did. He's going to look into it for me." Ed tells Joe, "hopefully, he'll find something out before me and Amy leave." Joe replies, "well, if he doesn't find out soon, I could always email you what I find out." Ed suggests, "or, you can take a trip down to the beach and visit us."

Joe mentions, "it looks like we're ready to get started. I'm giving the talk tonight, so I don't want to be too late." Amy tells Joe, "we were wondering who was going to give the talk tonight." Amy is glad that Joe is giving the talk this evening, as opposed to Rodney speaking to the group. The group heads into the room, taking their usual place along the back wall.

Mike Collins stands on the stage, and announces, "good evening. It's time for us to get started. Someone, please tell those outside that we're ready to begin." Everyone in the room stands up, waiting for those outside to come in and join the group. Once everyone gets settled, Mike opens the meeting with a prayer. The praise band takes the stage, playing a few numbers before today's talk is given.

This evening, as the praise band plays, Rodney is not on stage. Instead, Rodney stands off to the side, taking a place against the side wall with Donna, Theresa, and a few others. As opposed to walking around the room seeking out the scent of alcohol or tobacco, Rodney stands quietly, not saying a word. Rodney is secretly hoping that Ed did not make public knowledge of the incident that occurred last Friday when Rodney got caught slashing Ed's tires.

After the band is finished playing, Mike takes the stage and announces, "tonight, we'll be hearing from Joe Sugarman, who I hear has a very important message for all of us. Joe, please come on up." Hearing that Joe is giving the talk tonight, the members of the fellowship clap and cheer. It is not hard to figure out that they all love Joe.

Joe walks up to the stage, thanking his audience for the warm welcome, telling them, "thank you. Thank you. Good evening all of my friends and thank you for having me again today. Don't worry. You can relax. There will be no biochemistry lesson today. There will be a biology lesson instead. Today, I will be talking about fruit." The group laughs, always glad to hear Joe's sense of humor.

Joe, who is accustomed to speaking in front of a group, asks his audience, "by a show of hands, how many of you here are going to Heaven because you accepted Jesus Christ as your Lord and Savior?" Nearly everyone in the room raises their hand, with five people in the back of the room as the notable exception. Rodney, holding his hand up high, looks toward the back of the room seeing Ed, Amy, Pete, Jenny, and Brittany being the lone holdouts. Ed looks at Brittany and smiles. Brittany nods her head, signaling to Ed that Joe is really going to address the issue that has been weighing on his heart.

Referring to the five people at the back of the room who did not raise their hand, Rodney whispers to Dana, "see? I knew there was something wrong with those guys." Dana whispers back to Rodney, "I knew it! I just knew it." What Rodney does not know is that Ed and the four other people at the back of the room have had the discussion of "accepting Jesus Christ as your Lord and Savior" with Joe on several occasions. They know exactly what Joe is going to address tonight.

Joe continues, "well, I have some bad news for some of you. Nowhere in the Bible is it mentioned that the way to Heaven is by accepting Jesus Christ as your Lord and Savior. If someone is aware of the passage that says that, please let me know. I've never been able to find it." A few students frantically search through their Bible for an applicable verse, but come up with nothing.

Joe moves on to explain, "it seems that, in the modern day church in America, when a person gets saved, the scenario is always the same. The person walks down an aisle, answers a few questions posed by the pastor, fills out a card, and they're on their way to glory land. Occasionally, the new convert will meet with a deacon of the church and pray. That, my friends, is a very watered-down version of what salvation really is. In fact, what I just described will likely get you nowhere. Countless people who have walked the aisle and filled out the card are not on their way to Heaven."

Joe then boldly exclaims, "the creation does not tell the Creator what to do! The Creator tells the creation what to do! The creation does not make the rules! The Creator makes the rules!" Joe then explains, "if we want to be on the path to Heaven, we might want to carefully listen to what God has to say regarding the issue, not what man, the modern church in America, or tradition has to say."

Now having everyone's attention, Joe explains, "to some people, salvation is viewed as analogous to receiving a free ticket to a concert. When you arrive at the concert, the ticket gets you in the door. With salvation, it's not quite the same. While salvation is a free gift, there are certain prerequisites to receiving that free gift. But, before I address that issue, please allow me to address a few other important issues."

Joe explains, "first, let me say this. If you are in the process of being saved, God picked you. You did not pick God. There is nothing in man or woman that would move them toward seeking God or to follow Jesus. God extended an offer to you and, if you respond in the proper way, God will graciously grant you eternal life. If you do not respond in the right way, you might just end up in the eternal fire."

Joe explains, "let's take a closer look at this warped theology of today. You walk an aisle, say a prayer, and fill out a card. Monday morning comes, and you cheat on an exam. You steal someone else's homework assignment, copy it, and turn it in. You covet another person's girlfriend, boyfriend, automobile, or lifestyle. You post gossip or repeat gossip on social media. You lie to get what you want. When you don't get what you want, you destroy what someone else has. You remain sexually immoral. You continue to take recreational drugs without any intent to stop. You harbor bitterness and an unforgiving spirit. I could go on, but you probably get the picture."

Specifically addressing the topic of unforgiveness, Joe explains, "an unforgiving spirit is, by the way, stark evidence that a person is not on their way to Heaven. But, don't take my word for it. In Matthew, chapter 6, verse 15, Jesus said, 'But if you do not forgive others, then your Father will not forgive your transgressions.' If you do not forgive others, it is evidence that you are not saved and therefore not on the path to Heaven! It's right there in God's Word, in black and white. What can be clearer?"

Joe instructs the group, "please take a look at the Book of Revelation, chapter 22, verse 15. That verse lists a few practices that will also exclude a person from entering the Kingdom of Heaven. Included in that list are the dogs, which refers to those who are impure. Also, included in that list, are sorcerers. The original Greek word, by the way, that we translate to 'sorcerer' is *pharmakeia*, which is where we get the word 'pharmacy' today. Pharmakeia refers to drugs, specifically using drugs to obtain a distorted perception of reality. Murderers are also excluded from the Kingdom of Heaven, as are idolaters, and everyone who practices lying."

Without looking up the scripture, Joe then quotes Matthew chapter 7, verse 21, telling the group, "Jesus said, 'Not everyone who says to Me, 'Lord, Lord,' will enter the kingdom of heaven, but he who does the will of My Father who is in heaven will enter.'" Joe asks his audience, "just exactly what is the will of the Father?" Answering his own question, Joe continues, "the will of the Father is that we bear fruit. We can start by bearing the fruit of the Spirit, which is love, joy, peace, patience, kindness, goodness, faithfulness, gentleness, and self control. But, we have a little problem here. That is not your fruit. That fruit is the fruit of the Holy Spirit. You can't bear that kind of fruit on your own. In The Gospel of John, at the beginning of chapter 15, it clearly states that, in order for you to bear fruit, you must abide in the vine. That vine is Jesus Christ. If you don't abide in the vine, you will be gathered up and tossed into the eternal fire. What could be clearer?"

Joe then asks the group, "can you bear fruit outside the Spirit?" Five seconds go by, and Joe, answering his own question, tells the group, "of course you can!" Joe then asks his audience, "do you want to know what kind of fruit you can bear outside the Holy Spirit?" A few students reply, "yes," and Joe moves on to answering his question. But, before he gives the answer, Joe informs the group, "we must remember that there are only two kinds of fruit. The first is the fruit of the Spirit. The other kind of fruit is the fruit of the flesh. You and I can bear the fruit of the flesh quite well on our own. We don't need God's help to do that."

Now with everyone's attention, Joe explains, "if you turn in your Bible to Romans, chapter 1, verses 28 through 32, you'll find a description of the fruit of the flesh. Let me read it to you right from the text. The fruit Paul is talking about here is, and I quote, 'And just as they did not see fit to acknowledge God any longer, God gave them over to a depraved mind, to do those things which are not proper, being filled with all unrighteousness, wickedness, greed, evil; full of envy, murder, strife, deceit, malice; they are gossips, slanderers, haters of God, insolent, arrogant, boastful, inventors of evil, disobedient to parents, without understanding, untrustworthy, unloving, unmerciful; and although they know the ordinance of God, that those who practice such things are worthy of death, they not only do the same, but also give hearty approval to those who practice them.' Now, how does that contrast with the fruit of the Spirit?" Joe pauses for a moment, then summarizes, "so, there are only two kinds of fruit, the fruit of the Spirit, and the fruit of the flesh. In order for you to bear the fruit of the Spirit, you must abide in the vine."

Hearing what Joe has to say, a few people in the fellowship suddenly have a grave look of concern on their faces. Among them is Rodney, who is staring at the wall across from him, concluding that Joe's words are directed specifically at him. Dana, about to have another emotional breakdown, manages to hold her composure at least for the moment. And, Donna appears calm, justifying to herself that Dana is the one who generally starts the gossip within her social circle. But Donna, propagating the sin of gossip, is equally as guilty.

Joe then asks, "what else is the will of the Father? High on the list is that we, who claim to be Christians, love each other." Again, quoting scripture without referencing his Bible, Joe states, "in First John, chapter 3, verse 14, it states, 'We know that we have passed out of death into life, because we love the brethren. He who does not love abides in death.' That's also pretty clear, my friends, isn't it?"

Joe continues, "there is another requirement that is grossly overlooked by the walk an aisle and fill out a card theologians of the modern-day American church. That requirement is repentance. Repentance is turning away from sin. If someone claims to be saved, and yet continues in their same sinful lifestyle, you have the right to suspect that they may not have truly been converted. If someone claims to follow Jesus and doesn't repent of their sins, how is that congruent with what the Bible teaches? It's not! Now, I'm sure someone is going to say, 'Joe! You're judging people!' No, I'm not. As I mentioned before, the Bible states, 'you will know them by their fruits.' If you shall know them by their fruits, you should be looking at a person's fruit!" Joe then summarizes, "it is the will of God that you come to repentance, love the brethren, and bear much fruit."

Joe then digresses, and tells the group, "I mentioned earlier that salvation is a free gift, but there are certain prerequisites that must be met to receive that free gift. God called you. The proper response to God's call is getting sorry for your sins, repenting of your sins, abiding in the vine, that is Christ, which will lead to loving the brethren and bearing much fruit."

Joe then asks, "let me ask you this. How does that compare to the theology of walking an aisle and filling out a card? The only thing that walking an aisle and filling out a card will get you is your name entered into a computer somewhere. Walking an aisle and filling out a card won't get your name written in the Lamb's Book of Life. On the contrary, perseverance in abiding in the vine, repenting of your sins, bearing fruit, and following Jesus will get your name written in the Lamb's Book of Life."

Joe quotes Matthew, chapter 7, verse 13, orating, "Enter through the narrow gate; for the gate is wide and the way is broad that leads to destruction, and there are many who enter through it." Joe asks the group, "what is the sign over the narrow gate?" Nearly everyone in the fellowship answers, "Heaven." Joe smiles, and replies, "good! You all got that right." Joe then asks the group, "what is the sign over the wide gate?" Nearly everyone answers, "Hell." Joe smiles and chuckles, then tells the group, "no. The sign over the wide gate says Heaven. It just doesn't go there." Many in the group laugh, surprised that Joe caught them off guard. Joe then tells everyone, "get on the narrow path and walk through the narrow gate."

Joe then gives quite an unusual invitation, telling the group, "this is where your pastor would usually give an invitation, and tell you to come forward if you would like to join the church or accept God's offer of salvation. If you haven't already guessed, I'm not going to do that. If you feel convicted by anything I said today, your job is to get right with the Lord, and repent of any and all sin in your life. And, you must follow Jesus. And, if there is anyone here who is not currently following Jesus and wants to know how, please speak with me, or anyone else here after the meeting, and we will help guide you in your path."

Finished with his talk, Joe tells the group, "thank you for listening to me this evening. I sincerely hope I said something to encourage someone here tonight." Joe steps down from the stage and waves to the audience, receiving a standing ovation from the group. Joe walks to the back of the room where he receives hugs from his closest friends.

Not everyone, however, participates in giving Joe a standing ovation. Briskly walking to the rear of the room, hastily brushing up against those whom he passes by, Rodney storms out of the room, slamming the door hard on his way out. Showing her concern, Dana also leaves, chasing after Rodney. Ed looks out the door into the common area, and tells Amy, "Rodney is having a breakdown. Dana is trying to calm him down." Amy laughs, telling Ed, "as if Dana is going to be any help!"

Mike then takes the stage, and asks the group, "does anyone know what's wrong with Rodney?" Leesa Iron, one of Rodney's close friends, stating the obvious, replies, "he got kind of upset, and left." Knowing that Dana will not be much help, Mike asks Leesa, "will you check and see if he's okay, please?" Leesa replies, "sure." Leesa goes out and checks on Rodney. The praise band takes the stage, and begins their first number.

Outside the meeting room, Leesa finds Rodney and Dana both having a major league breakdown, where Rodney is angry and Dana is in tears. Leesa suggests to Rodney, "hey. Why don't you come back in and join the group?" Rodney exclaims, "I've had it with those guys! They're all out to get me! I'm never going back in there again!" Rodney errantly has come to the conclusion that Joe's talk this evening was directed specifically at him. Maintaining a level head, Leesa assures Rodney, "I really don't think anyone is out to get you." Earlier in the semester, Rodney preferred that Joe give a presentation that is more of a spiritual nature. This evening, Rodney got his wish. Apparently, the truth was a bit too difficult for Rodney to swallow.

Dana, quite self centered in thinking Rodney's problem has something to do with her, cries as she tells Leesa, "he's right! They're out to get us. They all know that I really wanted to go out with Ed, and now look at what they've been posting online!" Dana shows Leesa the pictures that Amy posted of Ed and Amy when they were at the beach, telling Leesa, "see?" Leesa reminds Dana, "Ed and Amy are getting married. They're not posting pics of them together to hurt you." Hearing Leesa say that Ed and Amy are getting married, Dana breaks out into a bigger crying fit. Realizing that she is not getting anywhere in consoling either Rodney or Dana, Leesa heads back in to join the fellowship.

As the praise band plays their last number, Mike walks over to Leesa, and asks, "what's going on with Rodney?" Leesa explains, "Rodney thinks everyone is out to get him, and said he's never coming back to the fellowship. And, Dana is having another pity party." Mike tells Leesa, "I'll ask the group to pray for them in just a moment." Leesa, who knows Rodney extremely well, whispers to Mike, "after listening to Joe tonight, I really don't think Rodney is saved." Showing his concern, Mike nods his head, fully understanding what Leesa is saying.

Mike closes the meeting with prayer and afterwards requests of the group, "if anyone knows Rodney and Dana well, please check on them sometime this weekend. Apparently, tonight, they're both very upset about something." Ed whispers to Amy, "I can't imagine what Rodney is upset about." Amy replies, "we see this all the time on the beach. Someone goes through a traumatic situation, and they're not quite the same afterwards. Maybe Rodney should see a doctor." Ed replies, "I agree. But, I'm not the one to tell him. I'm the last person he'd ever listen to."

Joe walks up to Ed, and asks, "are we ready?" Ed replies, "I'm ready. Let's go and get some dinner." Ed looks around, then asks, "where's Pete and Jenny?" Joe replies, "they're up in the front, filling Mike in on a few things he should know, such as Rodney's appearance of adhering to strict legalism and enforcing his beliefs upon others, and, on the other hand, living a lifestyle completely to the contrary."

Amy tells Ed, "you were right." Ed asks, "about what?" Amy reminds Ed, "when I first met you, you told me that Rodney was a Pharisee." Joe tells Amy, "that about sums it up." Over the years, Rodney, with his outward appearance of righteousness, has apparently fooled Mike as well. Joe, Ed, Jenny, and a few others, however, clearly see what has been going on.

Walking into the pizzeria, Ed and his group quickly find out that they are not the first ones from the fellowship who have arrived. Rodney, Dana, and Donna, waiting for their dinner to come out of the oven, are sitting at a booth sharing a pitcher of beer. Shocked at the anomaly in Rodney's behavior, Jenny whispers to Amy, jokingly asking, "should I like take a pic of him and post it online?" Amy laughs, and replies, "um, no. That's exactly what they want you to do. So don't do it." Jenny tells Amy, "I think you're right about that, girl."

Ed, Pete, and Joe go up to the counter, place the group's order, and return to the table with the drinks. Still a Pharisee of sorts, Rodney glances over at Jenny, seeing if she is having a glass of wine. Looking straight at Rodney, Jenny runs her tongue along the rim of her wine glass and takes a sip.

While they are waiting for the pizza to come out of the oven, Joe asks Ed and Amy, "so, how long are you guys going to be around?" Ed informs Joe, "the plan is to leave right before Thanksgiving break. Amy is going to start her job sometime around Christmas, when the snowbirds come down from the Northeast and Canada. And, I start on January 2, right when all the New Year's Resolution people storm into the gyms." Amy adds, "and, our wedding is right after Thanksgiving. So, mark the date on your calender, Joe." Joe tells Amy, "I got my invitation. The date has already been reserved. We'll definitely be there."

Jenny tells Amy, "I like can't wait for your wedding!" Amy laughs, and tells Jenny, "you like can't wait? Like?" Jenny laughs, and replies, "I do say 'like' all the time, don't I?" Pete replies, "you like say 'like' a lot." Amy laughs, and tells Jenny, "I can't imagine you any other way. You did that ever since middle school."

Jenny then tells the story, "I remember the first time I walked into the pizzeria here. It was right before the semester started, and the place was like really deserted. I saw Tony come out from the back, and I asked him, 'are you guys like open?' Tony looked at me and said, 'no. We're not 'like' open. We are open.'" The group laughs and, as somewhat expected, catches the attention of Rodney who is sitting in a booth a few tables over.

The pizza arrives and Ed and the group dig in. Over dinner, Brittany asks Amy, "so, tell us about your wedding. What do you have planned?" Amy explains, "it's going to be really simple. We're getting married on my beach. Then, we're going down to the Keys for our honeymoon." Quite puzzled, Brittany asks, "your beach?" Amy smiles, and replies, "yeah. My beach. The beach that I'll be working at when we get back from our honeymoon."

All excited, Amy adds, "oh! And we'll be living a few blocks from where I work. So, I can walk to work or ride my bicycle." Jenny asks Amy, "are you like going to buy the Jeep that you always wanted?" Amy replies, "no. Not right now. Honestly, I've survived in that town for two years with just my bicycle. That's all I really need."

Interrupting the conversation, Rodney walks toward Ed's table, telling Ed, "hey! I want my money back." Raising his voice, Ed tells Rodney, "junior! I'm eating dinner! Get out of here." Making a scene, Rodney tells Ed, "no! I want my money back for two of those tires." Ed replies, "sorry, junior. You're out of luck." Tony, the pizza shop owner, tells Rodney, "hey, you! Stop harassing my customers!" Rodney pays Tony no attention and continues to harass Ed.

Boldly crossing the line, Rodney grabs Ed's phone from the table, and tells Ed, "fine, then! I'll just keep this until you give me my money back." Ed grabs Rodney's arm, squeezing it like a vice. Rodney relinquishes Ed's phone, which falls onto the floor. Jenny whispers to Amy, "he's definitely drunk." Amy replies, "yeah. I'd say so." Seeing the commotion, Tony walks over to Ed's table, telling Rodney, "I'm going to have to ask you to leave!"

As Ed bends over to pick up his phone, Rodney jams his knee into Ed's face. Now angry with Rodney, Tony again tells Rodney, "I told you! You're going to have to leave!" Ed stands up and tells Tony, "I'll help you with that, Tony." Picking up Rodney and throwing him over his shoulder, Ed tells Tony, "open the door for me." Tony gladly opens the door for Ed, who hurls Rodney out onto the sidewalk. Tony yells out at Rodney, "if you come back in, I'm going to call the police on you, and let them cart you away in a wagon!"

Now that Rodney is out on the street, Tony tells Ed, "thanks for taking out the trash for me. You don't know how much I appreciate it." Ed replies, "no problem, boss." Tony informs Ed, "you know, that guy comes in here for lunch a lot during the week. He orders two slices of pizza and a beer, and sits alone in the back. He's usually very quiet. I really don't know what got into him today." Ed informs Tony, "I can tell you what got into him. He slashed my tires, and I made him pay for them. So, he's really ticked off at me." Tony shakes his head, and replies, "that would explain a lot. He hasn't been the same in the last few weeks." Ed informs Tony, "well, a few weeks ago, he hit his head on a diving board and got a concussion." Tony replies, "no wonder he's been acting a little strange recently."

Ed returns to his table, where Amy shows him the video of the altercation. Ed comments, "I don't know what's wrong with Steele. What did he expect me to do? Let him steal my phone?" Amy tells Ed, "he's just a self-righteous little brat." Joe tells Ed, "all you can do is give him the truth. What he does with it is his responsibility." Ed finishes his dinner, wondering why Dana and Donna have not left with Rodney.

Walking back to campus after dinner, Ed sees no sign of Rodney anywhere. Amy asks Ed, "can we go diving, please?" Ed replies, "sure." Amy explains, "we're out of here soon, and we won't get a chance to go diving for a while." Ed asks, "is the pool down at the beach open all year round?" Amy replies, "it is. But, in the Winter, the water can get a bit on the cool side." Ed tells Amy, "that's okay. We can take it."

At the University, the pool temperature is carefully kept between 77 and 82 degrees, for that is the regulation temperature range for competition. The temperature of the outdoor pool near the beach depends completely on the weather. A few cool overcast days can significantly drop the temperature of the water.

Ed and Amy arrive at the dorms, get their swimsuits, and head to the pool. On the way, Ed tells Amy, "guess what I found out." Amy asks, "what's that?" Ed explains, "Tony, at the pizzeria, told me that Rodney comes into the pizzeria for lunch during the week. For lunch, he orders two slices of pizza and a beer, and sits all by himself in the back." Quite surprised, Amy replies, "really? Rodney totally makes no sense." Ed tells Amy, "I didn't want to say anything back there to start any rumors. But, you're right. Rodney doesn't make any sense." Ed and Amy walk into the athletic center, confident that they will not run into Rodney at the diving area tonight.

Week Twelve

Heading Home

The following week, very late on Friday afternoon, Jenny asks Amy, "is there anything I can help you with?" Amy replies, "I think I got it all." Jenny tells Amy, "I'm really going to miss you, girl." Amy reminds Jenny, "we're only going to be three hours down the road. When Springtime comes, you and Pete are going to want to come down and visit us every weekend." Jenny replies, "you're probably right about that, girl." Amy announces, "okay! I'm officially all packed. Well, at least for now, anyway. We're out of here first thing in the morning." Jenny asks, "are you excited?" Amy replies, "yeah! I don't belong here. Now, I totally understand why God sent me here. But, I don't belong here."

Amy tells Jenny, "I'm going to text Ed and tell him I'm done packing." Jenny replies, "okay, girl. I'll text Pete. Why don't we head downstairs?" Amy and Jenny head downstairs, and wait for Ed and Pete before they head over to Amy and Ed's last time attending the Interdenominational Campus Fellowship meeting.

Arriving at the student center, Ed and Amy are told by their friends how sad they are that they are leaving. But, after listening to Amy's and Ed's talks to the group a few weeks earlier, their friends fully understand. Ed and Amy answer dozens of questions, a few of which make them realize they have a bit more planning to do.

Out in the common area, Jenny whispers to Pete, "isn't that Rodney all the way on the other side of the floor?" Pete looks one hundred feet away to the other side of the building, not quite sure whether it is Rodney or not. Walking to the other side of the building to get a better look, Jenny has peaked Pete's curiosity. Pete returns, and tells Jenny, "that's him, all right. It looks like he joined the meditation group. Dana and Donna are with him." Recalling that Rodney stole from the fellowship's funds, Jenny sarcastically comments, "I wonder if the meditation group is like looking for a treasurer."

Joe walks up with Brittany. After saying hello, Ed wastes no time asking Joe, "did you find out if Mr. Frazier is a real person?" Joe replies, "I did. And, the answer is not that simple." Ed asks, "really? How so?" Joe explains, "my dad put me in touch with the author. The author told me that Mr. Frazier's coaching abilities, personality, and the way he talks are, in fact, modeled after an actual person. But, here's where it gets interesting. In the series, Mr. Frazier's knowledge of track and field training methods is modeled after a completely different person. And, Mr. Frazier's past history is modeled after yet a third person." Ed surmises, "so, a coach like Mr. Frazier is theoretically possible. Mr. Frazier is not a totally made-up person." Joe replies, "it would seem that way." Giving Joe the impression that something important was riding on the answer, Ed replies, "that's really good to know."

Joe informs Ed, "not all fiction books are completely fiction. The author told me that every one of the classroom scenes during the high school years actually happened. And, get this. Angelo, the auto mechanic, was modeled after a real person. So was Vinnie at the auto body shop." Ed exclaims, "I knew it! A lot of stuff in those books just seems way too real to me! You just can't make some of that stuff up!"

Amy asks Joe, "how about Mr. Zunde? Mr. Zunde is really funny." Joe replies, "I'm sorry to say that Mr. Zunde is not modeled after a real person. He's totally a fictional character. But, get this. The author told me that Mr. Crum, the principal of the high school, in part, is modeled after a real person. In the series, Mr. Zunde's character was invented to keep the principal in check."

Joe asks Ed, "how far have you gotten in the series?" Ed replies, "I'm in the middle of *Eddie, The Collegiate Freshman*." Joe tells Ed, "wow! You've been really busy!" Ed explains, "since Amy and I decided to not come back to the University, we've had a lot of free time. I've been reading a lot." Truth is, Ed is studying Mr. Frazier and Mr. Zunde, for Ed wants to be a high school coach someday.

Amy tells Joe, "I'm stuck on the sixth book, *Eddie, The Mechanic*, in chapter one. That chapter has all my wedding plans in it." Joe replies, "really? I haven't gotten that far yet." Amy tells Joe, "I won't spoil it for you. But, when you get to that chapter, you'll be sure to get a déjà vu moment after seeing our wedding." Amy has found her perfect wedding plans in the *Eddie, The Mechanic* series.

Mike makes the announcement that they are ready to begin, and everyone heads inside to the meeting room. After the opening prayer, Mike announces, "today is Ed and Amy's last day with us before they move away. It's my understanding that Ed and Amy are leaving early tomorrow morning. If you haven't already done so, today is your last chance to tell them goodbye. Ed also asked me to announce that, if anyone wants to join them at the pizzeria after the meeting for dinner, please feel free to head there right after tonight's meeting."

As the band takes the stage, Mike asks the group, "is Dana here?" From the back of the room, Pete announces, "she's over at the meditation group with Donna and Rodney." Suspecting that Dana is gone for good, Mike announces, "that's a really big surprise. Okay. Does anyone feel that the Lord is leading them to lead our singing tonight?" Seeing no volunteers, a freshman, Cyndi Caldwell, raises her hand, and tells Mike, "if no one else wants to, I'll give it a try." Glad to have a volunteer, Mike tells Cyndi, "sure. Come on up." Cyndi takes the stage, and the band begins to play their first number.

Midway through the first number, Jenny whispers to Amy, "Cyndi has a really beautiful voice. Even if Dana comes back, they should keep Cyndi." Amy whispers back, "I know, right?" Jenny whispers to Amy, "now I'm wondering if Dana and Donna are like ever coming back."

Answering Jenny's question, near the end of the first number, Dana and Donna walk through the door and stand with the group and start singing along. Using the common intonation from the movie *Poltergeist*, Amy whispers to Jenny, "they're back." Jenny replies, "I see that. But, there's still no Rodney." Before walking into the fellowship meeting a moment ago, Dana and Donna attempted to convince Rodney to return to the fellowship, but Rodney would have absolutely nothing to do with returning to the group.

Finishing their third number, the band takes a seat on the floor with the rest of the group. Mike takes the stage and addresses the audience, telling them, "Rodney still has the sign-up sheet for our weekly talk. I have no idea who is supposed to speak this evening. Whoever that is, please come forward." A few seconds go by, and no one comes forward. Mike announces, "okay. This is not good. Let's do this. First, will someone please place another sign-up sheet on the table in the back, with dates for the remainder of this semester." One member of the fellowship announces, "I'll take care of that." Mike replies, "thank you."

Mike then announces, "okay. Now, on to problem number two. Would anyone here like to give tonight's talk?" A volunteer cannot be immediately found, so Joe, who always has some encouraging words, walks up to the front of the room, announcing, "I'll take care of problem number two." Mike is suddenly relieved, for he had nothing prepared to speak about tonight, and winging it wasn't on his list of things to do this evening.

Joe takes the stage, and begins, "so far, this semester, I've talked about biochemistry, and biology. This evening, I'm going to be talking about agronomy, specifically soil. More specifically, I'm going to be speaking about the four types of soil that Jesus referenced in the Parable of the Soils. This parable is found in Matthew, chapter 13; Mark, chapter 4; and Luke, chapter 8. If you would like to reference your Bible as I speak to you this evening, please refer to any of the three passages that I just mentioned. The story is the same."

Joe begins by holding up his Bible, and announces, "everything in the Word of God is seed. All you get are seeds. The seed is a Biblical truth. When you read the Bible, you obtain seeds. When you listen to a sermon, you may also get seeds. Maybe, if God wills it, you'll get a seed by listening to me tonight. If the seed is an acorn, that's what you'll get, an acorn. You will not get an oak tree. To get the oak tree, the acorn must be planted in a certain type of soil. Hopefully, you are the type of soil that will allow the acorn to grow into an oak tree."

Giving some preliminary information and history, Joe informs the group, "in the Parable of the Soils, Jesus was not instructing those listening to him on the technical details of how to plant seeds nor was He giving a seminar on agriculture. Trust me. Unlike many people today who think fruit comes from a grocery store, people who lived back then knew exactly how to plant seeds and cultivate crops. Their survival depended on it. In the Parable of the Soils, the people during Jesus' time knew exactly what Jesus was speaking about when he discussed the four types of soil."

Joe begins discussing the four types of soil, explaining, "the first type of soil is the soil along the road or a footpath. No one in their right mind would ever sow seed on a road or footpath and come back in four months expecting to find a plant. The seed likely fell there quite by accident. The seed here is the Word of God. As Jesus said, Satan immediately snatches away the seed that is sown in those who are represented by this type of soil. In today's modern society, this can be said to refer to the person who attends a church service with their extended family over Christmas, hears the message of salvation, and immediately goes back to their former belief that Christmas is all about Santa Claus and gift giving." Joe then raises his voice and points out, "in this case, the problem is not with the seed! The problem is with the soil!"

Moving on to the second type of soil, Joe explains, "the second type of soil is the rocky soil. No one plants seed in rocky soil and expects the plant to come to maturity. But, the seed will grow to some extent. The seed that germinated in the rocky soil has no viable roots. Once the weather becomes hot, the plant withers away. When torrential rains come, the plant is washed away. When freezing cold weather comes, the roots freeze and die. Now, in his explanation of this type of soil to his disciples, Jesus clearly explains that this inclimate weather is persecution and tribulation. The seed that fell on the rocky soil never matured to the point that it yielded any fruit. Again, the problem we have here is not with the seed. The problem is with the soil!"

Discussing the third type of soil, Joe explains, "the third type of soil is really a concern for me. A lot of college students fall into this category. So do a lot of people who go to church week after week in modern-day America. Perhaps you know a few people who are this type of soil." Mentioning the phrase "college students", Joe now has the attention of the entire group.

Joe explains the third type of soil, telling the group, "in this case, the seed fell among the thorns. The soil must be reasonably good since the thorns were able to grow in this type of soil. Again, like the seed that sprouted in the rocky soil, the seed that fell among the thorns sprouted to some extent. But, we have a serious problem here. The thorns grew up and choked out the plant. What exactly are these thorns? The Bible clearly tells us that the thorns are the cares of this world, the deceitfulness of riches, and the desires for other things not congruent with following Jesus. Once again, the problem is not with the seed. The problem is again with the soil! In this case, the soil is severely compromised because it is so full of weeds."

Giving a warning, Joe explains, "now, please listen to this. The Bible says the thorns choked out the plant and the plant yielded no fruit. The word 'choked' in the original Greek means to strangle completely. Some preachers errantly claim that those who are represented by the soil supporting a crop of thorns will go to Heaven. I do not believe that for a moment. Let me explain why. Just like with the seed that fell on the rocky soil, the seed that fell among the thorns never matured to the point where it yielded any fruit. The seed that fell onto the road or footpath never yielded any fruit either! So, we have three types of soil here, none of which takes the seed to maturity where it bears any fruit. These three types of soil are completely incongruent with bearing fruit!"

Moving on to the final type of soil, Joe explains, "coming to the fourth type of soil, we have quite a contrasting scenario. In this case, the seed, which is the Word of God, falls on the good soil. The seed planted in the good soil is described as growing up and increasing, and yielding fruit. Some plants yielded thirtyfold, some sixtyfold, and others one hundred fold. Persecution comes, and the plant still yields fruit. Tribulation comes, and the plant still yields fruit. Weeds may even attempt to sprout up, but the plant chokes out the weeds instead." Joe then asks his audience, "do you see the difference between the first three types of soil and the good soil?" Many in the fellowship nod their heads or reply "yes", indicating they are following Joe's explanation.

Summarizing the Parable of the Soils, Joe informs the group, "you are the soil. The seed is the Word of God. The roadside soil, the rocky soil, and the soil infested with weeds are not conducive to bearing fruit. Consequently, those people represented by these three types of soil will not be found in Heaven. In stark contrast, the fourth type of soil, the good soil, brings the seed to maturity and bears much fruit."

Joe then asks, "now, what exactly is this fruit that Jesus is speaking about?" Giving the answer, Joe explains, "to begin with, the fruit that Jesus is referring to is, in part, the fruit of the Spirit, which is love, joy, peace, patience, kindness, goodness, faithfulness, gentleness, and self control. When you read the Word of God, if you are represented by the good soil, the seed of the Word of God should bring forth that type of fruit in your life. So, that's a good start. And, if you were here the week that I discussed fruit, you should be able to see how bearing fruit ties in with salvation."

Joe then asks, "what else is fruit? The list is quite long, my friends. Fruit is that we love each other, care for each other in times of need, admonish each other when sin is present, and so on. I say 'and so on' because the list cannot be all inclusive. Bearing fruit comes back to abiding in Jesus, for He is the vine and we are the branches."

Joe then explains, "let me leave you with an example. If you are a follower of Jesus, you have been endowed with a spiritual gift. If you exercise your spiritual gift in the Spirit, you are bearing fruit. If, for example, my spiritual gift is teaching, right now I am bearing fruit if I am accurately teaching the Word of God. Your job is to take the seeds of that fruit, and apply it to your own life and bear your own fruit of the Spirit from the truths that you learn."

Joe concludes by telling the group, "thank you guys for giving me the opportunity to speak to you this evening. I hope that I said something to encourage someone here. And remember, the issue is fruit." Joe steps down from the stage, receiving a standing ovation from the group. Joe walks to the back of the room, rejoining his friends, who tell him that what he said was perfectly clear.

Standing outside the open door, watching and listening to Joe's talk from a distance, is Rodney, who previously made it understood that he wasn't returning to the fellowship. As the band takes the stage and begins to play, Rodney, coming to the stark realization that something is missing in his life, walks away.

As the praise band begins their closing set, Amy tells Joe, "that was really good! You know, Joe, your spiritual gift has got to be teaching. You make everything sound so simple." Joe smiles, and replies, "I try. I give it my best." Amy tells Joe, "well, you did really good." Amy then tells Joe, "Ed's spiritual gift is the discernment of spirits. That's how Ed knows that Rodney is a fake." Joe replies, "Ed might be right about that. Rodney had just about everyone fooled. The book of Jude speaks about it and, in Rodney's case, God revealed it."

After the praise band plays their final number, Mike closes the meeting with prayer. In the back of the room, Ed mentions to Amy, "wow! This was our last meeting here. And, now it's off to our last trip to the pizzeria." Amy agrees, telling Ed, "yeah. You're right. I'm not sure I'm ever coming back here again, unless Jenny and Pete or Joe and Brittany get married around here somewhere." Ed whispers to Amy, "is there something that I don't know?" Amy whispers back, "no. But, just look at them. It's easy to figure out where both of their relationships are going." Ed thinks for a moment, and tells Amy, "you're right. Joe and Brittany have been together since I've been at the University. And, I've known Pete for two years. I've never seen him this happy." Amy adds, "I've noticed that Jenny is really happy too."

Ed, Amy, and their friends head to the pizzeria. Knowing that Ed and Amy are leaving tomorrow morning, a few other members of the fellowship join them. On the way, Jenny mentions, "it looks like Rodney is headed to the pizzeria tonight with DDT," referring to Dana, Donna, and Theresa. Amy laughs, and tells Jenny, "the last time we saw Rodney at the pizzeria, he got kicked out." Jenny replies, "that didn't end too well for Rodney. And, I'll be like really surprised if Tony lets him back in tonight."

Arriving at the pizzeria, the group of twenty fellowship members combine several tables and take a seat. Since they are such a large group, the waiter comes over to the group's table and takes their order. Rodney and his crew walk in, taking a seat at a table uncomfortably close to Ed and Amy's going away dinner.

Knowing that this is the last time she is likely to see Amy, Dana stops, and asks Amy, "did you delete that pic of me yet?" Amy sighs, and replies, "please don't bother me with this crap anymore. Okay?"

Dana, clearly upset that Amy has a pic of her vaping, tells Amy, "you better delete it, or else." Amy sarcastically replies, "whatever."

The waiter returns to the table with the drinks. If anyone at Rodney's table was expecting to take a photograph of Jenny having a glass of wine, they are sorely out of luck tonight. Rodney, however, goes up to the counter and places an order for two medium pizzas and a pitcher of beer for those at his table. In sheer contrast to those at Rodney's table, no one at Ed's table seems to care what anyone in Rodney's group is drinking.

Over dinner, Ed mentions to Joe, "that was a really good talk you gave tonight. It was a whole lot clearer than many of the sermons I've heard." Joe tells Ed, "I try. A person is either good soil, or they're not. It's that simple. There's no reason to take something so simple and make it more complicated than it really is."

Since he will be working soon, Ed asks Joe, "how about tithing? That seems to be a favorite topic of many pastors." Joe replies, "tithing is a command given to the Israelites, and was paid only when they resided in Israel. In Old Testament times, only landowners and herdsmen tithed. Many craftsmen and tradesmen were not required to tithe. And, back then, there were actually three tithes, not one. The first was the Levitical tithe, which was 10 percent. The second tithe was the feast tithe, which was another 10 percent. Then, there was the tithe for helping the poor, which was an additional 10 percent, but only paid every three years. So, a true Biblical Old Testament tithe is not 10 percent, but rather 23 1/3 percent. So, unless you are a Jew living under the Mosaic Law, and a landowner or herdsman living in Israel, the tithe doesn't really apply. Give what the Lord leads you to give." Ed replies, "Joe, again you make everything sound so simple."

During dinner, Amy receives a text from one of her lifeguard friends, Angel, stating, "See you tomorrow!" Amy opens her phone, and replies, "Can't wait! ETA noon." Amy lays her phone back down on the table, and reaches for her second slice of pizza.

Seeing Amy's phone unlocked, Dana rushes over, grabs Amy's cell phone, quickly searching for the photo that she wants deleted. Exploding out of her seat, Amy grabs Dana's arm, wrestling with Dana to recover her cell phone. Ed rushes over to help Amy but, seeing Amy holding her own, stands by at the moment. Taking Dana down, Amy exclaims, "give me that!" Dana sobs and whines, "no! I want that pic deleted!" Recovering her cell phone, Amy returns to her seat, leaving Dana crying on the floor.

The commotion quiets down, this time escaping the notice of Tony, the owner. If Tony had seen the altercation, someone would have been thrown out of the pizzeria. Since Jenny videoed the altercation, the evidence suggests that it is Dana who would be out on the street tonight.

Locking her phone and putting it in her pocket, Amy finishes her dinner. Ed asks Amy, "are you okay?" Amy replies, "yeah. I'm fine. All that working out with you just paid off. But, Dana doesn't look too good." Dana pulls herself together, stumbling over to her table and taking her seat.

Right before Ed and Amy's group is ready to leave, Officer Richard Davidson walks in, who is promptly greeted by Rodney and Dana. Amy watches and listens as Rodney explains his one-sided view of the altercation to Officer Davidson. Jenny tells Amy, "don't worry, girl. I like got the whole wrestling match on video." Amy replies, "I'm not worried. But, I can't believe this. Rodney, or one of them, called the police on me." Reconsidering what she said, Amy corrects herself, telling Jenny, "on second thought, I was wrong. I totally can believe that they called the police."

Officer Davidson walks over to Amy and, pointing to Dana, asks Amy, "I'm sorry to interrupt your dinner. Were you in an altercation with a Dana McPherson, sitting over at that table?" Amy replies, "that's correct. Dana, the drunk underage girl at that table that you are referring to, tried to steal my cell phone. So, I grabbed my phone back from her." Officer Davidson asks Amy, "wait. The girl you had an altercation with is underage?" Amy replies, "yup. She is." Officer Davidson asks Amy, "how do you know this?" Amy replies, "her birthday is in January. She's twenty years old. I can show you. It's online." Officer Davidson replies, "I'll check her ID." After all, a date of birth found online hardly constitutes legal evidence.

Jenny interrupts, and tells Officer Davidson, "I have the whole thing on video, if you want to see it." Officer Davidson tells Jenny, "oh, really? Please show it to me." Jenny shows the video to Officer Davidson, who clearly sees that Amy was trying to recover her cell phone from Dana. On Amy's side, the evidence clearly shows the altercation stopped immediately as soon as Amy recovered her phone.

Officer Davidson walks over to Dana, telling everyone at her table, "I need to see everyone's ID. Please place your ID on the table in front of you." Rodney, Theresa, and Donna put their ID on the table, which are examined by Officer Davidson. Searching through her purse, Dana tells Officer Davidson, "I can't seem to find my ID. I must have left it in my dorm." Officer Davidson informs Dana, "that's okay, ma'am. We'll search your purse downtown." Fearing that she'll be taken away to the police station, Dana reconsiders her deceitfulness and, suddenly finding her ID, hands it to Officer Davidson and tells him, "oh. Here it is. I found it."

Officer Davidson examines Dana's ID, and asks her, "ma'am, are you aware that you must be twenty-one years of age to purchase alcohol?" Dana replies, "well, yeah. But, I didn't buy it." Officer Davison asks those sitting at Dana's table, "okay. Who here bought the pitcher of beer?" Rodney pipes up, answering, "I did. But, I'm twenty-two." Officer Davidson asks Rodney, "are you aware, sir, that purchasing alcohol and supplying it to a minor is a misdemeanor?" Suddenly struck with great fear, Rodney replies, "no. I never heard about that." Pointing to Rodney and Dana, Officer Davidson tells them, "you two, step outside with me."

As Rodney and Dana are being escorted out of the restaurant by Officer Davidson, Amy asks the officer, "are we free to go?" Officer Davidson replies, "unless you want to press charges against this woman, you're free to go." Breathing a sigh of relief, Amy tells Officer Davidson, "she didn't damage my phone. So, I'll let it go this time." Officer Davidson tells Amy, "then, you're free to go. Have a good evening."

Looking out the window, Pete mentions, "wow! Rodney is in handcuffs, and the officer is putting him in the back seat of his police car." Jenny mentions, "and, he's putting Dana in handcuffs too. She's like crying herself a river. Her mascara is running." Amy comments, "so sad. Too bad. With her leaky eye syndrome, she should have bought waterproof mascara." Not the least bit serious, Jenny asks Amy, "where's your sympathy, girl?" Amy replies, "it went down the toilet when she tried to steal my cell phone, and then called the police on me. But, I forgive her. I'm sure she's doing the best she can. Maybe she'll learn something tonight."

Joe tells Amy, "you were every bit as good as Erika back there." Amy laughs, and replies, "you might be right about that, Joe." Jenny asks Joe, "who's Erika?" Joe replies, "she's a character in the *Eddie, The Mechanic* series." Jenny replies, "I haven't gotten to her yet." Joe tells Jenny, "Erika briefly shows up in *Eddie, The Early Years* and shows up again in *Eddie, The Sophomore Year*. I won't spoil it for you." Jenny replies, "that's right! I remember Erika from *Eddie, The Early Years*! She kicked the crap out of that other girl, whatever her name was."

Heading back to campus, Ed reassures Amy, "when we get to the beach, all of these problems will be gone." Amy informs Ed, "we'll just have a whole new set of problems to deal with." Ed asks, "really? Like what?" Amy replies, "hurricanes, storms that suddenly roll in, and Spring break traffic on the strip." Ed tells Amy, "I'll take that over the crap that happened back at the pizzeria any day."

Arriving back at the dorms, Ed, Amy, Pete and Jenny hang out for a while. Wanting to get an early start to their day tomorrow, Ed and Amy call it an early night.

Amy wakes up early on Saturday morning, making sure she has everything packed. Jenny also wakes up early, not wanting to miss the chance to say goodbye to her best friend. As they are waiting for Ed to text Amy, Jenny tells Amy, "this all happened like really fast, girl. I can't believe it! You come here, and just like that, you're out of here! And now, you're getting married!" Amy tells Jenny, "when you know it's God's will, you have to go with it. I don't belong here. I belong back at the beach." Jenny sits on her bed, and replies, "I know, girl. You really do. But, I'm really going to miss you." Amy replies, "I'm going to miss you guys too." Amy then reminds Jenny, "you and Pete will be down at the beach every weekend when Spring comes." Amy and Jenny reminisce over the events of the last few months as Amy waits for Ed to text her.

Once Ed has all of his belongings loaded into his Jeep, he drives over to Amy's dorm and parks in front. Ed texts Amy, telling her that he is downstairs. Upstairs, Amy tells Jenny, "Ed is downstairs. I guess I'll start loading up my stuff." Jenny springs up off of her bed, and tells Amy, "I'll help you, girl." Amy and Jenny carry a load down, wishing that Ed could come up and help. Unfortunately, men are not allowed in the women's dorms until 10:00 a.m. on the weekends.

Once Amy's stuff is all loaded, Jenny tells Amy and Ed, "I'm really going to miss you guys." Jenny gives Ed a hug, and tells him, "keep in touch, okay?" Ed replies, "we will. And, remember. We'll see you guys in a few days." Jenny then gives Amy a hug and, shedding tears, tells Amy, "I'm really going to miss you, girl."

As Ed is making sure everything is secure in the Jeep, Jenny whispers to Amy, "thank you for inviting me to the pool that day. If I didn't go, who knows? I may have never gotten together with Pete." Amy whispers back, "when I look back, I can see that day at the pool was part of God's plan."

Jenny again tells Amy, "I'm really going to miss you, girl." Amy warmly tells Jenny, "I'm going to miss you too. But, we're only three hours down the road. It's really not that far. You guys can come down on the weekends." Jenny replies, "I would really love that!"

After a long goodbye, Ed and Amy get into Ed's Jeep. Standing on the sidewalk, Jenny wipes the tears from her eyes as Ed and Amy drive away to their new life together.

Appendix I
Mr. Frazier's Motivational Speech

Before the team heads out to the track for today's practice session, Mr. Frazier addresses his team, "in our last meet, as a team, we did not perform quite as well as we could have. Some of you, as always, delivered a world-class performance. A few others, according to our statistics, could have done much better than you did. Before we get out on the track today, some of you need to hear what I am going to say. Much of what you are about to hear I have said before. You may have heard what I am going to say several times but, this time, I want you to listen and take it to heart."

Mr. Frazier reminds his team, "the divisional meet is coming up in one week. Is there any reason why this team can't walk away with the gold medal in every event? No! There's not! There is absolutely no reason why we can't walk away with all of the gold medals! In fact, there is no reason why we can't walk away with all the medals! If you're up against someone who has beaten you in the past, do something! Mess with their head! A little psychological warfare might just be the difference between winning and losing! We, as a team, are going to have to do everything we can if we are going to emerge as the clear and undisputable winner of this year's divisional meet!"

Beginning his talk in a way quite familiar to the team, Mr. Frazier exclaims, "let me remind you of something we all need not forget. In any race, there is only one winner! In the Bible, in the book of First

Corinthians, in chapter 9, verse 24, the scripture reads, 'Do you not know that those who run in a race all run, but only one receives the prize? Run in such a way that you may win.' Make no mistake about it! There is only one winner! Whoever comes in second place is the first loser! If you come in second place, learn something! Work harder, learn from the situation, and figure out what you need to change to do better next time!"

Conceding the point that second and third place are worth something in a track meet, Mr. Frazier explains, "and, yes, I understand that they give medals for second and third place. That is how they keep score. Honestly, though, where in the world did that ever come from? But, that's how they've organized track and field in the world. So, we have to play by their rules. So, if you come in second place, your goal is to come in first place next time! If you come in third place, your goal is to come in second place or better! If you did not place, learn whatever you can from those who did! And, if you were the winner, you'd better not let your guard down because there are dozens of athletes out there who want to knock your ass off the first-place tier! If you came in first place, understand this! Your competition does not like you! They may act like they like you, but they don't. Remember this. When they are training, they are training so that they win, not so that you win!"

Rehashing one of his favorite stories, Mr. Frazier tells his team, "many of you have heard this before, but some of you need to hear it again. When I was in my early teens, it was very stormy outside, and my father was watching a track meet on television. As you know, track was my sport, so I watched along with him. I remember that day quite well, as if it were yesterday. My race, the 100-yard dash, came up. I carefully watched what the runners did before they got into the blocks. I watched them as they were waiting for the gun. I watched very carefully when the gun went off and they left the blocks. And, I watched every step as they raced toward the finish line."

Explaining when he first heard that there is only one winner in any race, Mr. Frazier continues, "once the race was over, it was clear to my father and I which runner took first place, but second and third place seemed to be a tie. While we were waiting to find out who came in second and third place, I asked my father, 'who do you think came in second?' My father turned to me and said, 'George. It doesn't matter. They both lost. Only one person wins the race. Everyone else is a loser.' I told my father, 'but, they give medals for second and third place.' He replied, 'so what. They still lost.'

My father wanted to teach me a lesson, so he told me, 'George, go and get your Bible.' I returned with my Bible, and my father told me, 'open your Bible to First Corinthians, chapter 9, verse 24, and read it to me.' I read, 'Do you not know that those who run in a race all run, but only one receives the prize? Run in such a way that you may win.' My father looked me straight in the eye, and said to me, 'George, there is only one winner. Everyone else is a loser. It's that simple.' I saw the deep conviction in his eyes when he told me that. His conviction was unmistakable! There is only one winner!

My father didn't stop there. He asked me, 'George, when you play football in school, and your team loses, do you go around boasting to everyone that your team came in second place?' Before I could answer him, he told me, 'of course you don't! Second place is nothing to be proud of, especially if there are only two teams playing!' If there are two runners in the race, or eight, there is still only one winner! There are many professional football teams. Only one team wins the Super Bowl! There are many professional baseball teams. Only one team wins the World Series! No one ever boasts about coming in second place!"

Explaining the value of time, Mr. Frazier tells his team, "there are 365 days in a year, 7 days in a week, and 24 hours in a day. No one can tell me there isn't enough time to train. How valuable is your time anyway? What is the value of one year? If you really want to know the value of one year, ask anyone who has been in prison for a year. What is the value of one week? If you want to know, ask a family who is looking forward to a well-deserved one-week vacation at the beach. What's the value of one day? Ask someone who is not expected to live more than a day or two. What's the value of one hour? Ask someone who flew into town, and can only see his wife for one hour before he has to fly out again. What's the value of one minute? Ask a football player whose team is down by six points with one minute left to play in the fourth quarter. What's the value of one second? Ask the runner who comes in second place in the 1,500-meter run. And, what's the value of one-hundredth of a second? Ask the runner who came in second place in the 100-meter dash."

Addressing a common problem with collegiate athletes, Mr. Frazier explains, "for some of you, the reason that you do not win has nothing to do with your training or abilities. The reason you do not win is because of that thing between your ears they call a brain! Someone has programmed your brain, and told you that you can't win. What bothers me is that some of you actually believe it! Why are you listening to what they have to say? If you convince yourself that you cannot win, no matter who or what you are up against, you will never win! Your competition on the track is nothing compared to your own mental obstacles! Get this through your head! The clock that's timing you and the person running next to you is nothing compared to your own mental obstacles! Do not, and I repeat, do not let yourself get in the way of achieving your goals!"

Addressing the subject of success, Mr. Frazier explains, "I am now going to tell you how to succeed at anything you do because some of you seem to have forgotten it. Whether it is on the track, in the classroom, or at your job when you graduate, the one principle leading to success is the same! Most of you have already heard this. If you forget anything else I say here today, remember this." Mr. Frazier pauses for a moment, then exclaims, "the one, and only one, attribute that will determine your success at anything you attempt is you must attack the challenge you face with no fear! Did you hear that? No fear!"

Citing a few examples, Mr. Frazier orates, "they said no one can run a mile faster than four minutes. Roger Bannister did not believe that for a second! They said a man is physically incapable of running 100 meters in less than ten seconds. Jim Hines did not believe that for a second! No one thought that the shot-put could be thrown farther than 22 meters. In 1976, Aleksandr Baryshnikov threw the shot-put using the discus technique, and did exactly what everyone said could not be done! They said no one can run 400 meters in less than 45 seconds. Otis Davis did not believe that for a second! They said no relay team is capable of breaking three minutes in the 4 by 400-meter relay. Robert Frey, Lee Evans, Tommie Smith, and Theron Lewis did not believe that for an instant! What's stopping you? What's in your way? Whatever is in your way, if you want to win, you must get rid of it!

What do all these athletes I just mentioned have in common? These athletes have in common the one, and only one, attribute that will determine your success at anything you do! They attacked the challenge they faced ahead of them with no fear! Roger Bannister. No fear! Jim Hines. No fear! Aleksandr Baryshnikov. No fear! Otis Davis. No fear! Robert Frey, Lee Evans, Tommie Smith, and Theron Lewis. No fear! If you are to win, you must do the same! You must attack the challenges you face with no fear!"

Mr. Frazier then asks the athletes, "I have a question for all of you. Who is the fastest sprinter in our division?" Eddie raises his hand, as a few athletes answer, "Eddie." Mr. Frazier chuckles, and informs the group, "well, maybe he is, and maybe he isn't. It depends on what race he's running." Getting very serious, Mr. Frazier continues, "but, I can tell you this. All of you seem to agree that Eddie is the fastest sprinter in the division. Anyone who steps onto the track and is up against Eddie has already been preprogrammed to believe that they will be up against the fastest sprinter in the division! If anyone believes Eddie is the fastest sprinter in the division, when they step onto the track next to him, at best, that makes them second best! They've already lost! When you believe that you are better, faster, and stronger than your opponent, then you will win!"

Reminding the team of Eddie's high school career, Mr. Frazier explains, "speaking of Eddie, when Eddie was a freshman in high school, Eddie won the silver medal in the 40-yard dash at the State invitational meet. During the following three years at the invitational meet, Eddie won the gold medal in the 40-yard dash. And, Eddie won the gold medal in the 100-yard dash at the Spring State invitational meet for four consecutive years! But, here's what you may not know. Eddie put all his gold medals in a box, where he couldn't see them. Left out on his dresser was Eddie's silver medal, where it served as a constant reminder to train harder. Second place was not acceptable to Eddie! Second place should not be acceptable to any of you either!"

Specifically addressing the seniors, Mr. Frazier tells those who will be running in their last divisional meet, "now, for some of you, this is the last season you will be running for this University. Congratulations to all of you who are graduating this year. In a sense, you will be crossing another type of finish line in just a few weeks. Over the last four years, you sat in classrooms, did homework, took tests, performed lab experiments, solved problems, wrote papers, and did whatever else they have you do around here. When you've taken enough classes and passed enough tests, what do they do? They give you a piece of paper, called a diploma, that tells you that you've taken enough classes, and passed enough tests! For all the work that you've put in over the last four years, you will receive a degree in the field of your choice. For some of you, that degree will be in exercise science. For others, your degree may be in science, the arts, communications, mathematics, history, or some field that you plan to work in when you graduate."

Addressing the seniors regarding what they have done in the classroom for the last four years, Mr. Frazier explains, "regardless of your chosen field, I will share with you today exactly what you need to know to succeed when you graduate and hit the working world. But first, let's back up a little bit. There are only three types of degrees offered by any college or university. Those three degrees are a degree in memorization, a degree in problem solving, or a degree in the arts. A degree in history is nothing more than a degree in memorization. A math degree is nothing more than a problem solving degree. A degree in music is one example of a degree in the arts. Many degrees, however, are a combination of the three types of degrees that I just mentioned. The only difference in the three types of degrees are the field of study in which you memorized information, solved problems, or developed your artistic skill. That would be the name of your degree that you will see on your diploma when you graduate in a few weeks."

Mr. Frazier then exclaims, "nothing they teach you at this University will determine whether you succeed when you graduate!" Mr. Frazier continues, "you already know how to succeed at anything you do once you graduate! I told you just a few minutes ago! Whether it is in sports, in the classroom, or at your job when you graduate, the one principle leading to success is the same! You must attack the challenge ahead of you with no fear! No fear! What have I been telling you all year? Whether it is on the track or in your job, the same principle leading to success is the same! You must attack the challenges you face with no fear! That includes the challenges you will face in the divisional meet next week, the challenges you face when you graduate, and anything else you do in your life!"

Moving on to the subject of success, Mr. Frazier continues, "now, when you graduate, society has programmed you that you measure success by how much money you earn. You don't measure success by how much money you earn! You don't measure success by what kind of car you drive! You don't measure success by the size of your house! It is of no value to wake up in the morning and drive to a job you hate. It is of no value to drive a luxury car when you really want to drive a Jeep or British roadster. It is of no value to live in a mansion in the suburbs when you really want to live in a bungalow at the beach. The only measure of success is how well you follow your passion and do what you love!"

Addressing the subject of passion, Mr. Frazier explains, "when you watch a professional football game, every player on the field has been told at one time or another that they'll never make it in the NFL. The same holds true for any sport, such as basketball, baseball, boxing, and so on. When you listen to music, every musician was constantly told that they will never make it in that industry. Some athletes, musicians, or whatever, have deliberately chosen to ignore all the negative talk, follow their passion, and chase after their dreams and goals. They are the ones who succeed! They have followed their passion, and attacked the challenges they were facing with no fear!"

Giving a real life example, Mr. Frazier tells his team, "I mentioned earlier to you that whoever comes in second place is the first loser. I am going to take that premiss and apply it to the real world that a few of you will be entering in just a few weeks. Some of you, when you graduate, will be in the sales field. If you put together a sales presentation, and get the customer to sign the sales contract on the dotted line, congratulations! You won! You came in first place! Now, let me ask you this. What does the salesman who comes in second place get?" Mr. Frazier pauses for a few seconds, then exclaims, "nothing! Absolutely nothing! In sales, there is only one winner! Second place counts for absolutely nothing! Do you finally get it?

There is only one winner! The winner puts food on the table! The loser winds up flipping burgers at a burger joint!"

Wrapping up his presentation, Mr. Frazier finishes, "now, we're all going to head out to the track and start our session today. When you get out there, I want you to train as if you are the salesman competing for that contract. I want you to train as if track and field is your passion. I want you to train as if first place is the only thing that matters. And, remember, there is absolutely no reason why we, as a team, can't walk away with all the medals. Okay! Let's get out there and get some work done!" The team gets off the bleachers and heads out to the track, highly motivated by Mr. Frazier's speech.

To read the entire *Eddie, The Mechanic* series, please visit www.eddiethemechanic.com.

Where Are They Now?

Amy Amherst
Amy moved to the beach right before Thanksgiving break, and got married to Ed shortly after. Amy got the beach wedding that she always wanted. Amy enjoys her position of lifeguard captain, and often spends the days out on a boat with her friend, Angel.

Edward Becker
Now married to Amy, Ed is enjoying life at the beach. Ed works as a personal trainer and landed a job at the local high school as the diving coach. Ed was highly motivated by Mr. Frazier, the gym teacher and track coach in the *Eddie, The Mechanic* series. After reading the entire series, Ed decided to finish college and pursue a degree in exercise science, looking forward to a career as a gym teacher.

Jenny Radcliffe
Jenny finished college, earning a degree in computer science. Shortly after graduation, Jenny got married to Pete. Jenny still indulges in an occasional glass of wine. Whenever Jenny does have a glass of wine, Pete can't resist taking a picture of Jenny running her tongue along the rim of the glass, and adds it to their photo album.

Peter Darby
After graduating with a degree in computer science, Pete opened his own company writing software phone applications. As Amy predicted, Pete and Jenny head down to the beach to visit Ed and Amy every chance they get.

Joe Sugarman

After obtaining his Ph.D. in biochemistry, Joe took a position with the University doing DNA research and teaching chemistry. Still working out at the University's athletic center, Joe keeps his body in top physical condition. Joe still looks forward to his two slices of pizza on Friday night.

Brittany Kramer

Brittany and Joe got married shortly after Brittany obtained her Ph.D. Brittany is now working as a professor of molecular biology at the University.

Rodney Steele

Rodney never could get his act together. Abandoning Christianity all together, as Ed always suspected, it is doubtful that Rodney ever followed Jesus to begin with. Rodney never did pay back the money he took from the fellowship's treasury.

Dana McPherson

Dana eventually graduated from the University, but never did obtain her Mrs. degree. Going from one crisis to the next, Dana's life continues to be status dramaticus after leaving the University.

Donna Ruff

Donna never did get to go out on a date with Pete. After graduation, Donna joined a church having a large single's program. Years after graduation, Donna still remains single.

Theresa Harris

After graduation, Theresa intentionally lost contact with Dana and Donna. Much happier now, Theresa wonders how she ever became friends with Dana and Donna.

Leesa Iron

After listening to Joe's talks about true salvation, Leesa abandoned the legalistic ways she learned from Rodney, and started following the Lord.